PRAISE

"Harlan Stone is the hero we all need, and *Tick... Tick... Tick...* proves why!"
JONATHAN MABERRY, NY TIMES BESTSELLING AUTHOR OF THE JOE LEDGER THRILLERS

"A spell-binding tale of intrigue and science fiction... Harlan Stone, is a splendid creation, a man caught in inexplicable crisis that belies the world he has known all his life."
ARMIN SHIMERMAN STAR OF *STAR TREK :DEEP SPACE 9* AND AUTHOR OF *ILLYRIA*

"An espionage farce full of sex, spies, sci-fi, and secrets with a serious message embedded at its core—and one we'd be well-advised to wake up to before the aliens do show up... But you might have to stop laughing first."
GREGORY FROST, AUTHOR OF THE RHYMER TRILOGY

"Time is literally running out for humans on Earth in this speculative fiction romp, masterfully weaving together aliens, geopolitics, fossil fuel gluttony and White House intrigue."
CHRISTOPHER CHAMBERS, ANTHONY AWARD-WINNING AND SHAMUS-NOMINATED AUTHOR OF *SCAVENGER* AND *STANDALONE*

"A wild, frightening, and entertaining take on global terror, and guaranteed to be one of the craziest, most inventive romances in espionage history you will ever read."
CHRIS BAUER, AUTHOR OF THE MAX FEND THRILLERS

"A chilling read; be prepared to shiver."
MERRY JONES, AUTHOR OF MAINCREST MEDIA AWARD WINNER *THE WOMAN IN THE CUPBOARD*

"A nail-biting thriller. Warning: This is no slow burn, best to buckle-up for a sling-shot ride!"
LANNY LARCINESE, AUTHOR OF *GET BEK* AND *FIRE IN THE BELLY*

ABOUT THE AUTHOR

Steve Zettler is a professional writer and actor. He has authored or coauthored eighteen works of fiction. He has worked extensively as an actor in New York, Los Angeles and regionally, and created a memorable role in a Pulitzer Prize-winning play. He has also worked on countless television shows and feature films and is a Marine Corps combat veteran. He lives and writes in Philadelphia, Pennsylvania.

stevezettler.com

TICK... TICK... TICK...

STEVE ZETTLER

www.vineleavespress.com

Tick... Tick... Tick...
Copyright © 2025 Steve Zettler

All rights reserved.
Print Edition
ISBN: 978-3-98832-139-8
Published by Vine Leaves Press 2025

No parts of this publication may be reproduced, stored in a retrieval system, or transmitted in any form or by any means, electronic, mechanical, photocopying, recording, or otherwise, without the prior written permission of the copyright owner.

This book is sold subject to the condition that it shall not, by way of trade or otherwise, be lent, resold, hired out, or otherwise circulated without the publisher's prior consent in any form of binding or cover other than that in which it is published and without a similar condition including this condition being imposed on the subsequent purchaser. Under no circumstances may any part of this book be photocopied for resale.

This is a work of fiction. Any similarity between the characters and situations within its pages and places or persons, living or dead, is unintentional and coincidental.

Cover design by Jessica Bell
Interior design by Amie McCracken

For Greta

"It's not down on any map, true places never are."
Herman Melville, *Moby Dick*

PHASE ONE
TICK...

WE DIDN'T START THE FIRE
ATLANTIC CITY, NEW JERSEY

Call them Manny, Moe, and Jack. Call them anything for that matter, because those are not their real names, which should have been more than obvious to the individuals they encountered. But in this mad, mad world of theirs, only a few caught on. Scarcely a soul bothered to look beyond the screen of their cell phone. There was a change in the air, but people, being people, shrugged it off. It can't happen here, not in my backyard, etc. 9/11 could never be repeated. And that was exactly what this trio of terrorists were counting on, the inability of Americans to see what was right in front of their eyes.

These interlopers didn't hail from the Western Hemisphere and their real names, after any feeble attempt at an English translation, would consist of a long string of useless vowels with a maximum of two consonants. And even then, these names would be totally unpronounceable by the average Joe. Therefore, they had adopted the names of Manny, Moe, and Jack, and had gone largely unnoticed until security caught up with them.

Not one of the three had ever been celebrated for an iota of originality. And two of them weren't tremendously different creatures, in looks, political beliefs, hairstyles, shoe size, or thought processes. One might call them somewhat cookie-cutter by US standards. Resembling a small, somewhat ruthless portion of political zealots, they were blunt, limited in English vocabulary, methodical in the extreme, and murderous to the point where they outright enjoyed and reveled in their line of work, which in fact, was just that—homicide. In the past, Manny and Moe had taken a great deal of pride in the sheer number of people they had eliminated, wherever they might have appeared. They enjoyed living the life of strong-armed thugs, the ultimate gangsters. Over the years they had appeared in quite a varied assortment of places, mostly in Europe. However, no previous operation resembled the massive scale of this current undertaking. Though, this US thing was a new ball of wax for them, and a way of life for which they had difficulty adjusting.

Jack? Well, Jack was not so much the killer. He was a bit of a poet, unpredictable. He'd been conscripted, and Group never fully trusted the draftees. There was no telling what they might do. Most of them were dreamers looking for a mild form of adventure and travel, or worse yet, something to write about. They were essentially bored with home life and had a burning desire to get the hell out of town. Group didn't pressure those who did not want to serve in far-off lands. Jack was just looking for something different. He found it, but he wasn't overly joyed with what he had found. He hadn't fully understood the demands before signing on. Tragically, for Jack, there was no turning back now. Going home on his own was out of the question. Group had him in their clutches, and Group was going to hang on to him for as long as it took to get the job done. At this point, Jack understood that if he didn't play along with Manny and Moe this could easily become a suicide mission.

The three had arrived in Atlantic City on a Tuesday afternoon in mid-July. They were on an operation that could have been accomplished by just one of them without much difficulty, but Group liked to have backup. "Always the friggin' backup," Moe would often grumble. He didn't relish having others constantly looking over his shoulder. But much to his chagrin, he wasn't in charge of this undertaking. And never would be.

Group was insistent on keeping records, detailed records, and had found that three renditions of any given event, or operation, provided the most thorough, reliable, and accurate reporting, leaving very little room for details to be *accidentally* overlooked, or worse, embellished upon. A practice for which Moe was notorious. When eradicating infestation, annihilating diseases, vanquishing enemies, detailed records of past failures proved to be very dependable roadmaps, scientifically. And at this point, failure was no longer an option. The timetable had been moved up. The clock was ticking, and ticking very quickly.

Interestingly, draftees, like Jack, often supplied more accurate and truthful interpretations of events. They were still somewhat innocent and drawn to the truth. Some at Group considered this a fault of over-exposure to liberal sensibilities, and the influence of Female intrusion into leadership positions. Manny and Moe tended to exaggerate, and Group was aware of this. They pictured themselves as heroes of a cause and believed they should be far more highly decorated than they had been. Nonetheless, they were efficient at what they did, despite their often-unorthodox methods. They were good foot soldiers and followed orders; not without question, but they followed directions to the letter.

Manny and Moe had been working together for so long that neither of them remembered what their first assignment had been. Their success ratio had been high, better than any other combo Group had sent out, and that's exactly why they were finally handed this North American part of the operation, an assignment at which every other team had failed. Miserably. Group realized that this was no time to rely on the inefficiency of amateurs. Year in and year out there had been small gains, but nothing significant had been accomplished, and the opposition numbers had done nothing but expand and multiply, and at an alarming rate as of late, a trait for which diseases were notorious. This disease, these people, were basically a cancer in their eyes, and these operatives were in the US to eliminate that cancer before it spread further. Group had grown weary of these vermin, and it was time to bring this conflict to an end; it had gone on far too long. A meticulously developed solution had become available, and now was the time to put it to the test.

And time was running out on Group. Recent evidence indicated that this disease was beginning to branch out, looking for new territory to infest. Probes had been sent to unexplored realms. Like all cancers, it was metastasizing. If that continued, if it was allowed to set up operational bases Elsewhere, there would be a total collapse of any environment Manny, Moe, and Jack were familiar with. And they understood that all too well—this had now become a life-or-death situation.

Despite having never visited Atlantic City in the past, boredom set in quickly for the trio. The room was dull, on the sixth floor, with no ocean view; it simply looked down on a parking lot that was consistently vacant. The Ferraris and Lamborghinis parked Elsewhere. The walls of their room were decorated with faded watercolors of overweight cats with neon eyes. The one armchair was frayed with age, and with only a pair of queen-size beds, two of them were forced to sleep together on any given evening. They would flip a casino token every night to determine who the unlucky ones would be. Each preferred to sleep with no clothing, which became dicey at times, their bodies reacting unpredictably to the steamy setting.

The city itself was still the gambling mecca it had always been, but people had become so inured to losing their life savings that even the suicides had diminished to near zero. Though the number of children roasting in overheated locked cars while parents became spellbound by slot machines remained steady. The restaurant in their hotel, though glitzy, served nothing but reheated canned entrees such as chili and Campbell's mushroom soup. Quite naturally, the gambling floor sparkled like an amusement park.

The three of them had never before gambled anywhere on Earth. They had no understanding of how it worked or why people wasted so much time on it or got so much enjoyment out of losing their life savings. Still, they quickly became fascinated with it all. Even for Manny, Moe, and Jack the lure was irresistible. Group had advised them to steer clear of the gaming tables. But it hadn't been a direct order, and the attraction was far too great. The lights and noises were mesmerizing.

These emissaries each had an uncanny head for numbers, and not long after arriving, by working as a team, they had determined the precise win/lose ratios and odds for every form of gambling the citywide casinos had to offer. Counting cards proved to be child's play. It was as if they could read the minds of the blackjack dealers. Craps, roulette, even the slot machines were no match for their mathematical prowess as they hopped from one machine to the next. One casino to the next.

As a result, within seventy-two hours of their arrival, they had accumulated a vast amount of money—and had been summarily banned from setting foot onto the floor of every gambling house in the city. Their photographs had been digitally circulated throughout town by a private security firm, along with unflattering descriptions of their physicality and poor clothing choices. They didn't take to the banning happily, and when alone in their hotel room, lounging in their nakedness, they spoke in their own language.

"These filthy creatures encourage you to bet, encourage you to win, throw their Females and booze at you, encourage you to wager higher, and then when you do win, they throw you out on your ass. You don't even get to keep the Females as a consolation prize."

"I've always liked the Female aspect of these operations, especially in Eastern Europe. They are so easy if you have enough money." Moe offered a lecherous smile. "The Jersey Girl thing is okay, but I do prefer the Estonian Females. It would be nice if things worked that way back home, though I don't see how it could be accomplished. I like dipping this organ of mine. It makes me feel wanted. Even if it is just a Jersey Girl."

Manny was only half in agreement. "Yeah, the Females are a nice bonus, but it annoys the hell out of me that Group won't let us eliminate people on this gig. That babe at the Caesar's blackjack table would have been number one on my list. That smug little look, the not-so-subtle nod to the goon who threw us out; I would have loved to put the touch on them both. Leave them gasping for air on the boardwalk while their blood oozed into the wooden planks. They wouldn't know what hit them."

Jack muttered, "Obviously," and rolled his eyes, wishing he could somehow escape these two morons. His thoughts were interrupted by an aggressive knock on their hotel room door, and he stood to answer it. "We need to be very careful how we play our cards." He then opened the door.

It was The Boss. Again, The Boss's actual name was so alien to the English language that there is little point in translating it. In the beginning, The Boss was simply referred to as "A." But she would, in the days to come, assume the alias of Angelica. This was done to blend in with the locals; though, in reality, she was somewhat ill-suited to blend in unnoticed. She was well aware that she was more highly educated than these three put together, and she resented being forced to deal with them. However, Jack seemed to be a bit more intuitive than the other two. When she spoke, she also used their native language.

"What's with the knocking, A?" Moe asked.

"In case you dopes have forgotten, we're becoming one with these people. Everyone in America knocks on doors before they enter so we will also knock on doors before we enter. It's that simple. Next, have you already forgotten that you've been wired? We've all been wired. This room has been wired. I hear everything you're saying. Group hears everything you're saying. Everything I'm saying, for that matter. What's all this talk about killing people?"

She studied the three of them.

"Yes, Manny, I'm talking to you. Did you think that comment would slide by unnoticed? We are not authorized to kill anyone. Get that through your thick head. I personally placed that in the operating instructions, don't *improvise*." She eyed the three of them closely. "We want this to run smoothly, without violence." Moe appeared confused. She added, "*Improvise*? Is that the word you're having trouble with, Moe?"

"Yeah."

"It means make shit up. It's an English word, perhaps not translated well, but I threw it in as a test. And you failed. The three of you should be spending your time working on improving your English, rather than pissing and moaning as if you were back at Base lounging in the enlisted man's club."

"I was only thinking of the old days. I wasn't going to do anything. I follow orders. You know that. It's in my record. I'm not killing anyone until I'm told to," Manny grumbled. "This too will change. And I'm looking forward to the time it does. Nothing's set in stone. Nothing ever is. Group's directives can change like the direction of the wind. And when they do, I will be ready. The Females will not be in charge forever. And I do hope they're monitoring, and I do hope they hear that. I hope they know where I stand."

"Should I take that as some sort of threat?"

He didn't respond.

"Good. Keep your opinions to yourself. Group is adamant about murder. And so am I. There will be no killing on this operation. That's a Female directive. Historically, freelance termination is where past operatives have continually gotten themselves into trouble, especially here in the US. And often Elsewhere. Remember when they ran to save the Europeans? Once we started slaughtering people these Americans instinctively fought back, no matter where we struck. They quickly developed a counterattack, which I needn't remind you, they are extremely good at. And in every past instance, they've fought back with intensity, successfully and lethally, and that's why they're still a thorn in our side, that's why we're still where we are, especially here in the Eastern States. Have these clowns never lost a war?"

"Vietnam?"

She switched over to English. "For crap's sake, Moe, don't take things black and white only. That's old-time stuff by their words. You should be spending your time working on English speaking. Learn to be as good in English as me. Read a book why don't you? There is a bible in that drawer." She pointed. "It doesn't make any sense, but you can learn English words."

"English is a shit, bastard language."

"There may be truth in that."

"I am now knowing improvise. Every day something new."

"Good for you, I report it to Group. Look, we're here to dispute a disease and that's everything. Murdering people is bad to the strategy. This new approach had been built up ages ago, but it took change in Group's leadership to perform it. Plus an adjusting in the technology. Now that we Females are controlling functioning, Group is going to design operations the Female way. We're permitting the science work. Give the disease nothing to strike back at, nothing to get its mutations into. It won't know what's going on until it's too late."

She paced the room for a minute. "Unless it passes the test. Which I doubt it can. In the end, there won't be much of a time changing between this strategy and the murder doing, or a war approach, which has failed badly in the past too. War has accomplished absolutely nothing. Makes me wonder what it's good for. With this new blueprint, the disease should be on its way to extinction. Eradication, by the time you boys are returning back to Base. Our function here is to execute the plan and disappear any attempts to challenge Group's goal. Without doing murder."

Jack raised his hand, looking much like a third-grade student.

"I follow all this, but I don't like the part about the gorillas. Isn't there some way to change that part of the blueprint? Leave the gorillas out of it?"

"Nobody likes the section about the gorillas, Jack. Understand what's true. It's how the machinery is working. The gorillas must go."

ONE

Harlan Stone was the Turk's Man, the best MPS operative the agency had known. The Turk being Charles Norcross, appointed head of MPS some fifteen years previous by President Logan. And even though Logan had been run out of office seven years prior for maintaining multiple mistresses in Bolivia, Israel, and Egypt, there was no replacing Charles Norcross. Simply because he was one of the few presidential appointments that the powerbrokers could all agree upon; he was a class act, truly irreplaceable, a take-no-prisoners leader. But in the end, it was the president's sole choice as to who held the leadership position at MPS. As a result, nobody crossed Norcross. To do so would be to directly cross the president.

Very few people knew that MPS existed, even in the Halls of Congress. The agency consisted of only a handful of employees: Norcross; field agents Stone, Walsh, and Perez; communications wiz-kid Olsen; and a dozen office personnel and research assistants. All reported solely to Norcross. Because of the small size of the agency, any potential leaks, or unintentional disclosures of top-secret information was nonexistent. The only classified information to leave MPS rested in an employee's head. All paper was embedded with trace elements designed to trigger alarms if it passed through an exit door. Agents and behind-the-scenes individuals were screened far more scrupulously than any other US agency.

MPS headquarters were housed in a nondescript section of the Food and Drug Administration in Silver Spring, Maryland. The lack of strict security personnel suited Norcross; no one paid much attention to what went on behind the locked doors labeled, *Logistics*. Though occasionally passing FDA employees would glance at the doors and say, "What the hell does go on in there?"

Norcross enjoyed his creature comforts. The MPS offices were decorated with original prints and paintings, most featuring naval battles or George Catlin portraits of Native American Indians. The furniture was high-end, plenty of wood and leather, all salvaged from the previous White House when the new FLOTUS decided to dump everything her trashy predecessor thought was stylish.

Harlan Stone was Norcross's most trusted agent; the one agent he called upon when he needed things done correctly, the first time, efficiently and clandestinely. And it was the Turk's Man who would be the agent sent to rural Pennsylvania to investigate what had become known as the *Mennonite Mishap*. Like many in government, Norcross had a soft spot for alliteration.

Harlan stepped from the Amtrak express train onto the Kindertown platform at two-oh-six on a Mid-August Thursday afternoon to the sound of a rather unhappy and lonely dog, barking. And as the train sped from the station, a billow of hot August dust was sucked past him in the wake of the departing stainless-steel beast that was to race on, all the way out to Pittsburgh. Mangey old dogs, he thought, dust, oppressive heat, more like Dodge City of the 1800s than present-day rural Pennsylvania. And he guessed that politically these folks held on to their old ways much like the western settlers of yore. In the previous election, the current POTUS did not fare well in this part of Pennsylvania, a part of the state referred to as Pennsyl-tucky by those highly erudite folks living in Pittsburgh and Philadelphia.

The summer had gone downhill quickly. Harlan was the only one to exit the train on this beastly hot Thursday. The temperature was not dropping any time soon; it had already hit ninety-eight. The platform was devoid of any signs of life, the withered and gray planks offered up sharp splinters to the unwary and parched doves searching for a drop of water.

Within seconds Harlan's polo shirt was clinging to him like a wet dishrag, so he moved off into the shadows of the station's overhanging roof and dropped his small case onto the weathered bench. A chip of overheated green paint fell from the bench's armrest to the platform in protest. This assault was possibly the first activity it had seen in weeks.

A short, round man in his seventies, bald, with an exaggerated, snow-white Fu-Manchu mustache emerged from the station and waved a carefully creased straw hat two or three times in front of his lined face before placing it back on his head. He was near the polar opposite of Harlan who stood six-two and carried himself like a prizefighter on a winning streak.

"Hotter 'n Hell out here," the old man said to the world in general, almost as though Harlan didn't exist. He made no attempt to look in Harlan's direction, concentrating more on his antiquated Pennsylvania Railroad pocket watch.

"Two-oh-six right on time though, despite the damn heat. Can't say that happens every day. You'd think all these newfangled laser gizmos would improve punctuality. Not a chance, but today she's on time, God bless her."

He dangled the watch and chain in front of Harlan as if he was trying to hypnotize him.

"Ever seen one? Only analog pocket-watch left in town, probably. Everyone has to have a damn i-Watch or i-Something or Fitbit, whatever the hell that is? Consume, consume, consume. Everyone wants the latest damn thing. Gotta get what the guy next to you's got. Toss the old one in a landfill like everything else. Worth a fortune, this baby of mine, but I ain't sellin'. No way. Had plenty of offers though. Real McCoy Pennsylvania Railroad watches are hard to come by these days. City people from Philly always comin' out this way lookin' to play us for rubes, but I ain't sellin'."

He placed the watch back in his pocket and removed his hat once more, pinched the crease at the crown until he seemed pleased with its appearance, and returned it to his head. He then sat on the bench next to Harlan's case.

"You lookin' for anything, or anyone, in particular, young man?"

"Doctor Jacobs."

"You sick?"

"Nope."

"I was gonna say, you don't look sick. You look like a pretty tough *muchacho*."

"*Muchacho?*"

"Only an expression I grew up with. My Granny hailed from south of the border. Everyone was 'boy' to her. No offense meant, but I can see why you might take it wrong. Some folks take things as a slight, when no slight was meant. The heat brings it out. But people talk that way around these parts. If folks can't get used to it, they'd be better off moving on."

Harlan remained motionless.

"Doc doesn't have office hours on Thursdays. Thursdays he goes out and sees folks, does house-calls. Hard to catch up with him on Thursdays. But that's also what people do around here, house calls. A far cry from any darn city doctor. Still doin' things the way we did 'em in my Granny's days. That's the way life is hereabouts. Change don't sit that well with some folks. Hard for city people like you to blend in with us locals."

Harlan read the comment for what it was, but he simply said, "He's expecting me."

"Yeah? How's come he ain't here to meet you? You'd think he woulda offered to pick you up in this heat. That's what I woulda done. If you was a friend of mine, sure thing, I woulda been here to meet ya. My wife woulda done the same, but she ain't with us no longer. Gone to the Great Beyond, she has. Almost ten years ago now. Lucky for her 'cuz she didn't never do well in the heat. She'd be on fire. Liked to say, 'This ole town is burnin' up.' Wonder what she'd think about today? She wouldn't recognize this world. The streets are meltin'."

The platform fell silent for two or three minutes.

"Ya know, it's a pretty good walk from here to Doc Jacobs's. Over on Hanover Street, he is. That's if he's there at all. Sissy Blackburn's expecting twins any day now."

Harlan checked the time on his cell phone and glanced around. "Well, actually, Mister?"

"Sonny. You can call me Sonny. Everyone else does. Not my birth name, mind you. And last names don't account for much here in K-Town. Specially if you're just blowin' through. Which I assume you are? Ya ain't planning on stayin', are you? Pretty small case you're carryin' for someone plannin' on stayin'. What's in that case, anyway?"

Harlan wasn't sure if Sonny was putting on an act for a stranger, was a blatant racist, or if years at a train station few people visited had ultimately turned him into the caricature of a small-town snoop. Harlan pushed the sweat from his brow through his dark hair.

"Well, Sonny, Doctor Jacobs did say he would meet me here. I guess I'll just hang loose until he shows up. Don't worry, I'm not staying long."

"I'm not the type of man who worries. Ya didn't say what's in the case."

"You're right, I didn't."

Sonny paused for a moment, turned his back on Harlan and glanced down the railroad tracks. "No offense taken."

"None intended."

"You want I should give Doc Jacobs a call for you? I got a phone in the station there. Happy to do it?"

"Thanks, Sonny, but I have my iPhone if I need to call. I'll give him another few minutes. I'm sure he'll show up."

Harlan debated whether to remove his case from the bench and sit next to Sonny, but the move seemed far too intimate for the setting. This was a part of the world where people cherished their personal space, and an invasion of that space by an outsider, especially a brown-skinned outsider, would not sit well, so Harlan stood. It wasn't the first time he'd found himself in this position. He had grown up standing while others sat. *Just as well*, he thought, the train ride from Washington, DC, through Philadelphia to Kindertown was enough sitting for Harlan for one day. Harlan wasn't a sitter; he worked best on his feet, always had ... always had to.

"We don't get many new faces here in K-Town," Sonny said with a small laugh.

Harlan got the distinct feeling Sonny was enjoying the fact that there was nowhere left for him to sit.

"Most folks that use the train come from The Village. Retirement spot. Old-timers goin' onto Philly to catch a show, have a lunch or a dinner with the ones who ain't out here yet. Have a meal at one of them fancy clubs I heard about. Or else it's the other way around. Family comin' out here to see the ones who's too rickety to make the trip into Philly themselves anymore. Nobody goes west to Pittsburgh, no point. But I don't guess you have any kin at The Village. Though there's some."

"I'm not one hundred percent white if that's what you're getting at. On the other hand, I'm not one hundred percent Black either. If that helps some?"

"I don't mean no offense."

Harlan gave him a thin smile and a nod. "None taken."

"You with the government? You look like you might be with the government."

Harlan leaned against the station wall, folded his arms across his chest and laughed.

"What makes you think I'm with the government?"

"Just askin'. The government's big on diversity these days."

Harlan let the comment pass.

"What would Doctor Jacobs want with the government?"

"Well, see, that's what I'm wonderin'."

He smiled. "No, I'm not with the government."

Lie number one, and not off the train five minutes, Harlan thought. Not a record by a long shot, but still fairly early on in any scenario, even for Harlan.

"Newspapers?"

"Newspapers?"

"You a newspaperman?"

"Nope. Is something going on in Kindertown that would attract government people? Or reporters from an out-of-town newspaper?" *Might as well find out who knows what,* Harlan thought.

"Naw, pretty sleepy around here lately."

Again, neither spoke for a few minutes, then Sonny broke the silence once more.

"What brings you around then? You're kinda the quiet type."

"I think that's something that's best handled by Doctor Jacobs. Let's just say I'm a friend of a friend who's come out for a visit."

"So you're a Philly kid, that it? You don't have the accent. Nah, no way you're from Philly. That accent always makes me laugh, like they got marbles in their mouths. Back East talk."

Harlan only smiled and shook his head.

"Say, you're not Doc Jacobs's nephew, are you? The one who served in the Marines? Went off to that crapshoot in Afghanistan? You that nephew? The one from Baltimore? Won all those medals? I heard Doc's sister married a Black guy."

"No, but we were in the same unit." *Lie number two.* Harlan liked to keep count of the lies. Until the number got too high, then he dropped it.

"Yeah, they got a funny accent in Baltimore too. He ain't dead, is he? Doc's nephew?"

"No. He's fine. He just wanted me to give something to Doctor Jacobs."

"Yeah? What's that? Something you got in that case there?"

"Well, again, I think I'll let the doctor fill in any details for you. If he chooses."

The two men fell silent once more, and after five minutes Sonny stood and walked back to the train station's door.

"Want to step inside? It's air-conditioned. Had it put in last year."

"No thanks. I'm fine."

"Suit yourself. I don't like the heat, never did. Guess I got that from the missus. But it just keeps comin' after you. There's no hidin' from it anymore. The world's burnin' up. It never seems to stop, only gets worse. That's why I finally put my foot down about gettin' air-conditioning. You don't stand up for yourself, nothin's gonna happen. But a young guy like you? I guess you Afghanistan vets handle it better. Say, you know I never thought about this, but is it hot or cold over there?"

"It can go either way. It's mountainous. North of India. Anything can happen. And anything did."

"Huh. How about that? I somehow thought it was down Egypt way. Say, did you know Egypt is in Africa? Crazy. Them Egyptians calling themselves Africans. They ain't no Africans as far as I can tell. I'll bet you have some thoughts on that. But I hear it's hot there too. Did you see that it's a hundred-and-two in Chicago today?"

Harlan nodded.

"Chicago, that's crazy. I guess we just gotta be happy we ain't in Chicago. I'm just a country boy in the end, but I can see what's happenin'. I don't need a weatherman to tell me this summer's hotter than last summer. My grandson just turned thirty, your age I'd guess, and I've been tryin' to tell him that we're burnin' this damn planet up. Gonna be nothin' left but cinders by the time he gets as old as me. Do you think he hears a word I'm sayin'? Hell, no. Blind as a mouse. I may be old-school, but I can see what's happenin' clear as day. I ain't no damn liberal, but they sometimes make sense. A category-four hurricane in June this year. Explain that to me. There's no way in hell we can air-condition the whole planet."

Sonny didn't wait for Harlan's response, just shook his head and disappeared into the building.

After another five minutes, Harlan heard the rumble of a vehicle pulling up on the far side of the station. The engine shut down, the door creaked as it opened and shut, and in a moment a man in his late fifties, rail thin with salt and pepper disheveled hair, stepped onto the platform. His face had a weariness to it, but his intense blue eyes gave him the appearance of boundless energy.

"Harlan Stone?" he said as he crossed the platform.

"Yes," Harlan answered. He immediately recognized the doctor's raspy voice from the recording he'd been given a few days earlier, but he added an obligatory, "You must be Doctor Jacobs?"

"Indeed."

The two men shook hands.

"Sorry to keep you waiting, but a young woman is expecting twins in a few days, and I wanted to look in on her."

"Sissy Blackburn."

"Yes, do you know her?"

"No, but I've had a little chat with Sonny. No last name offered. He's chattier than one might expect. Did you know Egypt is in Africa?"

"Christ. Did he actually say that?"

Harlan only smiled.

The doctor gritted his teeth. "Jesus, sorry about that. You didn't tell him anything, did you?"

"No. I suspect that would be a bit like handing it over to a *Times* reporter. And since you haven't explained a lot of it, I'm as much in the dark as the next guy."

"Well, Mr. Stone—"

Harlan held up his hand. "It's Harlan, since last names don't account for much here in K-Town."

"I'm fine with Bill, too."

Doctor Jacobs gave him a small smile, but his expression quickly turned more sincere. Harlan read it for what it was.

"Let me ask you this, Bill, if disease—"

Doctor Jacobs stepped closer, stopping Harlan from going any further. He then cocked his head toward the station door and Sonny. "Not here. The walls have ears."

Harlan nodded, retrieved his case and the two men walked around the building to the doctor's Chevrolet. It was perhaps twenty years old with signs of rust around the wheel wells. Harlan tossed his bag into the back seat, dropped into the front opposite Jacobs and said, "I guess I should tell you, I told Sonny that I was a friend of your nephew from Baltimore who's in the Marines and has a mother who married a Black guy."

"How did you know about him?"

"I love to say that I was that much ahead of the game, but for someone who probably fantasizes himself as being tight-lipped, Sonny's a fountain of information. Saying I was a friend of your nephew's seemed like a fairly innocuous cover."

"Good. It is. His name is Nick Ashcroft, if it should come up again, or did you know that too?"

Harlan smiled, shook his head, and lied once more. "No, I didn't know you had a nephew in the Marines. Though I was with the Marine Corps over there. It was a while back. When it first got cooking. But I never met Nick."

"He's a good kid."

"I'm sure he is. Feel like giving me some details on the cow?" Harlan said as he started to roll up the Chevy's window.

"Leave the window down. The air-conditioning is on the fritz. Certainly, not a good day for it to die. And *no* to any details with the windows down. It's a small town. I don't want to take any chances. People have a lot of faith in me, but I feel they also eye me with a great deal of suspicion. Too much education, that's my problem. It's crazy that people are now railing against liberal universities, but still expect to have doctors and nurses. Where do they believe we got our education?"

"That's the curse of mankind, isn't it?"

TWO

Doctor Jacobs's house had been built in 1883 by his great-great-grandfather, a man who arrived from Nova Scotia ten years earlier. He had been a blacksmith with a shop in the small barn behind the house. He'd done well for himself, and educated his sons, one of whom became a veterinarian, as did his sons after him. Bill was the first *people* doctor in the family, though he had started out as a vet, earning a degree at the University of Pennsylvania's veterinary school and interning at the New Bolton Center for Large Animals outside of Philadelphia.

The house was immaculately maintained on the exterior, with white clapboard siding, dark green shutters, and a wide front porch. Jacobs held the screen door for Harlan as they stepped inside. The living room of the old family home had been set up as his office, a small waiting area and a receptionist's desk, which led to an examination room with a reclining medical chair, a small cot with fresh linens, a scale, a computer desk, and an array of cabinets and drawers, all with pull handles and simple locks—pretty much what Harlan had expected to see. What he hadn't expected to see was what was through the next door, a fully outfitted laboratory, looking nearly as sophisticated as anything one might find at the CDC in Atlanta.

Harlan couldn't help but comment. "Pretty nice set-up you have here."

"I like to get my answers quickly. It can sometimes take the lab at General over in Lancaster a few days to supply test results. It's a good hospital but they don't always put priority on outside lab work from country doctors."

"Fair enough, but in our litigious society, I don't think I'd take that risk. Offering advice, or home-grown lab results, without a strong paper trail, or confirmation from a professional lab could be problematic, I'd think."

"And you call yourself a Marine."

"Oh, I've been known to take risks, sure, but not when it comes to encountering lawyers. I don't like the odds."

Jacobs laughed. "I know I'm playing with fire, but I also know all my patients like they're family. People trust people around here. An anomaly for politicos in DC I'm sure…" He waited for a reaction from Harlan, but none came. "Sit down, why don't you? You want a coffee or something?"

"If it's not too much trouble."

"I have a part-time nurse-receptionist who usually makes me a pot every day, but I gave her today off so we could meet in private. Apologies ahead of time for my home brew. It doesn't always pass the acid test."

"I've been treated to Amtrak coffee for a few hours. Not much could be worse."

Beyond the laboratory was a nice country kitchen, but one lacking a woman's touch. While Jacobs fiddled with the coffee maker Harlan sat at the small zinc-topped breakfast table.

"You know, Harlan, before we get into the nitty-gritty, I'm a bit confused. I mean, why the hell are you here?"

"You called the CDC."

"All I did was leave a simple voicemail and all of a sudden they send an agent out to meet me?"

"I'm hardly an agent." *What's that? Lie number eight?*

"What department are you with?"

"Poison Control." *Nine.*

"And you came all the way from Atlanta just because some country saw-bones left a voice mail?"

"I work out of the DC office. We're closer. Don't tell me that you're upset your government is taking your issue seriously?"

"Too seriously. That's what bothers me. Seriously enough to make me a bit suspicious. I'm guessing something bigger than me is going on. Not everyone out here is a hick. I find it odd that I'd be paid a visit. And so quickly."

Harlan only shrugged.

"Sorry about the DC crack."

"I'm not a politico. No offense taken."

"I figured that much. They're hardly subtle. Okay, let's go back. I'm trying to remember what I said that solicited such a personal and quick response." He poured two mugs of coffee. "Sugar? Cream?"

"Black's good."

He handed Harlan the larger mug. "Okay. Disease, fear of contagious disease, if that's what we have here, can panic people. Especially in a spot like K-town. Insufficient information in the wrong hands is like lighting a fuse to a powder keg, hard to stamp it out before it explodes. The damn Covid-19 thing sent the entire place into hibernation for three years."

Harlan gave him a small nod. "Right, I would have suspected vaccines weren't too popular in this neck of the woods." It wasn't a question.

"No, they're not. Once people started to drop with Covid this became a ghost town. That's how most folks dealt with it, just hunker down at home and don't see anyone. They're mostly farmers; they grow their own food. They can be self-sufficient and live off the grid if need be. But even the farm markets took a big hit. Nobody went out."

"I guess what we're looking at now is a bit different—cattle, not people. Still, until it's been pinpointed, and corrected, I'm with you, the less said the better."

"I've never seen anything that resembles it. That's why I made the call. And that's what concerns me, because I've pretty much seen it all."

Harlan looked down the hallway, past the refrigerator. "Again, I'll need more to go on. We picked up a real sense of urgency in your message, but the CDC can be a bit methodical at times, especially if the issue is isolated." *One more lie. No way in hell this issue was isolated.*

Despite the lies that had already taken place on Harlan's part, he could see that the doctor was an inherently honest individual, a man who was more concerned with the welfare of his fellow human beings than anything. It made Harlan want to be more truthful with him, but that wasn't why he'd made the trip to Pennsylvania.

"All I said in that CDC call was that one of the farmers had a bull that he suspected had gone sterile, and he wanted me to run some tests, which I did, and they showed no abnormalities whatsoever. Other than the fact that the farmer was right—the animal was not going to reproduce. I wanted to know if the CDC had received any similar reports from Elsewhere, people with which I could compare notes. That's just standard protocol. I've done it in the past, and not received a visit."

"That's pretty much how I remember it. That and the fact that you contacted Senator Samuelson. You had to know that was bound to get someone's immediate attention."

Jacobs smiled. "Stewart and I went to high school together. We're still close."

"Nice to have friends in high places. And I'm sure you're aware that Senator Samuelson has friends in even higher places. Like the Oval Office?"

"Still and all. That solicits a visit from an agent—a CDC representative? All I wanted was to have my call returned by someone in the know."

"We were just curious as to why this farmer with a bum bull would go to a GP and not a veterinarian?"

"I have serious veterinary credentials. Besides, many of these Mennonites think more of their breeding stock than they do of their wives and children." He paused for a second. "Wait, hold on a minute, is this about some 'practicing without a veterinary license' crap?"

Harlan laughed. "Not my department."

This time Jacobs didn't smile. "Well, what is your department? And Poison Control has a disingenuous ring to it. If you don't mind my saying so."

"You make a fairly good cup of coffee, Doc, anybody ever tell you that?"

"Jesus, you're worse than the IRS. Level with me. What's going on?"

Harlan took another slow sip from his coffee. "You tell me. You ran the tests. You phoned us. And the senator. Clearly whatever you discovered sent up a red flag or you wouldn't have called. You wanted some action, quick action. And you got it. Otherwise, you would have said, 'tough luck,' to the farmer and forgot all about it. It's not the first time in the world a cow has gone sterile."

"Bull." Jacobs crossed the kitchen and sat at the table opposite Harlan.

"Okay, this bull belongs to a man I've known for years. He's seventeen miles out of town. He's thirty-eight years old, has a wife and five kids, two hundred and seventy-five acres, and this bull has been producing offspring for six solid years. In the past three months, the beast has been shooting blanks, so the farmer came to me. You need to understand that these animals can be worth thousands of dollars, but if they go sterile, you're eating cheap rump steak for dinner. He didn't go to a vet because I'm his family doctor, he trusts me, he knows I worked at New Bolton, he knows I can do all the testing in-house, and knows I won't blab to the world that he's having reproductive issues with his bull."

"He only has one bull?"

"Yes."

"Any other local bulls with issues?"

"Not that I know of."

"So, there's no telling if it's contagious?"

"It's not."

Harlan cocked his head to one side. "You sound pretty sure about that."

"I ran the tests. I know what I'm talking about."

"Does this farmer have a name? I'd like to talk to him."

Jacobs shook his head. "No can do. HIPAA makes all this confidential. I'm pushing those guidelines as it is."

"Jesus, we're not talking about his wife and kids. I just want to talk to him about the damn cow."

"Bull."

"Right, bull ... I can get a warrant if I need to."

Jacobs laughed. "Good Lord, you're serious, aren't you? You'd really do that."

Harlan laughed as well. "I would, but there's no way in hell any judge would issue it, HIPAA and all. I was never that good at bluffing." *Small lie.* "Okay, what about the cows? Could this be an issue relating to the females rather than all the bulls?"

"Bull, singular, he only has one bull. You're thinking in plurals. You're giving yourself away." Jacobs smiled again. "You know, something tells me you already know the answer to that 'female question', and that I'm not the first person to have queried the CDC on this. But just to play your game, no it's not female related. Three of the cows he previously mated with the bull have since been successfully artificially inseminated. The Mennonites aren't keen on doing things artificially, but he's got to feed his family, so he went that route."

"But the cows were artificially inseminated by the same bull?"

"Yes, however, it was sperm from a bank, frozen last year. Nothing fresh would take."

"And no other farmers are having issues?"

"Okay, hold on, let's walk this back one more time." He stood, poured himself a second cup of coffee, and waived the carafe in Harlan's direction.

"I'm good."

Harlan finished his coffee, walked his mug to the sink, and ran some water into it.

"I'm not the enemy here," Jacobs continued. "I want some answers as much as you do. I did a little snooping on my own before I decided to call the CDC. I contacted every veterinarian within fifty miles and asked them if anyone had come to them with a similar problem. Well, guess what? They all told me exactly what I just told you, 'That's confidential information.' Nobody wants this to get out. Nobody wants his neighbors to know his stud's shooting blanks. But for the most part, I must tell you, the vets were very uneasy about being asked. Even over the phone, I could sense their trepidation."

"And you're absolutely positive this isn't contagious?"

Jacobs only nodded.

"What about horses? Anyone breed horses around here? Any problems with male horses?"

"Stallions."

"Whatever."

"I'm a step ahead of you. The only horses bred around here are draft horses or carriage horses. Horses gestate three months longer than cattle, about a year. People breed them in the Spring, so they're foaled in the Spring. The vets I spoke with said that all the horse breeding was on track. Same with hogs and sheep. So, this is definitely a bovine issue. Interesting that the vets would talk so freely about the good news but clam up about the bulls. Yeah, there's some paranoia in the air."

"Could it be something the bull ate or drank? He was poisoned in some way?" Harlan said, thinking out loud more than anything.

"I'd like to say yes, and I'm not totally counting that out, but I doubt it. I've taken blood samples, saliva samples, urine samples, sperm samples, stool samples. Any kind of sample you can think of from this beast, and his cows, and there's absolutely nothing alien in their systems. The sperm appears healthy, on the surface, through the scope, but just isn't doing its job."

Harlan cleared his throat. "I'm not sure what the veterinary term might be, but I assume the bull can still get it up?"

Jacobs laughed. "Yes. He's raring to go. It's more like the sperm seems to have no desire to stick, or even go to where it's supposed to go. It's not acting normally."

"Or something's preventing it from getting to the right place?"

"Then we're back to it being a female issue and I don't buy that."

Harlan paced the kitchen for a moment.

"Feel like driving me back to the train station?"

"Sure. But you got a lot more out of me than I got from you. I called the CDC to get some answers. All I got was questions. What the hell is going on?"

Harlan stuffed his hands into his pockets and leaned against the kitchen counter. "Okay. Do I get doctor-patient confidentiality? Am I covered by HIPAA? It seems like everyone else is."

"You're not a patient of mine."

"Make believe I am. Use your imagination. What I'm going to tell you can't go beyond that refrigerator over there."

"Shoot. I am now bound by HIPAA."

Harlan looked out of the window somehow expecting to see a flock of neighbors peering through the glass, but it was dead quiet, only a lonesome dove sat perched on the telephone wire across the street. The coffee was now leaving an acrid taste in his mouth and his stomach wasn't all that happy either. He sucked in the steaming August air and let it escape slowly. *Damn, it is hot around here,* he thought.

"Okay. Yours is not an isolated incident, and I knew the answer to the horse question, just wanted it confirmed. You got some special consideration because of your credentials and Senator Samuelson, thus, the visit. We've been tracking similar cases across the country for two months. However, the cases have all been limited to small, independent farmers. The big-time ranchers aren't having any problems."

"They're not having problems yet. If what you say is true,

our problems have just begun. Ninety percent of the Big Boys do everything artificially in this day and age. They're using sperm from grade-A bulls that was frozen and placed in banks potentially four or five years ago. Once those stocks go dry the picture's going to change, and real quick. You have my word on that. Ultimately, that's why I called. I knew damn well I wasn't the Lone Ranger out here." Jacobs took another long drink from his mug. "You're not a disease specialist, are you?"

Harlan was silent for a long minute, not sure how much he should give up.

"No, I'm not. I wouldn't know a sperm cell from an eight-ball. And that's about all I can offer. I will keep you posted. If you make any discoveries keep us informed. Via the CDC. But if we don't get some answers soon, and if it does jump to the Big Boys. Sell your McDonald's stock."

The two men drove back to the train station in near silence. As Harlan stepped from Doctor Jacobs's car he casually asked, "By the way, when are Sissy Blackburn's twins due?"

"Any day now."

"Give her my best, if that means anything?"

Jacobs cocked his head to one side as a slightly confused look crossed his face. It took him a moment to respond.

"Will do. Not many new ones on the way this summer. My guess is the young folks are getting worried about the future."

"Maybe they should be."

THREE

As Harlan settled into his seat on the three-ten express to Philadelphia he pulled his cell phone from his pocket and tapped the CNN app. This had become an hourly ritual in the last few months. At some point, this *Mennonite Mishap* was going to make the headlines and the folks in Atlanta wanted to be prepared. Along with the White House. So far, the number of reported cases in the US was limited. And as with Doctor Jacobs's assessment, the CDC had confirmed that whatever was going on, it was in no way contagious, as a result, there was no sense of panic in the air at the major health organizations. But cases were on the rise, and none of the researchers had been able to produce a logical explanation as to why they had appeared, albeit sporadically, throughout the globe.

The railcar was just as empty as it had been when he'd transferred onto it in Philadelphia on his way out to Kindertown. He found himself wondering how much longer it would be before this mode of transportation dried up completely. Dollars were spent widening the country's Turnpikes, not improving rail service. Compared to Europe, the US was an embarrassment. Someone needed to turn that around, and quickly, but Harlan knew full well it wasn't going to be Harlan Stone.

"Excuse me, but is the empty seat next to you taken?"

He glanced up from his cell phone and saw a strikingly good-looking woman with jet-black hair and haunting, black-as-coal eyes. His impulse was to stand, which he did, causing him to knock his head into the overhead luggage rack.

"Shit. Sorry. Ah, no, no one's sitting there."

He scanned the totally empty car.

"I'm happy to have you sit here with me, believe me, but don't you want to stretch out a little? Have some breathing room? Privacy? Not sit alongside the only other person on the train?"

"Trains scare me."

"Trains scare you? How can trains scare you? You know what should scare you? Cars. Cars should scare you."

"Trains move too fast. I don't like to ride alone. I'm not finding control. I had some trauma when I was a child. But if you want to be left lonely..."

"Not at all. Make yourself comfortable. I don't do lonely very well. Out of curiosity, why are you traveling by train if they scare you?"

"I don't conform to lonely well either. I wanted to be here with someone else. To be with me. To help me to not be scared, and I saw you."

Harlan scanned the empty car.

"I'd say you're lucky that even I'm on the train. It's kind of a slow day for Amtrak."

"It's a fast day. Time moves quickly."

"Okay. But again, if trains scare you, why not fly? Take a bus?"

"I don't know how to take a bus. I'm unfamiliar with buses. I don't know if buses scare me or not. They don't travel on rails."

"You're right about that, they don't. Well, you're not missing much. Where'd you go to school?"

"Why?"

"Oh, I don't know. School? School buses? You didn't take a bus to school?"

"I walked."

"Okay."

They both sat and she said, "Are you married?"

"No. Wait. What? Am I married?"

"You just seemed uneasy about having an overly attractive, unattached young woman ask to sit next to you on an empty railway car. I assumed you were probably married and feeling guilty because you were drawn to me. I mean in a sex kind of way."

Jesus, that's a lot to process. "No, I'm not married."

"Then you are queer?"

"No. Is this how you start out all your conversations with strange men?"

"You don't seem strange to me. I've seen strange men. I know strange men. I got on in Pittsburgh. There are strange men in Pittsburgh. A lot of them. Too many of them. The train was empty. There are no strange people on this train. The strange people are all still in Pittsburgh."

"It still is. Empty, that is."

Harlan laughed to himself, oddly thinking of a Willy Nelson song his father loved to sing when they rode on trains together—*Railroad Lady*. It continued to float through his head as he glanced down at her long, mostly exposed, and crossed legs. She was one of the more beautiful women he'd ever seen.

"Do you live in Philly?" he asked.

"Do you?"

"No."

"Then, neither do I live in Philly. Where's Philly?"

"Philadelphia. That's where this train is going."

"Oh, that's the same thing? Philadelphia and Philly?"
"Do I really need to answer that?"
"Are you getting off there?"
"Just changing trains."
"Then you don't need to answer that. Where do you live?"
"Silver Spring, Maryland. That's why I'm changing trains when we get to Philly."
"Wow, I don't live far from Silver Spring. I don't think there's any silver there."
"Probably not."
"Or springs."
"Nope."
"Just the Fleetwood Mac song. I researched that. I've never heard the song."

What the hell is happening here?

"So, logically, you'd be changing trains in Philadelphia too." Only half a question.

"Yes, in Philly?"

"Philly... Philadelphia. Same place," he said, shaking his head.

"Yes, I'm changing there. In Philly. What are you doing for dinner? My treat."

"Wait, hold on, this is a little too bizarre for me. Are you coming on to me?"

He shifted in his seat so that he was facing her. She was stunning to the point of taking his breath away. She smiled but said nothing.

"Listen, I don't want to sound rude, but I... well, okay, yes, I am drawn to you, which is kind of crazy that you should know that. But I need to write up a report before we get to DC, and then deliver it to my boss. In person. There's no way I'm finished up before ten or eleven tonight, so I'm afraid dinner's out. As tempting as that sounds. To me, anyway."

But Harlan had no desire to blow off a potentially good thing, and he followed it with, "I'm very happy you joined me. I certainly don't want to take responsibility for this train scaring you in any way, or making you go through any unnecessary flashbacks of childhood trauma."

She took his hand. "Thanks for holding my hand."

"Literally?" He pulled his hand free. "You know, I can't quite place your accent. I'm usually pretty good with accents. I think I'm hearing a bit of Scotland."

"My dad was from there. The country of Scotland. Not the United States of America."

"What part of the country of Scotland?"

"He never told me. We weren't very close. He died in a train accident."

"Huh."

Harlan pulled his laptop from his bag, lowered the tray table, placed the computer on it, and hit the power button.

"Well, again, I need to get some work done. Do you have anything to read?"

"No."

He reached into his case and offered her the current issue of *Time Magazine*.

"Nothing earthshattering in there. No news is good news, but it's all I have. Did your father ever mention to you that Scotland isn't really a country?"

"Once or twice. I don't think it makes any difference. Do you?"

"I suppose it does to the Scots."

"Philly's not a country either. Did you notice how hot it was on the outside of the train?"

"I did."

"We always wondered if the USA people knew how hot it was becoming. Or if they planned on doing anything about it?"

"We?"

"My father from Scotland and me."

After his computer came to life she glanced at the screen and said, "What's MPS?"

He shook his head again. "Do you have a name?"

"Angelica. I like Angelica. It's a good name. It starts with an 'A,' which is a good place to start. It's the first letter in the alphabet."

"Right you are. Nice to meet you, Angelica. My name is Harlan."

She grabbed his hand once again and shook it. "I liked meeting you, too."

"Yeah, well, you see, Angelica, this work I'm doing is somewhat confidential. This is why I offered you the magazine. So that you would have something to keep you occupied, rather than looking over my shoulder at my computer screen."

"Are you with the government?"

He laughed. "Yeah, well, that's the question of the day, isn't it? You're not a friend of Sonny's, are you?"

"Sonny?"

"Never mind. It was a bit of a joke."

"Oh, you mean the man at the station back there. No, we're not friends."

Harlan again faced her. "Hold on, if you got on in Pittsburgh how do you know his name was Sonny."

"I guessed. I saw him standing on the platform. Who else could you be talking about? He looks like a Sonny, don't you think? He was standing in the sun for a bit, so Sonny makes sense for him to choose that Sonny name. It must remind him of the heat."

"I guess you could say that. I'm not so sure I could." *It would require too much butchering of the English language*, he thought but didn't voice it.

"Or Sonny could be the man you drove off with? Is that who Sonny is?"

"I drove off with that man before this train got in from Pittsburgh."

She looked straight ahead for a full minute before responding. "See, this is why trains scare me."

Harlan lowered his head and turned his focus to his computer screen. "Okay, sure. I've got to get to work here, if you'll excuse me?"

"You didn't answer my question. Are you with the government?"

Without taking his focus away from his computer, he improvised another lie. "MPS stands for Motion Picture Scouts. My company looks for spots to shoot movies. I was *scouting* locations for a new film. It's called *Railroad Lady*." He had lost track of what number lie that was.

"Huh." After a long silence she added, "I've never seen a movie. Not a USA movie. Do USA people make a lot of railroad movies?"

"Not that you'd notice. Look, maybe we can get together this weekend and go to a movie. It would be an adventure. For both of us."

"That would be nice, but not a train movie. I've never had sex with an American either. That could be an adventure too."

And that was the last thing she said until their train stopped at Union Station in Washington, DC. They remained together until they got to the waiting room.

Harlan extended his hand to her. "I'd offer to share a Lyft or Uber with you, but I'm headed for the office and not my loft. Can you get home okay?"

"I'll be fine. The scary part is over."

"Would you like to give me your phone number?"

"I lost my cell phone in Pittsburgh. I'm going to get a new one with a new number. Too many creeps were calling me. I do that a lot, lose cell phones. And attract creeps. I have many numbers. Why don't you give me your number and I'll call you when I get a new number."

Harlan pulled an old Starbucks receipt from his jacket, wrote his name and cell number on it, and gave it to her.

"No business card?" she asked.

"No business card. I only give business cards to movie people."

"Huh."

She stared at the slip of paper for a second, then turned, walked through the station, and tossed the paper into a trash receptacle as she passed. Harlan's eyes followed her the entire way, along with every other man in the station. She walked like an angel. It was the first he'd noticed that she carried no purse or luggage of any kind; she was completely empty-handed.

FOUR

The Turk tossed Harlan's freshly printed report back onto his oak desk and grumbled a predictable Turk grumble.

"I read it on the computer. Well, that was a friggin' bust. Waste of paper. There's nothing there that we didn't know already. Sorry I pissed away your time, my time. There's nothing there to convince the White House this is not just another CDC issue, which, of course, is absolute bullshit."

He shouted bullshit loud enough to be heard by the entire eastern end of the complex.

"I'm sorry I even sent it over to them. It only confirms their suspicions. We need to dig deeper into this, with or without White House approval. Something's cooking, and we're gonna be caught with our pants down."

Norcross walked over to the far corner of the office where he had mounted a speedbag on the wall. The unit was totally foreign to the surroundings, and the painting of the Battle of Trafalgar that hung behind the dangling leather bag didn't soften the look one iota. He swatted at the bag for ten seconds and watched as it slowly came to a standstill in front of the painting. He seemed displeased with where the bag ultimately rested, and he adjusted it so that the *Everlast* logo was front-and-center, and he kissed it.

Harlan cleared his throat. "I found nothing solid with Doctor Jacobs, nothing I could grab onto. Other than he doesn't think it's a disease, and it's not contagious. Nice part of the country, though."

These debriefings with Norcross at Peyton Place, their sobriquet for the MPS office at FDA headquarters, often proved to be brutal as far as Harlan was concerned. The Turk always demanded more. And the speedbag was annoying as hell.

"This thing's not contagious, yet it's shown its face in almost every state in the country. I want to know what's behind it as much as you do, Boss—identify the enemy and go after the bastards, but there's nothing tangible out there. Who *is* our enemy? That jackass Polushin? God only knows what the Mad Russian will do next, but he hasn't played any cards. He's too busy pissing all over Ukraine and kissing North Korea's butt."

Yuri Polushin was the current president of the Russian Federation. He had lorded it over the Russian people for over twenty years. His power had become absolute, with control of the Kremlin, the courts, and the FSB. He was universally despised by the entire international community and a good portion of his own country.

"Yuri's off his rocker," Norcross snorted, "but there's a chance this issue has hit his homeland as well. Who the hell would know? Nothing comes out of that dump anymore. The CIA is worthless."

They were quiet for a moment, but Harlan opted to keep pushing.

"Or, in the end, it could just be an odd outbreak of some sort. Or maybe some other asinine rogue dictator. Or a loony-tune separatist mob in Idaho or Texas for that matter."

"Right. And that's if there is even an it, or a someone. I can hear the White House now, the damn cows ate some bad mushrooms, and that'll be the end of it."

"Bulls. Senator Samuelson isn't going to let this go away that easily. He's in Doctor Jacob's camp."

"Bulls, cows, I don't give a shit, if anyone over at Sixteen-hundred recognizes the difference, I'd be surprised. Someone would need to pull out a diagram and show them what balls are. The president isn't willing to confront the Kremlin or Polushin. Yuri made him look like a chump the last time they went head-to-head."

Harlan didn't respond. Norcross was one of those guys who had risen in MPS like a bulldog. Starting out as an agent and tearing apart anything that got in his way. Like all MPS agents, he spoke fluent Chinese and Russian, along with one other language. Though the Turk didn't stop at one, he also spoke Japanese, Korean, and six African dialects. The motive for MPS knowledge in Russian and Chinese? It allowed the agents to pose as Secret Service Agents, secretaries, janitors, bartenders, busboys, reporters, whatever. This allowed them to eavesdrop on high-level conversation while appearing to be only a low-level, one-language, employee.

Norcross had made his share of enemies amongst the few congresspeople who knew anything about MPS, but he got things done. He came out on top every time. No one in the White House, no matter which administration, nor any member of Congress, had the nerve or audacity to attempt to replace him, or cross him. He was straight out of Kipling; he could walk with kings but never lose the common touch. And this was a quality MPS looked for in all their personnel once Norcross took over.

"I'm certain a very big player is behind this," Harlan said as he retrieved his report. "I believed Doctor Jacobs when he debunked the contagious disease angle. But there's been no traffic dealing with cattle issues coming out of Russia, China, The Saudis—the usual suspects." Harlan's one backup language was Najdi Arabic.

"Then why haven't they gone after the Big Boys, the commercial ranchers?"

"I don't know. Some of these filthy-ass Russians and Saudis have investments tied up with the commercial ranchers in Argentina, India. and Brazil. Maybe it's another bi-annual yank the US's chain operation. Or maybe it's a move to drive up the market? Some hedge fund weasel is trying to make a killing?"

The Turk rubbed at his temples as he tapped a pencil on his desk for a full minute. Eventually, he broke the pencil in half and tossed it across the room. "But why go after the little guy? What's to gain? The White House doesn't give a shit about the little guy. And they don't supply enough beef to affect the market. You're just talking a handful of votes. Which he doesn't fetch anyway."

The two were quiet for another long moment.

Norcross pulled a second pencil from his desk and began tapping it. In a slow month he'd generally go through a full box of pencils. Harlan figured the *Mennonite Mishap* might bump that to a box a week. He never did understand why the Turk bothered to sharpen the damn things. He never used them for anything but aggression release.

"Yeah, see, that's why POTUS says this one's for the CDC and the disease geeks. Samuelson can push the Old Man all he wants, but as far as he's concerned there's no evil rogue nation out there. There is no bad guy for him to go to press with.

Nothing to bump up his approval ratings. Suck in the public. Woo the voters."

"Not yet."

Harlan stood, walked to the bookshelf, turned, picked up the broken pencil, and sat on the counter. He was tempted to go after the speedbag just so Norcross could see what a pain in the ass it was.

"I still think there's someone. This had to come from somewhere, and I don't think Mother Nature's behind it. What I don't get is how they were able to drop it into every corner of the country. Possibly every corner of the globe, so quickly and uniformly. The White House has to see that as an oddity. As a worldwide attack of some kind?"

"Christ, the Old Man's like talking to a brick wall sometimes, especially when he goes off on one of his shaggy dog stories. He only brought us in because of the senator. But you're right, I smell a rat. A big—goddam—rat." He was beginning to raise his voice. Never a good sign.

"First problem, we're talking about cows. The White House staffers can't see beyond that. Cows don't own cruise missiles, they don't invade other nations, they don't bomb the piss out of civilians, or torture POWs. Where's the threat? Where are the headlines? POTUS loses a few votes in Montana, who gives a crap. He didn't take Montana last election anyway. Christ, he'll never take Montana. The CDC will find an answer. If it takes them a year? So what if we lose a few cows in the process. There's a disease they haven't identified, and it is contagious. They just haven't figured out how it works yet. Or how it's traveled so far, so fast. It's the CDC's ballgame from now on. They need to come up with the answers. Case closed. As much as it pisses me off, that's the current White House position."

"They actually said that? Case closed? MPS is off of it?"

"Yes. Your 'I found nothing' report is just what they've been looking for. But screw 'em. I'm going to figure this shit out if it costs me my life." Norcross slammed his palm on his desk. "Ticks?"

"Ticks?"

"Maybe the cows were bit by ticks."

"Bulls. Jacobs didn't go there, however being a veterinarian I'm sure he considered it. I'll double-check with him." Harlan stood silent for a long minute, not sure how to handle this next bit of business. "Ahh … There is something else."

He took too long of a pause and Norcross picked up on it.

"What? What's that brain of yours chewing on?"

Harlan considered the best way to phrase what he was about to say, and then whether to even say it at all. In the end, he decided Norcross needed to be in the know. The Turk also had an uncanny way of reading Harlan's mind.

"I was tagged on the train ride back from Kindertown."

The Turk broke the second pencil and tossed it. "You were tagged? You were friggin' tagged? Why the hell isn't that in your report?"

"Because I can't prove she was an operative, but I'm almost certain she was. I've had women come on to me, but not like she did. She was clumsy. I don't think she'd played the game before."

He spent the next ten minutes explaining the oddities of his train ride with Angelica and why he didn't put it in writing. "It made sense to leave it out."

"Was she a looker?"

Harlan laughed to himself. The Turk missed life on the street and some of the fringe benefits that came with it. "She was absolutely stunning."

"American? Foreign?"

"Definitely not American, but I couldn't place the accent. And her speech pattern was loopy, to say the least. There's no way English was her first language."

"Guesses?"

"If I had to guess I'd say Saudi or Argentine. She did have that look, and she wasn't good enough to be a Russian or Israeli spook."

"Well, given the cow angle, Brazil would make sense, but the Saudis are generally up to some sleazy shit. It's always something with those bastards. Golf. Jesus, imagine putting all that cash out there just to corner the friggin' golf market? But either one of those countries may be thinking of a way to lower the competition, beef-wise. Manipulate the market. Eliminate some of the players. Maybe this is just some commercial shenanigans, and not the end of the world." Norcross seemed to think this possibility over for a minute. "No, I'm going up top with this. We're going to need some channels opened. I'd just love to hang some Saudi bastards by the balls after they chopped up Khashoggi."

Harlan couldn't help but laugh at him; the Turk could be so damn predictable at times. "So, it's no longer 'case closed?' That didn't last long."

"The playing field just changed. I'll make some calls." Norcross stood and walked to the window. He looked down at the steaming asphalt parking lot jammed with government cars and their sagging tires.

"If you've been tagged this early in the game it means someone knew who you were. And knew why you were going out to Hicksville to yack with a country doctor about cows."

"Bulls. Yep."

"Bulls. And it's a big enough undertaking to put an operative on your ass. Which means it ain't no damn disease unless it's man-made; there's a force behind it. And I'll bet good money they have someone on the inside."

"Definitely a possibility. But if that's the case, it's at the White House, or Senator Samuelson's office, or within the CDC. Everyone at MPS is clean."

"This bullshit is far from closed. Do you think this babe will try to make additional contact with you?"

"How could she resist?"

FIVE

At ten the next morning Harlan strolled across the already scorching, melting FDA parking lot. Heat vapors rising into the humid air created small mirages. He weaved in and out of the cars as he headed to Peyton Place and the Turk's office. The short walk already had him sweating. As he climbed the steps of the building his cell phone chimed. 'Probable Scam' was displayed on the screen. He stopped and tapped the green icon.

"Stone, here."

"Hi. It's me talking."

"Angelica?"

"Can we get ourselves together?"

"Sure. Sounds great."

He scanned the area half expecting her to be standing out on the asphalt behind one of the cars.

"Dinner?" she said.

"Dinner. Sure. I can pick you up. Give me your address."

"Let's meet at Lenny's Grill. Do you know where it is?"

"Yes. Uh, yes, I do." He waited for something additional from her, but nothing more came. He added, "How's eight o'clock work for you?"

"I was going to make the suggestion of eight at night in the p.m. See you there then. Bye."

And she was off the line. He tapped 'Recent Calls.' Angelica's number appeared nowhere. He walked back down the steps and trotted off to the far side of the parking lot half expecting to see her on the other side of the security fencing. She was nowhere, but he couldn't get past the feeling that she was somehow lurking in the area watching his movements. He glanced down the rows of cars. Nothing. He dropped his phone back into his pocket, strolled back to Peyton Place, climbed one flight of interior stairs, and knocked on Norcross's door.

"Sit," Norcross said as Harlan entered the office. The blinds were drawn to keep out the blaring sun from the east, but he suspected the Turk was being overly cautious for some reason. "MPS is back on it. I've drawn up a list—"

"She tagged me again. Just now. As I was walking into the building."

"She's outside? Now?"

"No, on my cell phone."

Norcross tossed his list onto the desk, walked to the window, and raised the shades. The brightness of the sun stung his eyes. He winced and turned back to Harlan.

"My list can wait. What have you got on her?"

"Nothing. That's it, just her name, Angelica. That's all I have, her first name."

"Address? Cell number?"

"Nothing."

"You checked 'Recent Calls?'"

"I checked. Nothing. It's evaporated. She's evaporated. It didn't even read 'Caller-ID Blocked.' But I'm meeting her tonight for dinner at Lenny's Grill."

Norcross groaned. "Jesus Christ, don't you ever get tired of that dump?"

"I didn't pick it, she did."

The Turk took a moment to let this tidbit sink in.

"Hold on a second, you eat at that dive, what? Two, three, four times a week? And with a thousand decent restaurants around DC to pick from, she just happens to choose Lenny's?"

Harlan shrugged. "Their fries are good."

"Sit," the Turk repeated in a tone that mimicked the reprimanding of a poorly behaved dog. Harlan obediently sat while Norcross swatted at the speedbag. When it came to rest, he again kissed it.

"At this point, I'm more concerned about the fact that we have a bad actor in-house than I am about the damn cattle. Someone's talking to your Angelica. She's the key, and that's what this list is all about, as far as I'm concerned. Screw the cows."

"Bulls." Harlan picked up the list from the Turk's desk and read it through. "I don't know any of these people. Who are they?"

"The first bull cases were reported less than two months ago. That's a list of all the new employees who may have gotten a whiff of what we've been looking into; no one here at MPS, like you said, they're all clean, but people at the White House and the senator's office. The staffers. The new faces. Someone in DC is working with these bastards. We need to grab whoever it is and squeeze like hell."

Harlan shook his head. "There's nothing that says it couldn't be an operative who'd been planted inside years ago, especially if it's Polushin and the Russians. Or they, whoever they might be, got to someone who's been around for a while. People get got to all the time."

"I know all that, but this is where we start. With those twenty people. Your Angelica appeared out of nowhere. She's new to the game, so I'm banking on the fact that the insider's also a new face. Our whale is out there somewhere. I will get the bastard."

"And you want me to look at all of these people?"

"No, I'll put Walsh on it. He's good at sniffing out bad players. I want you to concentrate on your new-found lover, Angelica."

"We're not exactly lovers."

"Make it happen."

Harlan laughed. "Take one for the team, is that it?"

"Ultimately, she's the shortest route to the top. If we can squeeze her, it saves a shitload of time." Norcross rubbed at his temples. It was getting as annoying as the speedbag and pencils. "Damn. I don't want to wait until tonight; I want to move on this, and now. Can't you meet her for lunch?"

"No contact number, remember?"

Norcross stood, crossed the room, and opened the door.

"Let's go down the hall and see what Max can suck out of your cell phone."

Harlan followed him out of the office and down the hallway. They walked into the communications lab together without knocking. The lab had more TV monitors than the average Best Buy with five separate keyboard terminals. The air was thick and had a metallic smell, as if something was overheating and primed to explode. Max Olsen sat at the middle monitor playing *Mongo-Jet* on one of the consoles. He was twenty-eight, overweight, with long red hair, a thin beard, and thick glasses. Max was a certifiable genius; he knew it and had little or no use for those he considered mentally inferior. And though he heard them enter, he was intent on his video game and didn't bother to look away from the screen.

"Ah, the Turk and his trusty Man Friday pay a visit to the bowels of the Earth. What is it this time? Can't find your car keys?"

Harlan glared at him. "Did anyone ever tell you that 'Man Friday' doesn't always fly with people of color?"

"Ooh, Mr. Sensitive."

The Turk cocked his head toward Harlan, who then approached Max with his cell phone in hand.

"Apology accepted. I got a call on this cell about ten minutes ago, but when I hit 'Recent Calls' nothing came up on the display. Not even, 'Caller-ID Blocked.'"

Max remained focused on his computer game and sighed. He continued to aggressively tap the keys as he spoke. He was in the middle of a World War One, air-to-air, dogfight.

"Hold the logic button down, press twenty-seven, and hit recent. It'll override any possible malware. All your in-and-out traffic for the last twenty-four will pop up. Is that all you wanted? I'm busy."

Harlan followed Max's directions. "Nope. Nothing. The last call recorded was to Lorenzo's Pizza at 2:14 a.m. last night."

Max finally tore his gaze from his computer. "Jesus Christ, Lorenzo's delivers twenty-four-seven?"

"Yep."

"Damn, I-did-not-know-that. They should put it on their flyers and menus. They're missing out on some real sales. All these late nights I've been dealing with friggin' Domino's and eating cold pizza. Here, give me that thing."

Harlan handed him his cell phone. He turned it over a few times. "What's your security code?"

"Zero-six-three-nine-zero."

Max punched in the code, then played with the cell for a few minutes. "Yeah, you're right. Last call showing was to Lorenzo's at 2:14."

"Thank you, I thought I might have been dreaming. Look, it must have registered something because it showed 'Probable Scam' before I answered it."

"Why do you even answer that shit?"

"I'm a curious type."

"Time to consult Lucy."

"Lucy?"

Max pointed to the ceiling. "Satellite. My baby in the sky. Nothing gets past Lucy." After he plugged the cell phone into his computer his fingers raced across the keyboard. Every ten seconds or so he would moan, shake his head, and try something new. Nothing was working.

"Come on Luce. Tell daddy something." His hammering on the keyboard became more frenetic. "You're positive a call came in on this cell phone after the 2:14 a.m. to Lorenzo's? And no other calls?"

"Yes. I waited outside for the pizza. The delivery kid never needed to call when he arrived."

"Lucy's just checked every cell tic, in and out of this entire installation, in the last thirty minutes. You're nowhere on the board. Damn, these FDA people live on Grubhub. Would it hurt them to bring a bag lunch? And our taxes are probably paying for that shit." He handed the cell back to Harlan. "Sorry."

"Explanation?" Norcross growled.

"I don't have one. Never seen it before." Max looked to Harlan. "I'd put it off to human error, but that's how my mind works. No offense but things don't just evaporate off cell phones. Unless someone works at it. Are you sure you didn't delete it? Put it in a file somewhere?"

Harlan only rolled his eyes.

"And you're sure you answered the call and spoke to someone."

"No. I'm making all this shit up just to annoy the hell out of you."

"Okay, okay. Are all your calls recorded?"

"Shit, I didn't think of that."

"Hit the logic button and—"

"I know how to do a play-back." Harlan went through the routine and his conversation with Angelica played back word-for-word.

Norcross looked over his shoulder. "Is it time-stamped?"

"10:21 a.m. Today."

"And her number?"

"Nada."

Max drummed his fingers on the desk. "Okay, the only thing I can think of is she used another type of device, not a cell phone and one that doesn't work on any US cell networks. Something like the walkie-talkie thingies they use at construction sites, you know, like the cops have. We developed a similar, much higher-tech, gizmo back in the eighties. It allowed the user to make untraceable calls into cell networks. The units never became fully operational because they worked on an extremely low frequency and the user needed to be within sixty yards of any cell phone they were trying to tap into—which became a little hairy for the agents working Sneaky-Pete in enemy territory."

"You're saying she was within sixty yards of me? I felt like I was being watched."

"Unless some bad players have developed a unit that has a longer range. But in that case, I'm sure Lucy would have nailed it and plotted a read-out for me. The signal would've been too strong. No, it had to be a short-range device."

"Why the hell didn't she just come up and talk to me in person?"

"She could have been outside the gate and still be within sixty yards. She couldn't get through security without swiping a pass-card."

The Turk began to pace the floor like a caged cat. Max and Harlan stood by silently and watched. After a minute he again put his palms to his temples. "No, we've got a bad player here. She wasn't anywhere near this installation. We're dealing with an adversary who's developed a communications network we've never seen before. And your Lucy's as much in the dark as we are."

Max began to protest but the look on the Turk's face persuaded him to keep his mouth shut.

Norcross turned his attention to Harlan. "You've got to be on your game tonight. We need a boatload of answers." He growled and smacked his hand into the side of a filing cabinet. It left a dent. He was clearly missing his speedbag. "What I can't get, what I can't wrap my head around, is why these bastards, whoever they are, are spending all this effort to neutralize a bunch of damn cows?"

"Bulls."

SIX

Monday nights were generally slow at Lenny's Grill, nevertheless Harlan arrived fifteen minutes early to be certain to grab the one secluded booth, in the back, away from the bar and constantly swinging kitchen door. Lenny's soundtrack, as always, was smooth jazz from the 1950s and '60s, played low, which did a fine job of keeping the atmosphere toned down: no televisions, no sports, no shouting, no idiotic bar games at Lenny's. The high ceilings were still covered in the original stamped tin from the 1920s, and two large fans rotated lazily above the bar. The feel was more like a subdued pub than a trendy DC hangout. If people got too loud, they were asked to hold it down or leave. There was a friendly string of regulars that spoke in civilized voices and several languages. It was a place where people swapped ideas. It wasn't a pick-up bar, almost everyone was attached to someone else, and generally a certain percentage of them were CIA operatives.

There were about twenty other diners, an equal mix of men and women, when Angelica strolled in at 8:00 p.m., on-the-dot, carrying a stylish red leather backpack. All conversation stopped as all eyes followed her. She seemed to float across the room as she moved to Harlan's table. She was dressed entirely in black with a skirt that barely covered what it was designed to cover. He felt as if he were entertaining Miss Universe and he stood as she approached.

"Very punctual. It's nice to see you again."

She dropped her backpack onto the seat on the opposite side and slid into the booth next to him. She then placed her hand on his thigh and kissed his cheek. "Sorry, I just can't seem to get nearer to you."

He made a small coughing sound. "Don't you want to sit on the other side? So we'll be more ... face-to-face?"

"Okay." She slid over and took his hand in hers. "If that's what you are wanting. We can change seating later. You're right, we aren't knowing each other as much as we need to. We can change that later too. We can do what you want, or we can do what I want. Maybe it's the same thing."

Harlan's mind was racing; she was so obvious it was becoming difficult to play dumb. The combination of her beauty and struggle with English made it impossible for him to read her. She was a total enigma. *What was she after? Who was she working with? Did she have anything to do with the cattle issue? Or were her motives driven by some completely different scenario? Something around the bend that he had yet to encounter. Or was she just an alien on the make looking to get a Green Card? A husband? An anchor baby?* He had been very intuitive at getting answers to these questions in the past, but Angelica was in another league.

"You know, Angelica, I'm not used to getting picked up by women. You're moving a little fast for me. I don't even know your last name."

"Jones."

He resisted the temptation to say, *I would have guessed Smith,* and said, "Ahh, now we're getting somewhere. What were you doing in Pittsburgh?"

"I was trying out for the Steelers' cheerleading squad."

Harlan was happy he didn't have a mouthful of beer. He might have choked to death. "How'd it go?"

"Okay, they said they'd be in touch. But I'm thinking they say that to a lot of Females."

"I can't imagine you'd have much competition."

"I had been thinking the same."

Even though she was possibly some sort of enemy operative and had very poor command of the English language, she was gorgeous, and he found her charming in an odd way. There was no denying he was attracted to her, however this required disregarding all the questions that were swirling around in his brain, and he was too much of a professional to disregard anything. The logical approach would be to convince her that she was working for the wrong team and then bring her over to his side, and he was tempted to be up-front about it. That's how the Turk would have handled it, with the delicacy of a backhoe. But he wanted to gain her confidence before he acknowledged he was on to her. *She may just cough up something unintentionally, they always do.*

Mackie, Lenny's round, and eternally jovial waiter, approached with menus and a Guinness for Harlan.

"Can I get you something from the bar, miss?"

"Just water, thank you."

After Mackie departed, Harlan asked her, "What do you do?"

"Do?"

"When you're not auditioning for the Steelers? Where do you work?"

"Oh, you mean to earn money to carry with me? I don't gamble. I have some friends who are very good gamblers, but they cheat. I don't cheat. Males like to cheat, have you ever noticed that?"

He didn't answer. She looked over his right shoulder as if she was checking a television monitor. Her gaze was so intense that Harlan turned his head to see where her black eyes were staring, but nothing was there, just the back wall of the restaurant and an autographed photo of Oscar Peterson.

"I work at Nordstrom. In Bethesda. At the spot where they sell perfume to people looking to buy perfume and smell nice."

He turned back to her. "I guess that's why you smell so nice."

"I do, don't I." It wasn't a question.

"You know, the more I listen to you, you don't really seem to have a Scottish accent at all."

"Oh. Okay. I'll be from Estonia. But my father was living in Scotland, like I said. That's why I tell people it's a Scotland accent. Maybe I shouldn't say that anymore? Maybe I need to say it's a different accent? I don't hear accents. It's all English to me."

"Whatever works." Harlan picked up the menu. "What would you like to eat?"

"I'll have what you're having."

"You don't know what I'm having."

"Yes, I do. You're having fish and chips. I could see the way you looked in the menu. You were staring at the fish and chips. But I'll have it without the fish. I've never had fish and chips. Is it good?"

"Well, without the fish, it's only chips."

Mackie arrived with her water and Harlan ordered two fish and chip dinners. "But hold the fish on one of them."

"Hold the fish?"

"Hold the fish."

"What are chips, anyway?"

"French fries."

"The fries are good here."

"How do you know that?"

"Some people were standing outside by the door when I came in and they said the fries are good here."

Harlan took a taste of his Guinness. "You know, Angelica, it seems like I'm asking you a lot of questions and you haven't asked me anything."

"I know all I need to know about you: your name, your cell number and where you work. I just don't know where you live. But ..." She patted her red leather backpack. "That's why I brought some overnight things. You can teach me all about American sex."

SEVEN

It had been a classic one-night stand. A good one, if Harlan had to rate it. They'd worked up a considerable appetite and ordered a large cheese pizza from Lorenzo's at 2:00 a.m. They devoured it in ten minutes. Though he offered to drive her home, Angelica left Harlan's loft the next morning by way of a Lyft. She never pressed him for information, if that had been what she was after. It was no different than any other woman Harlan had hooked up with. Still, her appearance on Amtrak, and insistence on latching on to him so quickly, made him certain she was after something. And whatever it was, it had something to do with the sterile bulls. It was all too damn coincidental to be someone looking for a Green Card.

On his way to work, Harlan stopped into the Parkway Deli for coffee and something to gnaw on. Any other day he would have ordered a take-out breakfast sandwich and eaten at his desk at Peyton Place, but there was too much churning in his mind, and he wanted to work out a few things before dealing directly with the Turk. So, he sat in a corner booth and ordered eggs, sausage, and toast along with his coffee.

As the waitress placed his breakfast in front of him a short man wearing an ill-fitting suit, new shoes, and a fedora sat at the counter with his back to Harlan. The man ordered coffee but didn't drink any. He never removed his hat, nor turned, but Harlan could sense he was being closely watched through his reflection in the mirror behind the counter. After he paid his check he thought, *might as well out this clown here and now*, and walked up and sat on the stool next to him.

"Excuse me, I'm Harlan Stone. You look familiar. Have we met somewhere?"

The man choked slightly. "No speak English."

His accent was, not so surprisingly, the same as Angelica's.

—

Harlan went directly to Lou Walsh's office at Peyton Place before approaching Norcross. Lou was Harlan's age, balding, with steely gray eyes, and the athletic build of a linebacker. He was writing up his report on the twenty people the Turk had asked him to investigate.

"I was just about to shoot this off to Norcross. I interviewed every one of these jokers yesterday. What a friggin' slog. All these people are beyond clean. Of course they're clean. They're all recent graduates of some US policy institution and had been thoroughly vetted by the FBI before they were offered their jobs. A total waste of time. Now what do you need?"

Harlan took a second to consider how idiotic his request was going to sound.

"You don't have to do this, you can pass it off to research if you want, but I need someone to contact the Pittsburgh Steelers and find out if one Angelica Jones auditioned for their cheerleading squad."

"You have got to be shitting me?"

"I wish I was. Also get someone to contact Nordstrom in Bethesda and find out if she works at their perfume counter. I'll be with Norcross."

As Harlan walked down the hall he braced himself for what was sure to be a salacious debriefing. The Turk was bound to ask for a detailed account of what had transpired over the last twelve hours, particularly the previous night, and any lurid details.

"Well?" Was all Norcross said as Harlan entered. His gaze was glued to his computer monitor as he scanned a series of urgent messages streaming in from Texas.

"I didn't learn too much more from her. A couple of sexual positions. She has quite an imagination."

Harlan was expecting the usual 'tell me more' reaction, but it was as if Norcross hadn't heard him.

"There was a major building collapse in Dallas last night. Ten stories high, no injuries. And I just got finished with a half-hour call from AW-CSA in Argentina. Ditto down there."

"I guess my extraordinary night with a potential Pittsburgh Steeler cheerleader is no longer our top concern. And the fact that she's not the Lone Ranger out there? She has at least one partner."

Norcross didn't even smile. He slid a paper across his desk to Harlan. "Sit."

Harlan sat. "I'm guessing these two events, in Texas and Argentina, are somehow connected to our cattle issue?"

"Bingo."

"What the hell is AW-CSA?"

"Animal Welfare-Central and South America."

"And there's now bull issues south of the border, I take it?"

"Big time."

"And the building collapse in Dallas?"

"The top five floors were occupied by one of the country's largest animal reproductive labs, and the largest bovine sperm bank in the world, Berger Solutions."

"You're not making that up, are you?"

"Berger with an E, not a U. It was founded by Lawrence Berger, still family-owned. Texas money up the ass. The Big Boys have been swept into the game, here and in Argentina. Probably elsewhere. The building collapse in Buenos Aires was the same type of facility."

Norcross glanced at his computer. "The Texas building was only three years old. It did not die of natural causes. NSA and FBI investigators are already on the scene. Senator Samuelson moves quick when he's agitated. There's nothing left of the place, flattened. Berger estimates a thirty-million-dollar loss in property damage and nearly as much lost reproductive units."

"Jesus."

"I'd say we're dealing with some seriously well-organized eco-terrorists. Your bull out in Hicksville was just a proving ground, a test site, see if they could neutralize cattle and leave no evidence. The next step is to get rid of the stockpiles and muck with the Big Boys."

"Why cattle?"

"What's the world's greatest producer of greenhouse gasses?"

"Human beings?"

"Okay, fine, smart-ass. But after that, it's cattle. Methane. Cow farts and belches and festering stacks of steaming manure."

Harlan stood and began to pace, making him resemble a baby Norcross, but he avoided the speedbag. "I'm trying to wrap my head around this. These eco-terrorist people go around chasing down whaling ships and carrying homemade signs and picketing the Capitol, they don't blow up buildings."

"There was no tangible evidence of any explosive usage. No one blew up shit. The FBI's forensics people are still trying to piece that together. They don't have a handle on what brought the place down. Thank Christ nobody was in there."

"These eco-people can't handle an operation of this scope. They'd need to have some serious money behind them. Or a foreign power..."

The pencil in Norcross's hand was clearly living on borrowed time.

"There are four possibilities. One: it's a disease. Two: someone's just playing games with the world in general. Three: a money player is trying to manipulate the price of beef. And four: it's eco-terrorism."

"The CDC has knocked disease off the list. And the likes of *Goldfinger* and *Dr. No* bringing rack and ruin to the world only play out for Ian Fleming and Hollywood."

Norcross snapped the pencil, dropped it into a nearby trash can, and moved over to his speedbag. He swatted at it twice and turned back to Harlan.

"What about that little girl? She's rubbed elbows with every foreign leader under the sun. And she's obsessed with greenhouse gas. She could have formed a coalition. Got all these piss-ant countries to band together and stand up against the big polluters."

"Little girl? What little girl is that?"

"You know, that one from Sweden or Norway or wherever. Greta something."

Harlan laughed. "Greta Thunberg?"

"Yeah, that's the one. She's a vegetarian, isn't she? Probably won't be happy until the whole damn world goes that way."

Harlan shook his head. "I don't think so, Boss. Whoever's doing this is breaking the law big time. I don't see Greta Thunberg doing that. She's probably on board with what's going on, but it's too far-reaching. And in the end, it's out-and-out illegal."

"I want her checked out."

"Okay. Anyway, this is now an international issue. Is Interpol in on it? If so, I'll ask them to bring her in for a few questions. If they don't laugh me out of the room."

"Yes. As of today, Interpol has been pulled in, but they have catching up to do. Jordan Bayless is on it; that's how serious they're taking it. I'll throw the Greta idea his way."

There was a short knock on the door. Norcross shouted, "Yeah," and Lou Walsh stepped in.

"Negative on both the Steelers and Nordstrom. They never heard of her."

Norcross raised his right arm and moved his index finger in circles above his head indicating he expected more details.

"I asked Lou to check on some stuff Angelica fed me last night. I figured it was all BS but wanted to be certain. I'm guessing you want me to go to Dallas?"

"Today. And don't tell this Angelica you're going. I want to see how slick she is. Leave your cell here and check out a new one. Use your back-up name and passport to book the flight to Texas. Nobody knows you left town. And I mean nobody."

"Check. And believe me, Angelica is slick, count on it. I wouldn't be surprised to find her in Texas trying out for the Cowboys' cheerleading squad."

EIGHT

The Berger Solutions Building was, or had been, on Jefferson Boulevard East, not far from the Dallas Zoo. It was now no more than a pile of rubble cordoned off with yellow caution tape, some of it reading *Police Line Do Not Cross*. The news teams were packing up, and FBI forensic experts were sifting through the debris, looking more like large rodents on a trash heap searching for scraps to eat. Dallas was burning up. The temperature had already topped one hundred. The heat wave had been going on for over three weeks. The Texas sun beat down on the team relentlessly but failed to dissuade the agents from their work.

As Harlan approached the devastation, he noticed a group of three men standing off to the side kicking at the debris. He recognized two of them—Tim Arnold, a seasoned FBI agent, and Christian Dodge, the top Interpol rep in the US. The third man looked slightly out of place, wearing a pair of pricy shoes, an ill-fitting suit, and a fedora; not the type of outfit for sifting through a heap of ravaged concrete, glass, and steel on a sweltering day in Texas. He was also more than a foot shorter than the other two, giving him the appearance of an out-of-place, overweight child dressed as a gangster for Halloween. He looked enough like the man Harlan had outed at the Parkway

Deli to make him suspicious from the onset. Arnold, Dodge, and Harlan exchanged handshakes upon meeting and Dodge introduced the round man with the pricy shoes.

"Harlan, this is Moe Jones, he's with Investiture, the insurance company that covered the building for Berger. I didn't know MPS was in on this."

"We've been on it for over two months. The CDC pushed hard on the Administration; the Administration pushed hard on us. You know how it works." Harlan turned his attention to Jones, thinking, *How hard is it for these bastards to come up with a different last name for their operatives?*

A Texas Dust Devil kicked up at that moment and left the four of them choking and covered in powdered concrete. Harlan wiped his nose and mouth clean with the back of his hand and focused on Jones. "Investiture took a bit of a hit on this one, didn't they, Mr. Jones?"

"It would be big hit, yes. If it becomes proven terror. Group knows, maybe? Group may settle other way. Maybe no. Too early."

Same accent as Angelica and the tail at the Parkway Deli. These clowns get around.

Harlan switched his gaze to Arnold. "Is that what we have here, Tim? Terrorism? Norcross has been putting his money on eco-terrorism. He's stuck on cow farts and the release of greenhouse gasses."

"He may well be right. The cattle industry's the target; there was nothing else in the building but small-time law offices, a couple of psychiatrists and a handful medical specialists. And an Asian massage parlor. One-stop shopping, Texas style. Gotta wash the dust off somewhere."

"Right. And you're also convinced it's terrorism, I gather?" Not really a question, Harlan knew it was an act of terror. Why else was every movement he made being tracked by these Estonians?

"Absolutely, but we have no idea what brought this baby down. So far forensics has found no evidence of any type of explosive. No residue whatsoever. People in the neighborhood heard nothing leading up to the collapse, just the rumble of the place coming down." He picked up some of the debris and rolled it through his fingers. "Look at this crap, it's as if the concrete turned to talcum powder, there's not a piece of it larger than a golf ball. It's a damn lucky break nobody was in there at the time. The security guard had just stepped out for a smoke."

Harlan looked at Dodge but kept Mr. Jones in his peripheral vision. "Is Interpol also looking at the collapse in Buenos Aires?" No reaction from Jones. It was as if he hadn't heard Harlan.

"We're on it. Almost the exact same scenario: good-sized building flattened, the main occupant was an insemination operation for cattle, hogs, and sheep. No explosive residue there either, concrete turned to powder. Tough, the building was close to fifty years old with a wooden substructure. Not a piece of wood was charred. It held up just fine. Our agent there said it looked as if the beams had been prepped for recycling, clean as a whistle."

"Any injuries or fatalities?"

"Negative," Dodge answered. "A lucky break or intentional? I'm guessing it's intentional and therefore eco-related. They don't want blood on their hands. All they want is to rid the world of the polluters. Starting with cattle."

"Noble of them. But it seems a pedestrian way to start scrubbing the planet. Did Norcross run his Greta Thunberg theory past you?"

"Jesus, was he serious about that? What was I supposed to say to him? It took all I had not to laugh in his face."

"Just tell him you'll look into it. He'll forget about it soon enough. But on that subject, why cattle? Why not go after the real bad guys? Why not go after the oil, gas, and coal industries? What's your take on this, Jones?"

"I'm only observing places."

"Clearly. I'd think you'd be interested in pinning this on some loony terrorists, you know, save Investiture from a multi-million-dollar payout? Call it an act of God? You never can trust God. He works in strange ways. Ever the scapegoat."

"I report back. We don't communicate with this God."

"Okay. Keep us posted if you do. I'd like to hear God's thoughts on this."

Harlan took the next few minutes to bring the three of them up to date on his trip to Pennsylvania where he'd questioned Doctor Jacobs, leaving out any details that might tip off Jones that he had his number, or any mention of Angelica. He finished with, "I'm guessing if you sniff around Buenos Aires, you'll find that most of the bulls, if not all of them, have been shooting blanks lately. And whoever's putting this together is not a bunch of fly-by-night eco-radicals. It's too far-reaching and sophisticated. There's got to be big money behind it. What do you think, Jones?"

Jones reacted as if he'd been in a deep sleep and had missed everything Harlan said. "Uh, I don't know. My only concern is getting claim settled. One way or another. And something's happening here."

"But you don't know what it is, do you, Mr. Jones? Or do you? You don't have a sister named Angelica, do you? Lives in the DC area?"

Moe seemed to freeze at the mention of Angelica's name. He stared intently at the pile of rubble as though he was transfixed by a horrific newscast. His look was so focused the others turned to see what had grabbed his attention. There was nothing there but crushed concrete.

"Angelica?" he stuttered.

"Angelica Jones. Are you related?"

"I don't know any person … Angelica."

"Skip it. There's no family resemblance."

Harlan realized he needed to get rid of Jones if anything constructive was going to come out of his trip to Dallas. "I'm not familiar with Investiture Insurance. Where are you out of?"

Jones appeared to be unsure of what Harlan was asking. "Is there a place to pee around here?"

"On the other side of the debris," Arnold pointed. "They've set up some porta-potties over there."

"Sorry, I have to go."

Jones trotted off and disappeared behind the pile of concrete. After he was gone Harlan looked at Dodge and Arnold. "You know he's dirty as hell, don't you?"

Dodge nodded. "Yeah. He showed up about twenty minutes before you got here. I'll get in touch with Berger and Investiture, see what's up with him."

"Save it. We don't want them running scared. Or going public."

Harlan then filled in the other two on Angelica, her accent and poor grasp of English.

"I can't figure out who these clowns are or who they're reporting to. They're dumber than dirt, and at the same time elusive as hell. But they're in this up to their necks, I know that much. Do you have anyone on the other side who can detain Jones?"

"Yeah, I've got an agent over by the crappers," Arnold said as he pulled out his cell phone. "I'll have her grab him before he wanders off."

As Arnold made his call, Harlan picked up a piece of concrete. He squeezed it between his fingers, and with no pressure at all it turned to powder and fell through his fingers.

Arnold dropped his cell phone back into his pocket. "Jones never showed."

"No surprise there, really. This Angelica seems to have a way of showing up unexpectedly. Whoever's set this up is way ahead of us." Harlan then looked at Dodge. "Is this restricted to the US and Argentina? Or is there an even bigger picture?"

"Interpol was only brought into it today. We've alerted our NCB offices in the countries whose economies rely heavily on beef production. If this is an organized attack, it's interesting that they've gone after Argentina and the US and left Brazil and India alone. Brazil pumps out a boatload of T-bone and India exports the most. Why haven't they been targeted?"

"Do we know they haven't?"

Dodge's cell phone chimed, and he tapped the green icon.

"Dodge … You're certain of that? Got it, keep me posted." He then returned the cell phone to his jacket and shook his head.

"India?"

"Brazil."

NINE

Harlan's flight out of Dallas/Fort Worth to Dulles International Airport was diverted to Kansas City somewhere over the Appalachian Mountains. Severe thunderstorms, hailstones the size of golf balls, and an EF3 tornado watch had shut down the DC airport indefinitely. He now found himself sitting in an airport sports bar in Kansas City that was outfitted with more Chiefs swag than Andy Reid's basement. There were six TV monitors all tuned in to sports channels. Next potential flight to DC was three hours off. Harlan ordered a Guinness, which brought on a hardy laugh from the bartender.

"No Guinness?"
"No Guinness."
"What have you got?"
"Coors Light or Bud Light."
"Vodka?"
"Smirnoff okay?"
"Do I have a choice?"
"Not really."
"Make it a double."

Sitting next to Harlan at the bar was a large balding man with a graying beard. He seemed to find the entire exchange too funny and laughed out loud. He then offered his hand to Harlan. "Tim Reynolds. You're with MPS, aren't you?"

Harlan shook Reynolds' hand but was a bit unsure how to respond. He simply said, "Harlan Stone."

"Nice to meet you. I'm with the FDA. I walk by your *Logistics* door two or three times a week. I've seen you go in and out. I was heading back to DC on the same diverted Delta flight. The weather seems to be rockin' and rollin' in DC. A tornado watch, that's a little crazy. We've got a few hours wait. I'd hold back on the double vodkas if I were you."

Harlan laughed. "One'll do me. Now that you mention it, you do look familiar. We must have passed a few times in the parking lot or something. What brings you to Dallas?"

"Same thing as everyone. Damage assessment."

Reynolds pulled his government ID and security card from his wallet and placed it on the bar in front of Harlan. "Feel like talking shop? I hold both Top Secret and Q Clearances. I think you guys could do with some help. You need to know what you're up against, and understand the potential public reaction. We're headed for a friggin' train wreck."

Harlan picked up his vodka and nodded to a small, secluded table in the corner of the bar. "Let's get out of earshot." And after they sat down, "The FDA knows what's going on?"

"We may share the campus and keep a low profile, but we're not asleep. We do tune into the news every now and then. Three worldwide facilities that are in the same agricultural business get hit with a terror attack, and we sit up and take notice. Some of us even have a good idea of what goes on behind your barricaded *Logistics* door. Look, I know MPS reports directly to the president and only the president. I hold that authority with the Commissioner of the FDA, and I'm in direct communication with the go-to persons at the NIH and CDC. I know they're shitting bricks. Everyone is. In three days, it'll be public knowledge and the whole world will be shitting bricks."

Harlan took a small sip of his drink. "Okay, worst case scenario. Every bull in the world is shooting blanks. What happens?"

"Is that where we're at? Every bull in the world?"

"Reports are flying in from everywhere. As you say, the CDC is shitting bricks. It just may well be the case."

"I gathered, but it's interesting to hear it from other corners. Okay, if every bull in the world is neutralized, ranchers will be forced to go the artificial route. Most of the big ranchers take that tack anyway. And they religiously restock what they've used. And by *stock,* I mean what's in the freezers, not livestock. If all the bulls are shooting blanks, there's no resupply channel at that point, and current levels will run dry in two ... max three years, and cloning becomes the only option. The problem with cloning is with each clone some minor natural attributes can be lost. It becomes a downward spiral, and eventually, it no longer becomes a viable option. Those collapsed buildings in Dallas, Buenos Aires, and San Paolo are going to be a serious setback. And you know damn well there's bound to be more."

"How much time do we have?" Harlan asked. "What's the average age of cows and bulls?"

Reynolds laughed. "I guess that was a serious question? Look, if we leave them alone they live fifteen to twenty years. But we don't leave them alone, do we? We slaughter them, then eat the poor bastards. Dairy cows usually dry up after five years. They don't produce enough milk, so they're also sent to slaughter. They're worth more dead than alive. Beef cattle are slaughtered at some point between a year and two years. Calves are slaughtered younger for veal and their rennet, which is needed to produce cheese. Thanks to mankind, cattle have a shorter lifespan than your average earthworm. My timeline is this—

given what semen's in the freezers globally, and assuming we don't have any more building collapses or similar issues, beef cattle are gone within four years. The species becomes extinct. Those are the hard facts."

Harlan appeared somewhat dazed.

"Right. Okay. Milk and milk byproducts are gone in five to six years. Though once the beef runs out, the price will skyrocket, and people are going to say, 'screw the milk,' and turn on the dairy cows sooner than expected for their meat fix. And if they do, the timeline on milk depletion speeds up. And if this issue relates to all bovines, bison are goners too. And don't think our appetite for meat will keep us away from bison once the cattle have evaporated. Water Buffalo and Cape Buffalo are bovine as well, there's no telling how that will play out. In six years, the vegetarians will be laughing their asses off."

Harlan had a strong urge to stand and pace the room as he digested this news, but he knew it would only attract attention. "So, the CDC has what? A year? Year and a half to come up with a cure?"

Reynolds played with a crumb on the checkered tablecloth. "I'm not convinced that's going to happen. I have a bad feeling this thing can't be reversed, and that we're already seriously screwed."

"Jesus. Where do we go without milk? If women can't breast-feed, how do they take care of their kids?"

"We should have swapped notes months ago. Why didn't you bring the health professionals in from the git-go?"

"We saw it as an enemy attack. Our mindset is to counterattack."

"Why doesn't that surprise me? Look, milk's not really a big issue. Most infant formulas have replaced real milk with a soy product." Reynolds smiled. "I hate to say this, but I haven't had a piece of red meat in six years. This may not be the end of the world. We may well be better off without the cattle."

"Yeah, well that's you, not America the Beautiful. We've got to fix this, and now. We don't have the time to screw around."

"Okay, but I think the only quick fix is to find out who instigated this and squeeze a solution out of them. If they even have one. Terrorists are not solution-fixated; they're damage-fixated. Waiting for the CDC could take well over a year. That's why MPS was brought in, in the first place, isn't it? The quick fix? I'd say the ball's in your court, not the CDC's. The only option now may well be your counterattack."

"Against who?"

"Whom."

—

Harlan was back at his loft by 3:00 a.m. He called the Turk immediately after setting up his computer on the coffee table. Despite the hour, and being awakened, Norcross's focus was razor-sharp. It took Harlan less than two minutes to relay his conversation with Reynolds.

"Shit." Harlan could hear the pencil snap in the background. "Okay, I'm going to assume that every country that's gone into panic mode about this crap is not our malefactor. Nothing's coming out of Russia. So, who knows if it's them or not."

"I think we can count them out as well," Harlan added. "If Angelica, this Moe character in Dallas, and the guy at the Parkway Deli are their operatives, it doesn't fly; none of them are remotely Russian. It's not a Russian accent."

"Listen to me closely. I don't give a shit if your Angelica is from outer space. You find that bitch and drag her ass into Peyton Place. I want some answers, and I want them now."

TEN

That evening Harlan once again went to Lenny's for dinner. He sat in the same booth he and Angelica had perched in a few days earlier. Mackie strolled over and handed him a menu.

"You good?"

"I'm good. You?"

"Yeah, I'm good. Guinness?"

"Why not." Not a question, simply a Pavlovian response.

"I recommend the burger. It may be your last chance. Apparently, the world is about to be turned upside down."

"So I hear. Jesus, there are no secrets in this joint, are there?"

Mackie only smiled.

Harlan placed his cell phone on the table and watched as the seconds ticked down, and at 8:00 p.m. on the dot Angelica walked through the door, looking like she had just stepped off a fashion show runway, wearing a dark red dress that clung to her as if it had been painted on. Not much was left to the imagination. She crossed directly to Harlan and sat in the booth opposite him. Her leather backpack was so stuffed it looked like a Thanksgiving turkey. Harlan eyed it.

"Going somewhere?"

"I hope so. I liked the sex thing. It was sort of enjoyable."

"Glad to hear it. Especially with such dramatic enthusiasm."

"So, we will do it again tonight?"

"Why not." Not a question, simply a Pavlovian response.

Harlan had made his decision two hours earlier. He wasn't sure if Angelica would pop into Lenny's, but he suspected she would, and that was why he'd arrived early. He wanted his booth, he wanted to talk. For the first time in his career as a MPS agent, he was about to buck a direct order from the Turk. He despised putting himself in that position, but he felt his route was still the best one and that Norcross was wrong—he wouldn't bring Angelica in, he wouldn't let her know he was on to her. *She'll slip up, I'm sure of it. They always do.*

"Like something to drink?"

"Water."

Harlan motioned to Mackie. He nodded and brought over a glass of water and another menu. After he'd walked off, Harlan returned his attention to Angelica. "Can I get your cell number? I'd like to be able to reach you if I want. Chance meetings have never been my thing."

She pulled a pen and a notepad from her backpack and spoke as she wrote.

"There's nothing chance about our now meeting. You are always here. I knew you'd be here and that's why I'm being here. Sex can be done with anyone, but I think it's better if you practice it with the same person on a regular basis, don't you?"

He nodded and she pushed a piece of paper his way. "I would have given you some number the other time, but I was waiting for my new cell to become active. Remember? The new cell came with a new number."

"Thanks. I assume this one works on an established American communications network?"

"Of course. Why shouldn't it?"

"Out of curiosity, if you left your old cell phone in Pittsburgh, what phone did you use when you called me the other day? Nothing popped up on my ID panel."

She again looked over Harlan's right shoulder as if a monitor had been placed there. Harlan turned his head. Just the same photo of Oscar Peterson.

"I was phoning with a friend's cell. I don't know what network he uses."

"Not Moe Jones's phone by any chance? Are you two related?"

"I don't know who that Moe is."

Harlan smiled to himself. Her expression told a different story.

"I just thought, you know, the same last name and all."

"Isn't Jones a popular last name in the US of A. Even Canada and England? Scotland?"

"It is."

"Maybe that's why we share it? I like it. It sounds normal."

For some reason, Harlan's mind became fixated on how beautiful she was. His entire train of thought seemed to have left him. He couldn't take his eyes off her eyes. He shook his head to regain focus, but there was still a fuzziness that had invaded his brain.

"The people at work are thinking of sending me to Texas for a month. Want to come with me?"

Her face again betrayed her when he mentioned Texas.

"You mean the Texas in the south part of the US?"

"The very same Texas. Ever been there?"

"No. I don't speak the Texas language. Why are you going? Don't you need to be working here?"

"It's flexible. They plan to shoot a movie about a cattle rancher in Montana but want to know if it would be cheaper to film it on a Texas cattle ranch." It wasn't much, but once more she gave herself away by averting his stare and looking down at her backpack. The word 'cattle' seemed to have triggered it this time.

"How could Texas be cheaper than Montana? You could take a train to Montana."

"You can take a train to Texas, but then I'd be missing you, wouldn't I? Because you'd be frightened to get on a train."

She thought this over for a moment. "No. I'm okay with trains now. I think you corrected me. Let's go to Texas."

"Not so fast, it's a union thing, this going off to Texas." Harlan thought, *This is crazy. She knows what I'm up to and I know what she's up to ... sort of. Let's just get it out there. And go back to my place and fool around.*

"Are you eating dinner here?" She said as she focused on the menu.

"That's kinda why I stopped in," he replied, a bit too facetiously. Though Angelica didn't appear to be very good at reading facetiousness. "Still, I'm happy you're here, as well. Dinner for two. No one likes to eat alone."

"I suppose sex alone is no fun, too?"

"Right. You could say that. A certain element is missing." He tapped the menu. "See anything you like? Or are you having what I'm having?"

"I don't eat cow meat. I'll have the chips and fish again. I liked it."

Rather than wasting time trying to figure out how she'd determined he'd planned to order a burger he chose to just move on.

"Is that an animal rights choice? The no-eating meat thing? Or is it for health reasons? It's a popular activity in Texas, eating beef. Do you have a grudge against people devoted to cattle consumption? Apparently, that's something that's going around."

"What difference does it make? Either way, it's a thoughtful choice, don't you think? Just go around killing things only because you're hungry? That's not very kind."

"Well, they are sort of already dead. Mackie had suggested the burger. He thinks there might be a beef shortage in our future. Get it while you can, seems to be the attitude of the day. Your backpack may end up becoming someone's collectors' item. Or lunch."

Angelica let out a short sigh. "I never thought of that. It's made from cow, isn't it?"

"Or bull. I guess it could go either way."

"It's made from a cow."

"You're sure?"

"I'm sure."

Mackie approached their table seemingly from nowhere. "Have you decided on anything?"

Harlan handed him the menus. "Two fish and chips."

"Hold the fish on one?"

Angelica smiled and said, "Yes, please."

ELEVEN

"Sit."

Harlan sat and the Turk stared at him for a full minute before saying another word.

"You're sure you haven't seen her?"

"She's not the type of woman you'd forget spending the night with." Harlan had spent too many years working closely with Norcross. He sensed the old guy knew when he was lying, but he kept up the front as best he could.

"She doesn't have her hooks into you, does she? It looks like she does."

"I just haven't seen her, what can I say? You'll be the first to know when she pops up."

Norcross moved some papers around his desk. There seemed to be no real purpose for doing so. He then pulled a pencil from the drawer and pointed it at Harlan in a particularly menacing way. "Do you have a picture of her? I'd like to circulate it."

"No."

"Next time you see her, get one. We may need to put someone else on her. Interpol reports that every one of their agents who've been digging into this crap has also been tagged at one point or another, even Christian Dodge. It seems the more senior the agent the tag has been one of these Estonian. You seem to be the only lucky one."

"Lucky one?"

"Your tag has been a lady. In all the other cases the tag has been some insipid dude." Norcross stood, put the pencil between his teeth, and approached his speedbag, while Harlan gritted his teeth.

The Turk moved the pencil behind his ear. "You should be pleased that you were tagged by Angelica. I'm guessing it means they think rather highly of you. Or you're a sucker. Which would be my assessment. They've obviously done their homework."

Harlan ignored the dig. "Right. Whoever they are."

The Turk belted the speedbag for ten seconds, then broke the pencil and tossed it across the room. "We've been monitoring every signal in and out of this country. If anyone's in contact with these clowns, it means they have developed a communication system we know nothing about. And sophisticated enough to bypass any of our scanners. On another front, your doctor from Hicksville?"

"Jacobs?"

"The same. He's been in touch with the CDC, and he thinks he's nailed this thing. According to Jacobs, and it's only a theory, it's being done with infinitesimal, nearly imperceivable sound waves, and we're looking at more invisible shit. We've had the technology forever, but we designed it to scramble people's brains. We've never used it. We haven't had to. Jacob believes that technology can now be honed and be directed specifically to destroy reproductive systems."

He spent another ten seconds belting the bag.

"He thinks the technology could allow sound to cover huge swaths of real estate in nanoseconds. It could then be shut down and detection is impossible. A device can be as small as a brick.

As a result, it would only take eight or ten agents to handle the entire US. Jacobs speculates that every bull on Earth is most likely shooting blanks and there's no reversing the process. Not an optimistic picture."

"Jesus. I don't know who has the wherewithal to handle an operation of this size. Even so, what's the motive?"

"Just to screw with the world in general, which is always an anarchist's motive. They probably don't give a shit if they never eat meat again. On the other hand, maybe the sound waves don't reach them, wherever they are. They've domed off their corner of the world and ended up with the only cattle on Earth? They corner the market. We need to take one of these tags and squeeze the hell out of them. Hook their balls up to a wind turbine until they talk."

"Angelica doesn't have balls."

"So, I gather. Nice to have observant underlings." He was quiet for a moment, then added, "Come with me. I want to run something past Max."

Harlan followed the Turk down the hallway and entered Max's lab. Once again, he was playing *Mongo-Jet* on his computer and so intent on the game that he didn't hear or see them enter.

Norcross looked at Harlan. "Give him your cell phone."

"What? What's this about?"

"Just do it, God dammit."

Max picked up on the intensity, turned away from the computer screen, and held out his hand without saying a word. Harlan dropped his cell phone into his open palm.

"Bring up all of his calls for the last forty-eight hours."

"Jesus. What are you looking for? Just ask me. There's nothing there. I've been upfront—."

"What're you looking for?" Max interrupted.

"Specifically? Angelica's cell. Or any number that's not in his address book."

"This is crazy. I haven't seen her or spoken to her."

Clearly not true, but he had yet to have any phone communication with her; his cell phone was clean. But Harlan was attacked with a strong case of self-doubt. *Was she playing me? Was she wooing me? Was she trying to bring me over to her side?*

"Nothing unusual here, Boss. Lorenzo's again at 4:38 a.m. And then I guess it's the Lorenzo's delivery guy at 5:03 a.m. Huh, not bad, twenty-five minutes. I'm going to have to check out Lorenzo's. Domino's really sucks. I waited forty-five minutes for a delivery last night and it was stone cold."

The Turk studied Harlan long and hard but spoke to Max.

"Give me a playback on that call, the one to Lorenzo's."

The three of them listened as Harlan ordered the pizza.

"Sounds like you worked up quite an appetite. A large cheese pizza at 4:30 a.m.? I'm guessing you were feeding two. No pepperoni, no anchovies, no extra cheese. Strange, I generally go for something saltier after I've been screwing all night long."

"I was hungry. I was just trying to fill the void."

"I want the two of you in my office tomorrow by noon or you're out of MPS. And facing an internal investigation, and disciplinary action. And I'm not kidding in the least bit. I want some answers. I don't care if she has balls or not; I will get my answers."

The Turk turned and walked out.

PHASE TWO
TICK... TICK...

TWELVE

Angelica felt the cosmic change in the atmosphere while standing in the dingy hallway, long before she knocked on the door, and it was not a good feeling. Even by Atlantic City standards, the air was thick and gloomy, and heat more oppressive than she could remember. She knocked and walked in.

Manny, Moe, and Jack looked like petrified statues from an ancient Egyptian crypt as they stood side-by-side against the far wall. It seemed she was about to witness a firing squad. In the room with them was a rail-thin, extremely tall stranger with long snow-white hair tied back behind his narrow neck. He spoke in a deeply accented monotone. A directive from Group to speak only in English had been put in place, and he appeared annoyed that he was forced to communicate in a strange new language. However, he knew full well he was being closely monitored, so he played the game.

"There have been immense changes at Group. Giant changes. Changes you know nothing about. I'm here to illuminate you."

Angelica looked him up and down. She chose her words carefully. Her instincts told her this was her new enemy.

"Sorry, but I don't know who you are intended to be."

"Call me Cain. I am your replacement. From now on you will refer to me as The Boss. You no longer hold The Boss position.

Cain is fake name; it comes from the book that was supplied with this hotel room. Group gave me the name. They believe it will make me blend in better. I like the name. It is good you don't learn more."

"I've read that book. I can think of quite a few better name choices. Why would I be believing you represent Group?"

She looked to the other three for any signs that would confirm that he was legitimately representing Group, but they remained stony-faced and fearful. She turned back to the stranger.

"You're going to need to show me physical proof that you travel from Group. And official replacement orders."

He reached into his jacket and removed his Group credentials along with a small metal plate that resembled a credit card. Angelica confirmed that he outranked her and scanned the card with her cell. He was legit. She was out. He was in.

"What is going on?" was all she could think to say.

"Moe, explain to her. I still am not yet perfecting this shit language."

Moe took a step forward. "There has been regime change at Group. The Females are no longer in charge. I'm not sure why that has become true. Something unusual has come to be. It all happened very quickly. Maybe—"

He stopped himself, realizing that everything he was saying was being monitored by Group. He opted to play it safe.

"All Female operatives are being recalled back to Base, including you." He looked to Cain. "How many Females were here?"

"I will not answer that," he nearly shouted. "Females are no longer to be given restricted information."

Moe trembled and continued. "The new commanders at Group now feel that Female leadership here was mistake. It was experiment. It failed. Your unwillingness to resort to liquidation has slowed progress. It would have been better warning to kill some people in that Texas place. They also think you've been compromised by locals. Not you personally, but apparently some Females have wandered, so all Females are being recalled. You have two days to return to Base."

She directed her response to Cain. "But we're on the schedule, operationally. How much faster did they calculate us to move? They are seeing their results. They knew this plan would take time. But the disease is on the run, just as we suspected."

He nodded to Moe, who continued.

"Don't forget that Group works with a different clock. New leadership is impatient—" Moe stopped mid-sentence. "Ah, sorry, not impatient, bad English word, they just want to move faster. The new leadership doesn't trust Females. You know that, you know the opposition has never trusted Females." He then said, to ensure his status within the operation was solid, "And who can blame them? Many feel that way. Your favorability ratings are dropping."

"So, the entire nature of the enterprise is changed? Altered in some fashion? Liquidation is back on the offering? From historical knowledge, we know that only creates aggressive resistance."

"Liquidation is most definitely back in play. The Males aren't nearly as sympathetic toward these people, but they do still see that the basic concept that you and the other Females created is a viable one, so it will stay in place and play out as designed. They believe the long-range Female plan is still a working way to gather the desired end-stage results. The disease will be curtailed. But they want all Females returning to Base now to serve as analysts. However—"

"Enough," The Cain groused. "She is no longer to be given classified information. I thought I made that clear, Moe."

"Sorry, Boss."

"Did you win a cell while here?"

"Win a cell?"

"He means buy. Did you buy a local cell phone in this country?"

"No," Angelica lied, hoping they wouldn't search her. "I only have Group communication ability."

"Give your Group cell to Jack. Any communication you have with locals here for your hours remaining in the USA will be of the speaking-in-person kind and will be monitored. You are aware of the route you must take to return to Group?"

"Yes."

"Good. Do not alter that route or it will prove fatal. Be back at Group within two days."

Angelica handed the Group cell to Jack who surreptitiously slipped a small piece of paper into her hand.

"We're going to miss you," he said. It almost appeared as if he was going to cry, which Angelica knew to be an impossibility. These three did not shed tears.

"Now leave." The New Boss checked the time. "When you return to Group, you will be offered another, less demanding post in the analytical department. Mistakes were made. They will be corrected. Group recognizes the advancements you have generated, and they are grateful. For now. They're looking forward to your return. There's nothing more for you here." He placed his hand on her back and literally pushed her out the door.

Angelica stood there for a moment completely dazed. She then trotted down the six flights of stairs and stepped out into the sweltering summer air. She walked five blocks to the north and strolled out onto the Atlantic City beach, removed her shoes, and waded into the hot water. Well out of reach of any visual monitoring apparatus. She pulled Jack's note from her jacket pocket. He had written it in their native language. It read: *Do not report to Group. Cain explained that all the Female operatives who have traveled here will be liquidated upon arrival at Base. I doubt if any other Females have been warned. If you stay, you may be the only one. Remember the chip. You are now the outcast. Do what you must to survive.*

THIRTEEN

It was highly unusual for Harlan to be called directly to the Oval Office without swinging by Peyton Place and first meeting up with the Turk. Only then would they venture over to the White House together. It was now seven in the evening. He'd received the ASAP text ten minutes earlier. He could only assume Norcross was already with POTUS and something big was in the works.

He had left Peyton Place at 5:00 p.m. and called Angelica the moment he stepped from the complex. She didn't answer. He'd tried her three more times before he reached the White House security gates, still no answer. His mind continued to wrestle with how he was going to handle her, and he wasn't looking forward to sitting side-by-side with the Turk in front of the president of the United States without having been briefed or having the Angelica situation settled.

After clearing security, a Marine guard escorted him directly to the Oval Office. No words were spoken. The White House was nearly empty. Harlan remained standing alone in the office until the president arrived. Norcross was nowhere in sight.

"Have a seat, Mr. Stone," POTUS said as he entered. Harlan sat. "How long have you been with MPS?"

"If you count university training, and some overseas work with the Marine Corps ... fifteen years, sir."

"You're young, then."

Harlan shrugged. "Everything's relative, sir. I've been around the block a few times." He looked for Norcross. His absence was unsettling.

"Yes. Things are indeed relative." POTUS took his seat behind the Resolute Desk. "The Turk has spoken very highly of you in the past, and despite your youth, he felt you would be the best possible choice to replace him if things should ever come to that."

Harlan shifted on his feet. "We've had our differences at times, but yes, we work well together. I'm not sure what you're getting at, sir."

"Charles Norcross was killed a little over an hour ago. He fell from the balcony of his condo. Apparently, he had been drinking."

After Harlan had processed this, he spun the numbers. Norcross had left Peyton Place at five. He always walked home, probably taking him twenty minutes, assuming he didn't stop along the way. That meant he had less than thirty or forty minutes to get blotto enough to fall off his balcony. Harlan didn't buy it.

"I don't buy that, sir. Charles wasn't a heavy drinker."

"That would have been my assessment too. The FBI is looking into it. I assume you know who to follow up with at the FBI?"

"Yes, sir."

"If he was killed, do you have any ideas as to who? Or why? It smells like something Uri Polushin and the goddam Russians would pull off. Was he working on something to do with those jackasses?"

"No, sir. I'd have to assume it would be connected to the issue we've been assigned to investigate. There's an off chance it might have a Russian connection, or even be a Russian operation. We're looking into that angle, but nothing's in stone. We were in the middle of preparing a briefing for you. It's not a rosy picture." Harlan paused for a moment. "Sir?"

"Yes?"

"I will find out who's responsible for Charles's death, I assure you. This isn't Russia, and people don't just fall off balconies or out of windows."

"Good. We need to be on the same page as the FBI. I'm appointing you as temporary head of MPS. It will require minor congressional confirmation of course, but I don't foresee any pushback. In fact, I'm not at all certain we have the time to deal with those clowns. Though a few may question your age." He let out a small laugh. "Screw 'em. Congratulations."

"Thank you, sir."

"I have to assume Norcross has positioned a *Warrior's Package* somewhere in his office. My personal contact information will be there. If for some reason he didn't set up the package, contact my secretary, Mrs. Albright. She'll see that you get what you need. Pick up her card on your way out."

POTUS stood. They exchanged a handshake, and the Old Man walked out, leaving Harlan alone in the Oval Office. He sat and mumbled, "What a goddam mess," before considering that he was most likely being recorded. He then left the White House by the same route he'd used when he entered and strolled all the way to Lenny's to clear his head.

Exactly seven minutes after he'd entered, at 8:00 p.m. on the dot, Angelica came in. She was wearing an olive drab outfit that made her look like a 1960s Central American revolutionary.

She quickly trotted over to his table and placed her hand over his mouth before he could say a word. She passed him a handwritten note she had prepared earlier. It read: *Don't say anything. We're being monitored. We need to get out of here before they can pinpoint any background noise.*

She then took his hand and dragged him out of Lenny's. They walked the two miles to Harlan's loft in absolute silence. He chose a residential route where no business traffic and noise might be recognizable. She had insisted that a Lyft, taxi, or Uber was out.

Once they were safely in his loft, Angelica pulled a Walgreens package from her leather backpack and opened it. It contained a scalpel sealed in a sterilized glassine envelope, a kit containing surgical thread and needle, tweezers, rubber gloves, gauze pads, and adhesive tape. She then stripped to the waist and handed him another prepared note: *Between my shoulder blades you will see what looks like a small dark mole. You know where it is. It's not a mole. It's an implanted device, a microchip. Remove it.*

She handed him the envelope containing the scalpel.

He shook his head, *no*, crossed to his desk, and returned with a pen and a yellow legal pad. He wrote: *This needs to be done under sterile conditions. I know a doctor who can do it. He's nearby. And he can be trusted.*

They continued their conversation in silence, passing the yellow pad back and forth.

Just do it. My life depends on it. I don't have much time. Once they know I've run off they'll generate the tracking function of the device, and we will both be killed.

And again, who the hell are they?

I will answer all of your questions once the chip is gone.

Jesus, Angelica, there's no anesthetics here. I can't do this to you. It's going to hurt like hell.

She scooped up her drugstore purchases, walked from the living room and into his bedroom. She then dropped the surgical equipment on the bed, stripped naked, and reclined, face down, next to them. Harlan followed and placed the yellow pad next to her.

Okay. Let me know how you're doing. It ain't gonna be fun—for either of us.

He went to the kitchen, scrubbed his hands for a full minute with anti-bacterial soap, and grabbed a bottle of rubbing alcohol from the bathroom. He returned, squeezed his hands into the rubber gloves, and arranged her paraphernalia out on a freshly washed white towel. He then pushed her hair off to the side and scoured the back of her neck with alcohol. Angelica gripped the sheets preparing herself for the pain, as Harlan tore open the scalpel's glassine envelope. The noise made them both shiver.

He had witnessed field surgeries while serving in Afghanistan and now thought, *Watching is a hell of a lot easier than doing.* Nevertheless, he picked up the scalpel, tapped on the mole to prepare her, took a deep breath, and cut into her flesh. She grabbed onto the sheets as the pain surged through her body. Harlan worked as quickly as he could. The chip was small, but easy to locate, not deeply implanted, and not intertwined with tissue, which would have been the case if it had been there for many years. It came out with no resistance, and he placed it on the yellow pad for her to see. She reached for the pad and wrote.

Destroy it.

I'm going to close you up first.

No. Destroy it now.

I'm running this show. I'm closing you up first.

As Harlan wrote, he smeared a sizable amount of blood over the legal pad, and she passed out. He took a gauze compress and mopped up the incision site with alcohol, sutured her up, and dressed the wound. As he cleaned up the area around her prone body Angelica's eyes opened. She turned and she sat up on the bed. Harlan took the pen and wrote.
You know, you really do have lovely breasts.
She smiled, pointed to the chip, and wrote, *You must destroy that now!*
He retreated to the kitchen and returned with a small vial marked—hydrochloric acid. He picked up the chip with the tweezers, dropped it into the vial, and they watched as the chip disintegrated to nothing but vapor.
She had a much-changed look on her face. It was as if the removal and destruction of the chip had made her a different person.
She smiled at him. "I'm almost afraid to ask this, but why are you having a vial of hydrochloric acid in your kitchen?"
He kissed her. "Because you never know when a situation just like this might pop up."

FOURTEEN

They made love with Angelica perched on top so as to not disturb her fresh sutures. They hadn't done much talking; the image of the chip seemed to still hang in the air. At 3:00 a.m. they ordered a cheese pizza from Lorenzo's. It arrived twenty minutes later.

"You're going to turn me into a vegetarian yet, aren't you?"

She smiled. "You may have no choice."

"Yeah, well, I hate to ruin sex and a good pizza by talking business, but I think you have some explaining to do. Now that no one else is listening in. What the hell is going on? If I just saved your life, I think you owe me a little honesty."

She was quiet for a long moment, and then said, "I lied to you. I've never been to Pittsburgh."

Harlan choked slightly on the piece of pizza he was gnawing. "Well, that's a start. Not a great one but neither have I—been to Pittsburgh, that is. You missed a perfect opportunity to make up a whole bunch of shit about the place and I would have never known the difference. Though I have heard of the Steelers and Falling Waters."

"Falling Waters?"

"Skip it."

He tucked into another slice of pizza and waited for her to offer some further explanations beyond Pittsburgh. When it was obvious she didn't plan to do so he said, "Okay, that's getting us nowhere. How about this? I'm going to be totally upfront with you. I'm going to tell you exactly what I do. For real. And then you do the same thing. Though, I have a distinct feeling you know everything I'm about to say."

He dropped the slice of pizza back into the box.

"I work for a government organization called MPS. It's a highly covert agency that few people know of. I report directly to the president of the United States. And as of a few hours ago, I was promoted to head MPS because the previous director died. And it wasn't an accident." He waited to see if that would register with her. It did.

"I was afraid that would happen once I was replaced. I suppose he was murdered by one of my associates. They'll come after you next if you've taken over that position. And me. They said they'd be altering procedures. They really are bloodthirsty. The Males. I didn't think it would happen so quickly. I was hoping it wouldn't happen at all. They're far more impatient than me. No one is now safe."

"Okay, that was a lot of non-information packed into one murky statement. Let's start with this once again: who is they?"

She didn't respond.

"You know this means I'll need to bring you into the FBI for questioning. I have no choice. You're the only link; the only person who can explain all this crap."

He moved to hold her hand, but she instinctively pulled back.

"I'm a professional, Angelica, I need to do what's right. I've taken an oath and I'm not about to betray it no matter what my feelings might be."

"You don't know what's going on."

"Clearly. That's the understatement of the evening. Your English is getting a lot better, but it's not helping you talk your way out of this. I need to do what's right. It's my job, my obligation, so fill me in. There's some abhorrent activity worldwide and I need to know who's orchestrating it. You're on my side now and you know damn well you can't go back to your side."

She stood and turned her back to him and nearly shouted, "No."

"This would go a lot more smoothly if you'd put some clothes on." *Jesus*, he thought, *the Turk was right, she does have her hooks into me.*

"I've got to do this."

"No," she again shouted. "At this point, I'm the only one who can turn this right. Stop the killing. If that can even be done. And I can't do it sitting in an FBI jail cell. And sex would also become challenging, wouldn't it?"

"Well, there is that."

"I will make your loft my home base. It will be my jail. I won't leave. We will find a solution together. But I suspect there isn't one. The killing will go on and the end will be inevitable."

"Who do you work for, who do you answer to."

"I can't answer that."

He laughed. "Okay. Another good start. Let's try this, a simpler one, what was the chip I just destroyed? Who put it there?"

She fiercely shook her head, *no*.

"How about this: Why neutralize all the cattle?"

She thought it over for a full minute, then touched the bandage on her back and turned to face him.

"This quest is strictly environmental in nature. We will clean up the atmosphere, continue to restore the ozone layer, and remove the threat of all greenhouse gasses. Eliminating the cattle is a necessary first step. Ultimately it was an experiment, but it was completely successful. This is a peaceful operation. It will be painless."

"Are you forgetting that one of your associates threw my boss off a ten-story balcony? Besides being my boss, Charles Norcross was my mentor and a close friend. It clearly wasn't painless for him, and it hasn't been painless for me."

She crossed over to Harlan, sat next to him, and gave him a soft kiss.

"I'm sorry that happened. It wouldn't have happened if I were still on top. But I need to have the free movement to prevent it from happening again. If I still had the chip in me, I would have been able to monitor their moves. But they would also know my whereabouts and probably would be with us, in this room, right now, with an intent to incinerate us. Your Norcross learned something, and he was done away with. It's how they work. That is now my fate. And I fear yours too. You need to trust me."

"You said the cattle were the first step. I assume this is some ridiculous attempt to reduce the methane released by these animals?"

"Yes."

"What's the second step?"

"I can't tell you that."

"Why doesn't that surprise me? I feel like I'm talking to a fish tank. You know what, Angelica, eliminating beef will have its effect, no question about it, but it's a baby step. I'm sure you and your associates, must have thought beyond that? Once the cattle are gone, the lamb and pork producers are going to move to fill the void. They'll take over the grasslands and you're right back where you started. Pound for pound those animals are no different than cattle when you're talking about the release of methane and other gasses. And let's be real, the big culprits in all of this don't have four legs. You would have been better off freezing the engine blocks of every petroleum-powered vehicle on Earth. If that was a possibility."

"We have developed that technology. And we considered it. The Males thought it would be the best way to go, and from their viewpoint, quick and highly entertaining. But we Females considered it too cruel."

"Cruel? In what way?"

She laughed. "How would you get your pizza tonight? Except for your farmers living in Pennsylvania who live off their land, you'd all starve to death in a month. Your markets would get no deliveries, your fishing boats would go idle, people would be stuck in their cars on interstate highways out in the boiling desert. All transportation would stop instantly. Planes and helicopters would fall from the sky."

"Okay, fine, I see your point. But that doesn't change the fact that all animals bred for food, pound for pound, produce nearly as much methane as cattle."

She said nothing, only sat there with her hands in her lap, and it all finally dawned on him.

"That's it. That's the next step. Eliminate all meat. Jesus. Just tell me who's orchestrating this. Give me a hint, for Christ's sake."

She shook her head. "What's so wrong with that? You Americans immediately jump to, 'Who's responsible? Who's out to get us? And we're going to get even at all costs.' Capital punishment on a grand scale. Someone must die; debts must be paid.

You need to understand, there is no getting even. In the end, what's wrong with the Earth becoming a land of vegetarians, if that's what it takes to save the planet? Your bodies are designed to handle that. Most apes are vegetarians."

"I need to stop it."

"Stop the senseless killing, yes. We'll work on that together to bring an end to it, but you want some honesty? Okay. We weren't understanding if this tactic would work. Biologically. It was an experiment, and we had to start somewhere. But it has worked, so the long-range plan was for the second phase to be implemented yesterday. I'm sure their distrust of me ... all Females in fact, and my rushed removal from leadership, was for fear I would obstruct Phase Two. It's too late to make changes. But maybe we can save lives. Save pain and suffering."

"You say it like this will have no effect on you. Like you're immune to the consequences."

"I'm a vegetarian. In the end, my existence will be greatly improved when the ozone is completely healed, and CO_2 gasses are drastically reduced or better yet, removed."

"And how long is that going to take? Decades? I doubt that you'll be around to enjoy any of it."

She shrugged.

"You know, Norcross had this wacky idea that you were a Russian, Chinese, North Korean, whatever operative of some sort. I disagreed with him, but now that a few cards have been put on the table I don't know what to think. Who's behind this?"

She laughed hard enough to stretch the sutures in her back, and the laugh quickly gave way to a sting of pain.

"Well? Answer my question." Harlan attached no sympathy to it.

"You need to trust me. You need to let it play out. Leave it at that."

FIFTEEN

Harlan entered the Turk's office shortly after 8:00 a.m. He sat at the teak desk for less than a minute before standing and crossing over to the weathered speedbag. He worked on it for twenty seconds, went back to the desk, pulled out a pencil, broke it in half and tossed it across the room as a final salute to the Turk. He then turned on the computer and called in Lou Walsh. The agent arrived two minutes later. When he entered, he stopped short and looked at Harlan seated behind Norcross's desk, then at the still swaying speedbag and broken pencil. He was a bit shocked.

"Jesus, it didn't take you long to settle in."

"Then you heard?"

"The head of MPS jumps, falls, is thrown, off a ten-story high balcony in Silver Spring, Maryland before the sun goes down, it tends to make the news. Are you just testing out the chair, or is there something else I should know?"

"The Old Man called me in yesterday shortly after the Norcross situation was reported and bumped me up. Temporarily. It requires some half-baked congressional approval, which we don't have time for. I'm recommending you fill my position."

Walsh opened his mouth to speak but Harlan held up his hand. "Before you say anything, I have it on good authority the

Turk was murdered. I'm sure you must've come to the same conclusion. This puts me, and you, if you accept the bump, directly in the crosshairs. He was on to something and paid the full price. The FBI is on it. We're dealing with some serious, and very driven and dirty personalities here. They have their eye on something. It seems to be pointing to environmental terrorism, with a tree-hugging resolution for all mankind."

"I don't doubt the Turk was murdered. He wasn't prone to accidents or suicide, and he wasn't a boozer. But now I'm just mildly curious who your good authority might be?"

Harlan stumbled. "Yeah, right, maybe I phrased that poorly. Like you say, there's no way in hell he killed himself."

Walsh seemed to buy it. "Do we know who they are?"

"No. Obviously that's our job. Norcross must have figured it all out."

"Any ransom demands? Threats of impending violence?"

"Not here. I'm meeting with Christian Dodge at Interpol in an hour. Maybe you should come along. Get a look at the big picture. Interestingly, there seems to be no serious malice behind it all. Unless you're addicted to cheeseburgers."

"Or get caught in a building collapse, or live ten stories up. What do we have so far?"

"Nothing solid, but it is a worldwide operation, and clearly well-funded."

Harlan unlocked the center desk drawer and pulled out an envelope reading, *Tickets to the Warriors Game*. "Thank Christ, I was afraid this might not be here."

"Why wouldn't it be there? That's how the game's played."

"Norcross and I had some disagreements yesterday. It was a bad way to end the day. Usually, we walk out the gates together, but he left me in the dust. I didn't know if he was having second thoughts about who should follow him in this chair. On the other hand, maybe he knew what was about to happen and wanted to handle it alone. It could be he was meeting someone."

"He liked a good fight."

"Indeed, but it would have taken a tough son-of-a-bitch to get the best of him and toss him off the balcony. Despite his age."

"Was his apartment busted up?"

"Negative."

Harlan spent the next twenty minutes bringing Walsh up to speed, leaving out any direct references to Angelica and the fact that a phase two had already been implemented. He then opened the Warrior envelope, retrieved the codes, and punched them into the Turk's computer. All of his files and notes became immediately accessible.

"He must have been onto a way of undermining this operation. Otherwise, why would they have gone after him specifically?"

"Maybe he was more concerned about the sabotaged buildings. Realizing it was too late to reverse course on sterilization. You know, preserve what workable stock remains before any more setbacks hit the industry?"

Harlan scanned the computer files looking for anything that might lead in that direction. After a moment he found it.

"Here it is. You're a genius, Lou. It's a directive to the FBI and NSA telling them to advise all facilities handling that type of product to expand security and offer them government assistance when needed. Including National Guard protection if necessary. Whoever they are, they did not want this directive going out."

Harlan then pushed his chair away from the computer as if he'd burned his fingers on the keyboard.

"What's up?" Walsh asked.

"He never sent it out. It's dated today. He intended it to go out first thing this morning. I guess whoever the hell they are, they're toasting to Mission Accomplished right about now."

Walsh sat opposite Harlan. Both their minds were spinning. Lou spoke first.

"So, he didn't meet with POTUS at all."

"No, it's an electronic approval. And the time frame doesn't work. He went straight home. He must have called The Old Man before he left yesterday and sent it over to him. POTUS cleared it after we left at five."

"Is it possible one of our cell phones has been tapped?"

"No, I doubt it. You know what this place is like, every one of these things are monitored twenty-four/seven."

"Remember, someone screwed around with your cell phone, and we still haven't solved that issue."

"I'll have Max run some line tests to be sure. I don't understand why POTUS didn't mention this letter when we met in the Oval Office."

He stared at the computer screen for another minute.

"Well, POTUS approved it. That's all I need. It goes out now. To hell with the consequences. Screw their Mission Accomplished."

Harlan made some adjustments to the message so that it would go out under his name rather than the Turk's. He included Jordan Bayless and Christian Dodge of Interpol on the list of recipients and hit the send button. He then took a moment to reconsider everything he'd learned from Angelica and decided some of it needed to be out in the open.

"I have a strong hunch that these people aren't going to stop at cattle."

"Meaning?"

"Meaning other meat supplies are going to be hit. If they haven't been already. They're trying to shut down methane gas entirely. This warning needs to be sent out to facilities that store content for the pork and lamb industries as well."

Walsh chuckled. "Sounds unlikely if you ask me. Don't you think we should gather some facts before we hit the panic button?"

"If we let this play out naturally it will take a month, maybe two, before they recognize they've been hit and have issues. They need to start testing these animals now, and seriously scale up their security."

"Do you have any idea how paranoid you're sounding?"

SIXTEEN

Interpol NCB offices in Washington, DC were in an innocuous building on E Street that looked more like a dormitory for a cut-rate business school. And even though Interpol agents were technically part of the Justice Department, they often fancied themselves as beholding to no one other than the International Criminal Court in The Hague and therefore globetrotting vanquishers of evil.

After Harlan and Lou passed through the metal detectors, a young man, who appeared to be no more than a college intern, emerged from a side room, asked them for ID, and escorted them up to Jordan Bayless's office on the second floor. Christian Dodge, the senior American Interpol agent, was standing by as well.

They waited for the receptionist to leave before exchanging greetings. Bayless spoke first.

"Good morning. Have a seat, gents. Things have literally gone off the Richter Scale in the last twenty-four hours."

"I gather. There seems to be no reversing the effect on the cattle industry."

"That's not the half of it, Harlan. In the last day or so there's been thirty-seven reported building collapses or cases of arson relating to facilities operating as reproductive storage centers throughout the world. The death toll is nearing eighty, with many more injured. I got your note about securing these businesses, however, I had moved in that direction worldwide as of one this morning, GMT. Sorry to jump on your alert, but I felt it needed immediate action."

"Absolutely."

Harlan considered whether to tell them that the lamb and pork industries had been targeted as well. It seemed absurd that there was a rogue nation out there fixated on turning the entire human race into vegetarians, and willing to kill to make sure it happened. But that appeared to be the case.

"You know, I was nearly laughed out of my office this morning by Lou for suggesting that whoever was orchestrating this was going to focus on other livestock. And now that I think more on it, the poultry industry may not be safe either."

"We're ahead of you on that, too," Dodge replied. "We've presented that theory to the CDC and their sister agencies in every country. They've all been stunned to the core, and they are going to begin testing as of today."

"And cranking up security?"

"That too."

"What's the scattershot on these collapses and arsons? Are they focused on any specific countries?"

"No. It's pretty much worldwide. No one seems to have been spared."

"Any notable exceptions? Russia? North Korea? Saudi Arabia? China?"

Bayless shook his head slowly. "When was the last time anything worthwhile came out of those dumps? We're working our informants, but internal, and particularly external communication, might as well be on blackout. Russian Interpol NCB, and individual agents, will work with us to a certain extent, but we've been unable to establish a secure avenue. Since Yuri Polushin started dicking around in Ukraine, Russian NCB communication began to slowly peter out. His arrest warrant has them all freaked out, because technically, by charter, they should haul his ass in. Clearly no one has the gonads to do that."

Harlan stood and walked to the window. He spoke as he looked out at the stalled traffic on E Street, keeping his back to Bayless, Dodge, and Lou.

"I have a contact that may be able to provide some answers. I can't share the contact. If the contact spooks, that's it, they're gone, and we have nothing. I need to work this one solo."

"Can he take us to the top?" Bayless asked. "Because this isn't a local or even a US issue. It's worldwide and we need to snuff it worldwide. And now. Corralling a few local bad players isn't going to cut it. If we need to negotiate—" He took in a long breath and let it out slowly. "I think we've reached that point."

Harlan wanted to scream, *It's too damn late, don't you see that?* But he knew it would cause more confusion than good. The objective at this point was to save as many individuals as possible. Reduce the collateral damage. Angelica must take him to whoever was orchestrating it all and set up a meeting. It seemed the only viable route.

"Give me twenty-four hours to work on this contact. At this point we need to protect the people who are working at these facilities and secure what inventory is salvageable. Let me ask you this, this Moe Jones character down in Dallas? Did he pan out as legit? Did Berger confirm if he was with Investiture Insurance or not?"

"The guy just disappeared, no trail at the airport, train or bus station, or rental car agencies in Dallas. We didn't bring it up with Berger because we didn't want to spook him. So, no, there was no significant follow-up. The guy evaporated."

"But you know he was a tag?" Harlan didn't wait for them to answer. "Have either one of you been tagged? I mean personally?"

"They've left me alone for some reason," Lou tossed in. "I'm guessing they don't have limitless personnel."

The other two both nodded, but it was Bayless who answered. "We've all been around long enough to spot these clowns. But as obvious as they are, these guys are damn elusive. I have to assume you've been tagged by someone, Harlan? I think they believe they're more subtle than they really are. They're sloppy as hell."

"I was tagged by a someone too," Dodge offered. "I can't swear to it, but he spooked the moment I outed the bastard."

"And that's my point, this is a colossal operation. Think on it, every senior agent, operative, whatever, who's in on this has been tagged. Mostly by totally nondescript individuals. This is crazy. Who has the wherewithal to pull this off? It requires a boatload of people." Harlan took a beat and added, "I have a feeling that as they get more aggressive the tags will be increased. Just a hunch."

"It could go the opposite way. If they feel they've got this situation locked up, everything under control, they may start pulling agents out, cut the trail cold. Leave nothing behind. Get the hell out before we pick one of them up. And in reality, they may be only ghosting the heavy hitters: us, Moscow, Beijing."

Harlan's cell phone chimed. He looked at the readout. "POTUS."

"Take it."

After listening to a nearly one-minute furious monologue he slipped the device back into his pocket. "Well, somebody's pissed. He wants some answers."

"Don't we all."

His cell phone instantly chimed once more, and he pulled it back from his pocket. "The FBI. Tim Arnold."

"You're a popular guy."

SEVENTEEN

The FBI headquarters on Pennsylvania Avenue, the brutalist J. Edgar Hoover Building, was something Harlan always considered a Washington, DC eyesore. He wasn't alone. He didn't like driving past it, let alone stepping into it. But this seemed to be the norm when it came to DC structures, they were either magnificent examples of exquisite architecture or downright aesthetic failures.

Tim Arnold's office was on the fourth floor, and after clearing security, Harlan scaled the stairs, knocked on the door, and entered. All the furniture was metal; there wasn't a piece of wood or textile to be found. On the institutional green walls hung photos of past FBI directors mingled with a few presidents and senators—all white men, making Harlan feel as if he had been transported to a hoods-off Klan meeting.

"Thanks for stopping by, Harlan. Looks like that crap in Dallas was just the tip of the iceberg."

"Who does your decorating?"

"God only knows. It came this way. Changing it involves more red tape than I care to deal with. Clearly, we don't have a personal connection with any former First Ladies like you guys."

"Well, it's inspirational. Anything on what brought the Dallas building down? Or the others, for that matter?"

"Zippo. But it was well coordinated. In each instance, the concrete was turned to dust. And there's an irony to that. In an average year, thirty billion tons of concrete are produced, and a shitload of carbon is released into the atmosphere in the process, eight percent of the total worldwide emissions of CO_2, to be exact. Rebuilding these buildings is going to make cow farts a moot point."

"Nobody said terrorists look at the long picture. But, yeah, it is a bit ironic. Though there's a distinct possibility that there may be no point in rebuilding them. It's beginning to look like the industry's dead."

"Let's hope not. Same mystery with the arsons. We've found no trace whatsoever of an accelerant being deployed. The scenes are devoid of evidence. The security cameras that survived have revealed nada; no intruders of any kind. Have a seat."

Harlan sat in a stainless-steel chair across from Arnold. He somehow felt as if a bright light was about to be shown into his face, and he was soon to be put under intense interrogation while some smiling masochist slipped bamboo needles under his fingernails. It turned out he wasn't far off the mark.

"And of course, the same old question lingers—who's behind it all?" Arnold didn't respond. "I assume you're on the Norcross situation too, because that was a flat-out case of murder. Anything on the security cameras in his apartment building?"

"Another division is on it. But shit—" He let out an exasperated sigh and walked to the window.

"What?"

"They want to question you. Since you and I are friends, I asked them to let me investigate. Before they dragged you in."

Harlan sat up a little straighter.

"What the hell? They think I did it? They think I took out Norcross?"

"Hold on, they're just checking all possibilities. You were the last person to see him alive. Where'd you go after you left Peyton Place?"

"This is bullshit. Someone at the FBI thinks I had something to do with, *anything* to do with, the Turk's death? Who the hell is that brain trust?"

"The director. That's how high up it goes. Don't forget they were good friends. I'm trying to help you out here, Harlan, but my ass is also on the line now. I've become the one who's required to debrief you and submit the initial report. You stood an awful lot to gain with Norcross out of the picture."

Harlan shook his head in disbelief and stood.

"This is crazy. I'm not going to listen to this crap."

"Sit back down. Walking out of here isn't going to make it go away. Better me than someone up on the fifth floor. Just fill me in. Where'd you go after you left Peyton Place at 5:00 p.m.?"

"How do you know when I left?"

"We've already reviewed the security cameras and interviewed Walsh."

"Jesus, you guys are serious. Maybe you should be putting more time into tracking down the people who're altering life as we know it?"

Arnold ignored the dig. "Walsh said you and Norcross had a serious disagreement before you left at 5:00 p.m. He said the two of you generally leave together, but that Norcross blew you off and left alone. What was that all about?"

"Christ. It wasn't a serious disagreement." Harlan paused, thinking of what Angelica had said: *I can't operate sitting in an FBI jail cell.* "We just had a difference of opinion on how to proceed regarding a certain informant. That's all it was."

"Who was the informant?"

"That was the disagreement. Norcross wanted to drag in the informant for a working over. I didn't think that was the best approach because the informant could clam up if they felt threatened. I felt they needed to be massaged. We don't do torture at MPS. We leave that to the CIA."

He studied Harlan for a minute. "Okay, I can see your side of it. Sometimes it's best to keep these clowns out in the cold. I've never been one for the heavy-handed approach either. You lose more than you gain, and they start making shit up just to get you to lay off. But that was the Turk's way."

Arnold sat and scribbled a few notes on a legal pad, while Harlan thought, *You don't call what you're up to right now heavy-handed?*

"Where'd you go after you left Peyton Place?"

"Home ... I walked it."

"Did you talk to anyone? Stop anywhere? Can anyone verify where you were, and when?"

"This is getting ridiculous. The security cameras at my loft are time-stamped. Check them out. They'll tell you exactly when I got home."

"They were checked out. They've been disabled."

"Jesus Christ, you guys have done your homework. It'd be nice if you worked this quickly on shit that mattered." Harlan ran his fingers through his hair, thinking, *Did they grab Angelica while they were there?*

"Okay, look, I don't know what's going on with the goddam cameras at my loft, but do the math on this. There's no way in hell I leave Peyton Place at 5:00 p.m. go to Norcross's building, kill him, go home, and then show up at the White House at 7:00 p.m. It's impossible. Plus, the cameras at Norcross's place would have captured me if I'd been there."

"Those cameras show nothing."

"They're disabled too?"

"No, they're working, there's just no movement at that time. Other than Norcross arriving home, and a couple of his neighbors."

"There you go. There's the proof that I never entered his building."

"Someone did."

"It sure as hell wasn't me. I'd say there was someone there waiting for him. How far back did you go on the security cameras?"

"Twelve hours. Only verified residents came and went." Arnold stood. "So, from what you're saying, there's no confirming that you actually went home at all, which leaves you plenty of time to pull this off."

"Come on, Tim, you know damn well I didn't go after Norcross. I would've resigned before I pulled a stunt like that. We were friends, have been friends for a dozen years. MPS Agents are not assassins. We're not armed. I don't go around killing people. We're not even authorized to make arrests. And why would I want to get rid of the sharpest mind at MPS in the middle of a national emergency? Listen, these bad players worked around my cell phone, contacted me without leaving any electronic trace. No footprint at all, no trail. They're ten steps ahead of us. They're not concerned about the concrete production. You can bet your ass they have an answer for that. Clearly, they bypassed Norcross's security cameras somehow. They've bypassed security in Dallas and everywhere else in the world where they've pulled off crap. How obvious is that? They killed the Turk, not me. Obviously, he had figured out their game and planned to put an end to it."

"Well, we don't know who they are, do we? Sorry, the director and POTUS aren't convinced. POTUS has bumped up Walsh. He's now running the show at MPS. You're not to set foot in Peyton Place until this is all sorted out. Direct orders from up top. Your entry pass has been deactivated. Take some time off. Go fishing. You're on administrative leave. You'll be on full salary until we sort this out."

"The entire world is falling apart and you're telling me to go fishing. Jesus. How do you know Walsh didn't go after Norcross?"

"Walsh has an alibi, you don't."

EIGHTEEN

When Harlan returned to his loft that afternoon Angelica was standing at the kitchen sink filling the teapot with water. She was completely naked. She had removed the bandage covering her wound. It was healing at a surprisingly quick pace. When she saw him, she placed the teapot on the stove, crossed over to him and latched onto him.

"For some reason, I was worried about you. I don't know what's going on. I'm having strange feelings, feelings I don't understand. Something is wrong."

"Is this why you've decided to forgo clothing?"

"The costumes I have are uncomfortable."

"And the bandage?"

"That was uncomfortable too."

"Aren't you—chilly?"

"I'm not—"

There was a long pause before Harlan said, "Not what?"

"A cold or hot person."

He found himself wanting nothing more than to jump into bed with her but managed to brush aside the urge.

"You wouldn't know anything about the security cameras in the stairway, would you? They seem to be malfunctioning."

"I disengaged them."

"Clever. Why didn't I think of that? Any particular reason you disengaged them?"

"The chip you removed allowed me to avoid security cameras. It had a blocking mechanism that scrambled images. I could make them unproductive when I passed. Without the chip they can found me. And I don't want to be found."

"Right. And so it is. Here we are back to the same old question. Who is they?"

"The ones who put the chip there in the first place."

"Of course, why didn't I think of that?"

She pushed herself into him. "Why am I now frightened? Fright is new to me. I don't understand fright. I had to Google it. That's how I knew it was fright."

"Why aren't you answering my one simple question?"

"What difference does it make? It's over and done with. There's no reversing it. Relax and enjoy your new life as a vegetarian."

"I see you've also developed a sense of humor." He put a light under the teapot. "Because the stairway security cameras are broken, there's no proof that I was here when Norcross was killed. They think I might have done it. They essentially fired me."

"This is a good thing. Now they won't try to kill you, but we should leave the cameras not working."

"There are cameras all over the city. Are you going to spend the rest of your life in this loft?"

"But they can't watch them all. And if I go outside, I can wear something with a lid on top."

"A hood, it's called a hood. As long as you wear something more than what you're wearing now it will tend to attract less attention."

NINETEEN

The fact is, Harlan did go fishing. They rented a small cabin in Pennsylvania's Endless Mountains and essentially dropped out for two months. Both had been ousted from their positions and were feeling useless. And avoiding security cameras seemed a wise route for Angelica to take.

Though she didn't know it, Group had put a price on her head after she failed to return to Base. Group couldn't quite figure out how she was able to neutralize the chip in her neck. Their minds never went to—just cut the damn thing out and stomp on it. Instead, after a month they assumed she had been picked up by Interpol, tortured, killed, and disposed of. Probably in the sea, which would have made her chip much harder to trace, and eventually destroyed by the salt water. That's how the Males at Group would have handled it. Especially if they had captured her after she had eluded them for so long.

The mountain cabin they'd rented was rustic with no other homesites in the near vicinity. A wide brook ran through the property, which was stocked up-stream with trout and there was a small market six miles to the north, which catered to vegans and vegetarians; though at this point, most markets had little choice but to go that route. There was no television, and cell phone service was hit-or-miss due to the mountains.

They purposely avoided discussing the worldwide situation and focused on enjoying one another's company. As a result, they had pretty much lost interest in keeping up with the news of the day. But the news of the day generally catches up with everyone sooner or later, no matter where they are.

The general public saw beef prices in the markets soar. Investigative reporters ferreted out the truth of the situation with remarkable swiftness and quickly thereafter a panic run ensued on all meats. Lamb and pork producers had determined that their breeding stock had gone sterile as well. In-home large-capacity freezers were cleaned out of appliance stores within a week. People began hoarding steaks and roasts of any kind. Venison had become a hot commodity, and several states that in the past had been overrun with White Tail Deer were rethinking their culling operations.

What first surprised Harlan, and most government people in authority, was that people didn't question the how and why of the situation. Sure, they panicked and hoarded, but no one seemed to see it as the end of days. They assumed, that as with disease, floods, famine, gas prices, acts of nature, inflation, acts of God, et cetera, the government would eventually get a handle on it, and everything would be back to normal. Angelica and Harlan knew better.

Meanwhile, MPS, Interpol, and security agencies worldwide had essentially locked down every business dealing in livestock propagative storage and breeding. This required twenty-four/seven manual, in-person, armed monitoring at each facility. Security cameras couldn't be relied upon because whoever had destroyed the buildings in the first wave of collapses and arsons had managed to evade any detection by the cameras. Only Harlan and Angelica knew that these agents had been implanted with programmed microchips.

Over the weeks there were furious and incessant calls by conspiracy theorists to government agencies, news outlets, talk radio shows, and anyone who would listen, demanding to know, "Who the hell was doing this, and why has there been no significant action by the powers that be?" Initially, these people were few and far between and seen by most as loonies from the extreme right and extreme left. But as the weeks rolled by, anxiety and panic were creeping into people's lives. The government was doing nothing from their point of view, and more and more people were demanding answers.

There was no way of keeping sensationalist news of worldwide confusion and panic from reaching a remote cabin in Pennsylvania's Endless Mountains. It was October and getting chilly. Angelica spent her days setting a fire in the large stone fireplace. It turned out she was a pyromaniac and would become somewhat mesmerized by the flames.

But reality was closing in on him. There was no avoiding it. He was not built to do nothing. He knew Angelica held the answers, and it was far beyond the time for her to explain things.

"You know what's going on, don't you?"

She simply stared into the blaze, holding her knees close to her chest.

"Well?"

She stood. "Okay, let's go back to Washington. I can see what's on your mind. Let's see what is going on. Maybe it can resolve itself. Without us. I need to observe. But I don't want to go back. I like it here. I want to stay here. This is a safe place for me. I'm not comfortable in your world."

"I'm afraid avoiding my world can't happen. Yes, we need to go back. I have work to do. We have work to do."

TWENTY

When Harlan and Angelica returned from the Pennsylvania Mountains it was late October. They were mostly silent for the ride back to Silver Spring, but he would push her every now and then.

"You need to give me some serious answers. I can't go on living in the dark. I need to know who these people are. I need to find their headquarters. I can't tackle this situation without more from you, a lot more."

"I want to explain it to you face-to-face. I need to be certain you understand the gravity, and the possibilities. Perhaps things can be worked out, but I don't want to talk about it while you're dodging bears and raccoons on the highway."

Harlan went from dodging raccoons and bears in rural Pennsylvania to dodging cokeheads and lunatics on the DC beltway.

They dropped their bags off at the loft. The security cameras had yet to be repaired, and even though he was exhausted from the long drive, they walked Silver Spring by night, mostly just observing the stillness. The streets were nearly deserted. The few people about seemed in a state of shock; it was far worse than they had anticipated. Harlan shook his head in bewilderment as they settled into their booth at Lenny's. It was only then that she let the sweatshirt hood drop to behind her head.

"Who would've thought that going cold turkey on meat and becoming a vegetarian would turn people into zombies?"

"It was a decision they didn't make. They're confused. They're frightened. Their enemy is invisible, so they're fighting amongst themselves. They want to fight an enemy, but they can't. They don't know what's next, and they're trying to survive any way they can. And they don't see an end to the dilemma. Their world has become a terrifying place. They don't know what lies in the future."

"But you do?"

Lenny's was nearly empty. The printed menus had all been discarded more than a month earlier and entrees were now displayed on a chalkboard above the bar. They changed with each passing day, depending on what became available from the suppliers. Lately, it was totally vegetarian dishes. Even fish and chips was hit-or-miss. Potatoes were always popular, and chicken was still available, although rivaling the price of caviar. Many people came into Lenny's simply to consume alcohol. Nothing on the menu excited Harlan and Angelica so they passed on ordering any dinner and only had a Guinness and a glass of water. Angelica looked around to see who might be able to hear what she was about to say. There was no one.

"Where do you want me to start?" she said, leaning her chin onto the palms of her hands.

"Let's try the beginning."

Angelica took a long drink from her water glass. He could see she had grown weary of concealing the truth, tired of going it alone. Ultimately, Harlan had saved her life. She appeared a different creature, physically and mentally.

"There is no beginning. There is no end. At least not in my lifetime. Nor yours. It started long before you were born, it will end after you die. I'm no longer able to go home. I've become the outcast." She took his hand. "I don't want you to die."

Harlan shrugged. "We're all going to die. It's a simple fact of life. Some sooner than others."

"I suppose. I guess I've never really been confronted by mortality. I'm just now beginning to understand it." She sighed. "I guess I'll start with this—I'm not an American."

He smiled. "I know that."

"No, I mean I'm not from here."

"I know that too."

"Listen to me, Harlan. I'm from Elsewhere."

He sat silently for a moment, considering what she wanted to tell him.

"And Elsewhere is—where exactly?"

"It won't make any sense to you."

"Try me."

She turned in the booth so that she was facing the bar and not him, then rested against the back wall and stretched her legs out on the leather cushion. She folded her arms across her chest. "I wish I didn't have to wear clothing. It's so constricting."

"Life can be cruel."

She smiled. "Okay. Let me go to the beginning you asked for. The closest beginning I can think to put on it is 165. I'm not an expert on this. It was before I was born. I've only been instructed in it."

"165? Is that code for something?"

"It was a long time ago, for you. But not for us."

"Ahh, as in the year 165? As in the year of the Antonine Plague?"

"Yes. We killed five million people. Well, not me. Like I said I wasn't born yet."

"Right. Well, neither was I. I only read about it in the ninth-grade world history class. Crazy how stupid crap like that sticks in your head. And who might this We be?"

"That's the hard part to explain. Do you know you're destroying the Earth? And it's not good. The consequences are becoming irreversible."

He laughed. "We're back to cow and lamb farts?"

"I'm trying to be serious with you. Don't make it hard for me."

"Angelica, I feel as if you're talking on this level—" He held his hand a foot over his head, "And I'm down on this level—" He moved his hand to his chest. "I have no idea what the hell you're talking about. The Antonine Plague? What's that got to do with anything?"

"All of them. What you call the Plague of Justinian, 541, twenty-five million killed; the Black Death, Bubonic Plague, 1346, a hundred million killed; the Cholera Pandemic of 1852, another million. I was alive for those, but I had nothing to do with them. I was too undeveloped. Even so, I've always been against the killing. I helped develop the Alternative. That's why I arrived here. To be certain the Alternative ran according to the plan we Females designed."

"Well, that explanation certainly clears things up."

"The Females developed the Alternative. But apparently the Males became impatient. I wasn't there. I was here. I don't know what happened. It was supposed to be painless, but the Males started the killing again. They change things without notice. It's their way. Every death has been a result of Male aggression."

"Sorry, Angelica, I'm not keeping up with you."

"We've been trying to kill you off for two thousand of your years," she nearly screamed, "but you keep coming back, you keep reproducing. You find solutions. And you multiply. And now your billionaires are sending probes out to other realms. We can't allow that to happen. You must be stopped before you infect other worlds."

"Of my years? You say that as if they're not your years."

"My clock is not your clock."

"No kidding."

"Don't you understand what I'm trying to tell you?"

"I can be a little dense at times, but if I'm following you, I'm starting to get frightened. Like everyone else around here."

"And you should be."

She turned to face him and began to move the place settings around the table.

"Okay. Say this sugar bowl is your sun. And these knives, spoons, forks, and salt and pepper shakers are the planets of your solar system."

"My sun, my solar system ... and not yours?"

"Right. Not mine."

"Okay, yes, you've frightened me."

"That's not my intention, I just want you to see what's going on. No one will kill you. I'll make certain of that."

She adjusted the table settings and then removed the pepper shaker, which was five or six inches from the sugar bowl, placed it off to the side, and knocked it over. Pepper spilled out onto the table.

"If you look at this set-up, it's similar to your solar system or one of your oxygen atoms, but it isn't oxygen, it represents an element you haven't discovered, and probably never will—."

"Stop right there. Hold on. Are you trying to tell me that you are not human? That you really are from Elsewhere? You're some sort of alien?"

"Yes, that's what I've been trying to say. I am from Elsewhere. Elsewhere exists."

"You mean all this time I've been making love to an alien?"

She couldn't help but laugh. "That part has been enjoyable, definitely, even for me, though I find this somewhat startling. Here I am trying to explain to you that your entire world is crumbling to pieces, right in front of your eyes, and all you're concerned about is where you've been sticking your reproductive organ for the last few months."

"It is a little unnerving."

She took his hand again. "You'll get over it."

"I'm sure I will, as long as you're around. Let's get back to the pepper shaker."

"Okay. This atom I've laid out on the table, that vaguely resembles your oxygen atom. It has a name, but skip it, it doesn't translate to American, and it would be unpronounceable for you even if it did. But let's give it an American name, say—Sigma."

"Sigma's Greek, but I'm still not following you. I was shitty at chemistry in college. You've laid out nine objects there. Can't you explain all this using a different analogy? Say baseball? It has nine players. I understand baseball."

"What's baseball?"

He laughed. "Yeah, well okay, if you had only mentioned that on the Amtrak train, we could have saved a lot of time. I would have known you were an alien from the start. Okay, back to Sigma. I'll try to keep up."

"It's just a name. These Sigma atoms exist in various places throughout the cosmos. They're not organic, but within each of these Sigmas, there can be a rogue electron that has the ability to develop exactly like your Earth; it can develop an atmosphere capable of supporting millions of living creatures, plant and animal. And if that rogue electron overdevelops, and then dies, in any one of the Sigma atoms, if the ozone layer and atmosphere collapse due to a proliferation of greenhouse gasses, if it then warms to irreversible temperatures, if all forms of life, plant and animal, die off. If the fish boil in the seas, the electron will then continue to heat to an unsustainable temperature, and it will implode, forcing the atom to implode, which can cause a massive nuclear reaction, which in turn, would be devastating, catastrophic in fact, to our way of life. We cannot live without sigma atoms."

"Like the Big Bang Theory?"

"Your scientific minds have wasted too much time on that. And Steady State, and other absurd theories. You're never going to make it that far along. Especially if things don't change dramatically. It only becomes wishful thinking on your part."

"I think I need another beer."

Harlan motioned to Mackie who brought over a fresh Guinness and a new glass of water.

"When you say our way of life, you're not talking about life on Earth, you're talking about your way of life, as you know it—Elsewhere?"

"Yes. I'm sorry."

"Does Elsewhere have a name?"

"You couldn't pronounce it."

"Okay, let's make one up. Sigma's already taken. How about Perigee? Has a nice ring, don't you think?"

"Perigee. Sure. What's it mean?"

"Technically it would be an extreme point in an object's orbit. Thus far and no further."

"I'm sorry, Harlan." She squeezed his hand tighter. "Try to look at it from our perspective. Human beings are a cancer to us; you're a disease we need to eliminate. You always have been a cancer. That's your behavior. You eat up your surroundings and leave a wasteland in your wake. You consume, consume, and consume until nothing is left. We must eradicate you for our way of life to survive. We cannot coexist. These plagues you've weathered over the centuries, The Black Death, the Cholera epidemics, Yellow Fever, AIDS, COVID-19, the influenzas of 1889 and 1918?"

Harlan sat there, a bit stunned. "Yes?"

"We introduced them to your Earth. Try to look at those waves of death from our point of view. They all have been generated by our researchers. In our laboratories. They are our vaccines, ones that we have introduced to eliminate humans from the Earth. To kill the cancer that you are. But like most diseases, humans have become resilient and developed your own antibodies, vaccines, and remedies that have prolonged your existence. You fight back to save your skins, it's only natural, disease or not. Every disease behaves like that. But in the last two hundred years your destruction of the Earth has accelerated at an astounding rate, far more quickly than the years before. Your Great Salt Lake is drying up, Greenland is nearly three degrees hotter than it was thirty of your years ago, ocean water in Florida reads over one hundred degrees. Howler monkeys in Mexico City are dropping dead from the trees due to the heat. Your atmospheric storms become more and more violent. Savage hurricanes form earlier every year. You have driven this destruction to a point where you must be stopped immediately. Your energy industries won't listen to common sense. We can't wait and rely on the feeble efforts of your impotent environmentalists to correct the destruction. You must be stamped out or we all die. This is why the Females developed the Alternative."

"Sorry, this is a lot to process."

"I know."

"And there are operatives like yourself infiltrating every Sigma atom in your cosmos? That sounds like a huge undertaking."

"Sigma atoms are not overly prolific, but there are enough of them, and they are crucial to our way of life. We must protect every one of them. They react with other atoms and elements and create a compound that fuels our way of life. Efficiently. It's like oxygen is to Earth and its inhabitants. Perigee would cease to exist if there were no sigma atoms. As I said, these rogue electrons in some sigma atoms are capable of sustaining life as you know it, but not all have progressed as far as your Earth. Once they do, once these electrons show any signs of biological or botanical activity, they then begin emitting a signal of sorts. This is an anomaly, but we have instruments capable of picking up these signals."

She took a long drink of water and gave him a caring look.

"When we identify these active sigma atoms they are constantly monitored. Your Earth is the only sigma electron that has developed to such an extent that it has become a threat to our way of life. We have found no other Sigma atoms where the apes have evolved into human beings and created these cancerous conditions, so we have left the others undisturbed. For now. We only study them. But very closely."

"And you've given up on diseasing us to death with your vaccines? You've decided that ridding the Earth of methane gasses, and eliminating CO_2 emissions is enough to preserve the planet and we all go on living happily ever after. But as vegetarians, and therefore halting the warming of the globe? Is that it?"

"You're not listening to me. Your environmentalists are no match for your corporate leeches, your ignorant politicians. Greed and consumption are winning the battle. Every cancer has the same blueprint."

She pulled her hand from his and stared down at it for a full minute. Harlan eventually asked, "What?"

"It will be painless."

"What will be painless?"

"The Alternative—Phase Three."

TWENTY-ONE

Manny, Moe, and Jack had developed different opinions of their new boss, Cain. Manny followed orders. He always would. Cain was his type of boss, a ruthless survivor. Of the three, he was the most cold-blooded; he enjoyed the hunt, he enjoyed the slaughter. Manny missed the old days of planting deadly diseases and watching the humans die a slow agonizing death, their flesh falling from their bodies like discarded paper napkins. Disease versus disease. Humans were creatures that would turn on one another in the blink of an eye, which made the game even more exciting. They would take sides and kill any of their own kind who refused to agree with their way of thinking. They would develop religions and use them as an excuse to butcher one another. They would shun the diseased and let them die in the streets rather than risk getting close to these infirm creatures. They would hoard their possessions and wealth, foolishly believing it would buy them a few more hours on Earth. They never grasped that they were only specks of dust in the wind.

Oh, sure, there were the ones who aided the dying and found the cures that allowed the species to continue, but they weren't the norm. Most were happy to step aside. Only the strong survive played out on Earth just as much as it did for the Males back at Group. For Manny, the humans were great entertainment, and although Group had a formula for instigating the human wars, they had never implemented it. Humans handled that well enough on their own, so they were left to their own folly when it came to wars.

Manny would have loved to have tried to get a good war fired up, and he had suggested the possibilities often, only to be turned down by Group time and time again. War's rudimentary weapons were just another way of adding to the pollution of the planet, thus counterproductive. Nonetheless, he was always thrilled if a good war was up and running when he'd made his past visits. He also didn't think very highly of his two partners. He thought Moe was a wimp for collapsing the Dallas building when it was empty, and Jack was just plain hopeless. But that was to be expected of the conscripts.

Moe, on the other hand, was not a wimp. He had waited for the Dallas building to vacate before bringing it down because those were the orders of the day. The Females oversaw operations when that event transpired. As much as he would have loved to have watched a few humans get crushed, he understood if he were to go against Group's orders, he would have been crushed as well. He'd been around far too long to do something so stupid as to disobey a direct order from Group, even if Group was commanded by a bunch of Females.

Nonetheless, the Females weren't running the show any longer. Cain was now The Boss, and Moe was delighted to watch the six humans burn to a crisp in the building he had torched two months earlier in Denver. Unfortunately, that incident prompted the Americans to double down on security and they alerted other nations to do likewise. It had now become impossible for any of the three to approach new targets.

Bypassing security cameras was a snap, avoiding trigger-happy SWAT teams and National Guard troops was something else altogether.

And then there was Jack. At this point, all he wanted to do was go home. He was becoming repulsed by the entire operation and rued the day he'd decided to go off on this folly. He didn't necessarily have a soft spot for the humans, far from it, he understood them for the disease they were, and the dangers they posed to his way of life. It was just that he didn't want to take part in the killing of them, even if the humans were an affliction that threatened to destroy everything he knew and yearned for.

In the few operations in which Jack had participated, he'd opted to take a back seat, claiming he was too new to the configurations, and was still in the learning stage. He didn't appreciate that Cain presented things strictly in black and white, and that everything had to be done exactly as he would prescribe it. Jack saw no reason for the needless killing; they were going to die off anyway. He much preferred the proposal the Females had laid out in the beginning, and the implementation of Phase Three. It was viable, there was no pain, and there were no gruesome deaths.

But the final decision on executing Phase Three would eventually approach, and he believed Group may still alter or ignore the Females' basic premise and move ahead without running the prescribed testing. There was no question that, if it were up to Cain, Phase Three would have kicked off long ago. As a result, Jack spent most of his days trying to develop a workaround. He also spent a fair amount of time wandering the boardwalk, creating poetry and wondering what Angelica's fate had been, if she had heeded his warning.

Manny sighed dramatically. "I'm bored crapless."

"Shitless."

"What?"

"It's an idiomatic expression the Americans use," Jack explained. "You can't just replace one adjective or adverb with another that has the same meaning. The humans will find you out. I suggest you stick with the playbook and don't go around making up your own words, or expressions. We'll all be screwed otherwise."

The other two may be bored, but Jack had totally run out of patience with these goons. He didn't understand why they all couldn't return to Base and come back to Earth once Group decided to move into Phase Three. After all, Phase Three was still five years off. Granted they were Earth-years and in the grand scheme of things less than a second of his actual life, but he believed that no matter whose clock was in play, this was a colossal waste of his time - *Who the hell wants to spend five years in Atlantic City, New Jersey?*

Manny sighed as if reading Jack's mind. "If you're barred from the casinos, Atlantic City is a class-A dump. All you can do is swim and eat crappy food on the boardwalk."

There was a knock on the door and Cain stepped in.

"I hope I'm not disturbing your grousing, Manny. This operation requires patience. Don't make yourself miserable by staring at the clock ticking away. I don't like it any more than you do, but if it helps, Group is getting impatient also. They're considering moving the testing date up by a few human years. If they do, they're certain to fail, and we'll be out of here once we implement Phase Three. Needless to say, the Females are against shortening the timeline. If it had been up to me, we would have run tests a long time ago. Never even bothered to test in the first place. After all, what's the point? Just go straight to Phase Three and hit the road."

"Can we go to Phase Three without Group's go-ahead?"

"Do you want to find yourself in the same position Angelica was in?"

"We don't know what that position is," Jack offered tenuously.

"I would say long gone and only dust remains of her, thus no signals from her implant. And, by the way, have you all once again forgotten that you are being monitored by Group?"

The three fell silent. The statement about Angelica from The Boss seemed a thinly veiled threat, though they weren't certain if the threat came from Cain or directly from Group, which was a distinct possibility.

TWENTY-TWO

When they arrived back at the loft, Harlan noticed that the security cameras had been miraculously repaired while they were at Lenny's. Their little red lights were flashing once again, and he pointed it out to Angelica.

"Why don't you pull up the hoodie until we get inside? There's no telling who's monitoring these damn things, your people or my people."

"My people aren't people."

"Right. Still, it's odd they'd get repaired the moment we hit town."

Once they were safely behind closed doors Angelica removed the hoodie along with the rest of her clothing.

"I don't know why I find all that stuff so restricting. Wearing clothing doesn't bother you, does it?"

"My parents were into clothing. I must have picked it up from them at an early age. It's a habit that's hard to break."

"How about me being naked?"

"After a couple of months, I'd like to say I'm getting weary of it, but you'll get no complaints from this side of the room. There is wonderful art in the female form."

"I think you are right about that. You probably wouldn't be as attracted to me if I was to appear to you in my Perigee form."

"Ignorance is bliss. I like you just the way you are."

"And that's exactly how diseases multiply so quickly. It's in their system, they have no control."

"Ever the romantic."

After settling back in, Angelica lit two candles on the dining table, and they sat down for a homemade pasta dinner with a bottle of Pinot Grigio, though she still only drank water. Over the months, Angelica had become quite a good cook, and he wondered if removing the chip had somehow changed her disposition. Or tastebuds.

After they finished with dinner, he gave her a long, serious look. "Well, here we are, back in the mix. I hate to destroy the atmosphere, but here goes—what does Phase Three look like?"

"Can't we just let that go until tomorrow morning? Clean up the dishes and lie together in bed? I just want to sleep with you."

"No. I need to know what's going on."

"It's not a good ending. From your viewpoint."

"I figured it wasn't going to be any bed of roses since you've been putting off talking about it for months."

Angelica took his hand. "You're smart, Harlan. I'm sure you can figure this out. Group is working to eliminate Earth's polluters; they're trying to save the planet, save this sigma atom, albeit for selfish reasons. It must be done. It's not an altruistic move on our part. I know that, but if Earth dies, we die. I'm sure you can see that."

"So, more disease, more famine until the biggest polluters of all, the human race, are finally eradicated. I'd hardly call that painless."

She finished her glass of water, walked to the sink, and refilled it.

"Do you think the cattle are feeling any pain? The sheep, the hogs? We simply sterilized them. They don't know what's going on. The ones that aren't slaughtered by your people will live out their lives until old age takes over. And you will still be able to have sex. We're not taking that pleasure from you. It's just that nothing will come of it. No more babies."

Harlan leaned back in his chair and pushed his fingers through his hair. It had finally dawned on him.

"Christ, you're going to sterilize the humans as well."

"Just the men. That's all that's necessary. And your reproductive equipment is much more easily targeted. Females are far more complicated creatures."

"So I've heard."

"It will be painless. You will all live out your lives in a normal fashion. Some of our vaccines ... or what you call diseases, that we introduced in the past have already been withdrawn, so fewer of you will suffer from them and die a painful death. We're trying to do this as gently as possible. This is the Females' Alternative. We're not monsters."

"Aren't you forgetting that humans have frozen sperm banks as well?"

"Those supplies won't last very long. And we're counting on the fact that most of your Females won't want to bring a child into a world that has no future."

"A world with no future ..."

"The only downside is that the technology isn't flawless, it requires us to sterilize all primates. We are unable to focus it on just the humans. As a result, the great apes and chimpanzees, along with most monkeys will have to die off as well. But you will still have your chickens, turkeys, ducks, and all. And your fish. We have only had success adjusting the reproductive capacity of Male mammals. Which means dolphins and whales could potentially disappear if we worked on it, but we're not going to go there. The technology can't penetrate the sea. And they're not a threat to the environment. In fact, they're beneficial. Whales are the picture of environmental stability, the perfect machine. In all likelihood, we'll stop at primates. There's no reason to go beyond that." She offered him a bit of an odd smile. "Too bad, really. I find gorillas to be charming, peaceful, lovable creatures. Chimps? Not so much, but we can't take any chances. If we allow chimps to survive, they will once again develop into humans, and we're right back where we started. Just a different variant on the same disease."

"And so that's it then. End of story."

"You're not focusing on the fundamental issue: human beings. Are. A. Disease. I've been saying this over and over. Every other species is beneficial and contributes to the well-being of the planet. Even if Perigee didn't exist, even if we had no interest in what happens here, you humans are an infestation and a threat to all other living creatures. You have been from the beginning. You can penetrate the seas, and you have. You still hunt and kill the whales. The ant, the termite, the lion, the hawk, and the whale, they all live their lives in harmony. Do they kill one another? For food, sure, but the lioness doesn't feel the need to control or own the entire veldt, nor does she kill out of revenge or pleasure. She doesn't domesticate, or enslave, other creatures. Or enslave her own species as humans have. She doesn't build cities, endlessly burn fossil fuels, and pollute the air all animals must share. The pride the lioness lives within has its domain, but there is no desire in lions to spread their seed across the face of the Earth like a cancer. Man is the only creature that does this."

After a moment Harlan let out a frustrated sigh. "Pathetically, my first reaction to all this is: how do I stop it? How do I stop Phase Three?"

"It's the survival instinct. You're predisposed to fight back. It's the same with all diseases."

Harlan reached for his glass of wine but set it back on the table without drinking any. Angelica took his hand once again.

"We did build in an escape of sorts for the humans if it makes you feel any better. It was in the strategy we Females laid out in the beginning. But there's no telling if the new Male commanders at Group have changed it. They're impatient, I know that much, and they really have no desire to give you a second chance. But without the chip, I have no way to determine what their current plans might be."

"Just to humor me, what is, or was the escape?"

"Our idea, the Females' idea, that is, was to give it some time and test to see how much the carbon and methane emissions had diminished once the livestock was removed. At first, we believed it would take fifteen years for them to die off. And if the emissions levels showed a significant drop, we would hold off on sterilizing the humans; we would just monitor them from that point on. But when we realized that the humans would devour the poor beasts out of panic and greed, the fifteen-year plan was scrapped."

"Well, you were right about panic and greed. We humans are very efficient when it comes to greed."

"That's how cancers metastasize, we should have realized that. Anyway, the test date was moved up sooner, to five years from now since the livestock will be gone by then. It was our compromise with the Males. And I'm assuming they haven't changed that timetable, but who knows?"

Harlan shook his head and smiled at her.

"There's nothing like having an outrageously beautiful, naked woman explain doomsday to you. It's sexy as hell."

"I knew you'd understand."

"Your clothing choices make a bitter pill to swallow that much easier, what can I say?"

He finished his wine and refilled the glass.

"There's no way in hell your Group is going to see any major change in carbon and methane levels in five years, even with the elimination of all livestock. Then it's still going to take thirty or forty years for the ozone to repair itself significantly, and that's if we go cold turkey on fossil fuel consumption tomorrow. Which I gotta tell you, ain't gonna happen. And at this point, is the warming of the Earth reversible? Current indicators would say, no."

"Our instruments are far better at projecting and pinpointing improvement than the toys your scientists use. Any changes can be easily detected and charted. But you're right, Group will be factoring in human coal, gas, and oil use, and they would need to be convinced it was dropping off at a rapid pace for them to call off Phase Three. Waiting for coal and oil to run out isn't an option. Humans would need to fast-forward wind and solar energy production and totally pull the plug on fossil fuel. Like, yesterday."

Harlan let out another exasperated groan. "I've always been an optimist, but I don't see that happening. The crypto-currency miners are raping the power grid, everyone needs a bigger gas guzzler, a second and third car, a trip to Disney Land, a bigger house, more air conditioning, a weekend in London. There's no way in hell that behavior turns around dramatically in five years. The first Earth Day people began rattling their swords in 1970. They've been ignored ever since."

They sat quietly for a few minutes; he sipping his wine, she spooning up her pasta's remaining tomato sauce. He broke the silence.

"You know, I've never thought much about having kids, but the more I look at you, and the more I realize that it will never come about, the more I want them." He poured himself another glass of wine. *Might as well kill the bottle. What the hell?* "What happens to us? More importantly, what happens to you? What if you don't return to Perigee? If you can't return to Perigee? Do you die here on Earth as a human? Of human old age? Or Perigee old age?"

"I honestly don't know." She gave him a warm smile. "I can't have children with you, it won't work. This body of mine is just a loaner. It didn't come with any extras—like ovaries."

He laughed. "I suspected as much. I may be a dumb Male, but I do know we've been saving a small fortune on tampons."

"Tampons?"

"I rest my case. Nothing you need to worry about." He stood, moved their dinner plates to the sink, and began playing with the espresso machine. "What does happen to you? Do you go back to Perigee? Or do you stay here with me?"

"I can't go back. Jack warned me against it. There's no telling what the Females in Group know about the situation here. I have no idea what they've been told, and returnees have been eliminated. If the remaining Females have been removed from any positions of authority, then they've lost the ability to monitor any of the field operatives. Time and space. I guess the choice is mine. This Earth of yours, this solar system, is a mere atom, smaller than a drop of my blood if I were to return to Perigee. I probably wouldn't remember you, and if I did remember you, I would find you totally alien and physically repulsive, I'm sure."

"Thanks."

She didn't seem to hear him. "I would live a normal Perigee life and die of old age, just like here. My operating system would eventually become obsolete and shut down. It would be many centuries of Earth's time, but it would just feel like a normal lifetime to me. My understanding of time, of a lifetime, is the same if I leave or stay. It's just how and where I choose to spend it. And whose ticking clock marks my days."

"Then, it's possible that you could return five or six centuries from now and observe the changes?"

"Yes. Possible ... I suppose. If the Males forgo any changes in our directive."

"That's kind of wild. Why don't you go for it? If you can."

She stood and approached him from behind. She then wrapped her arms around him causing him to spill some coffee grounds.

"It will be interesting to see if I age like a human. I may be stuck in Perigee time, roaming the Earth, looking for the rest of the Females who have opted not to return. And there's another big if. Other Females. But I suspect I'm the only one."

TWENTY-THREE

It was a restless night for both Harlan and Angelica. And when they stumbled out of bed the next morning, without engaging in any conversation, they had reached the same conclusion; something had to be done. The night had seemed to spawn a sympathetic streak within her. There had to be a formula for these two civilizations to coexist, but clearly Group held all the cards. Nothing could be adopted without Group's input and approval.

"I don't even know where Group stands," were the first words Angelica uttered that morning. "It's driving me crazy. I don't know if the Males have changed the timeline. It could be too late for any adjustments."

Harlan took her in his arms. They were quiet but the wheels in their brains were spinning out of control.

"So, you're on my side now?"

"I really don't know whose side I'm on."

"Okay. We'll work with that. How do we open a dialog with Group?"

"I can't go anywhere near them. I've known operatives like Cain. He'll liquidate me before I can present anything to Group. He's not about to let a Female upstage him. And in reality, I'm not certain I can physically return to Perigee without the chip in place. I'm in total limbo."

"Well, the chip had to be implanted after you assumed human form."

"You don't understand the technology. No, the chip was embedded in Perigee and traveled with me. I remember that very clearly."

"Fine, whatever, it still says to me that you can return, chip or no chip. You do have a choice. You weren't born with it."

"And they kill me?"

"You don't know that."

"Yes, I do."

"Okay. Are you sure you want to pursue staying here?"

"Do I have a choice?"

"Yes. In the words of the FBI, 'You can go fishing.' You liked it up there. You don't need to risk everything for a culture and race that threatens to destroy Perigee. A disease. Or you can remain loyal to your tribe and stick with the solution you yourself developed. You owe us nothing. I'm sure there's a way around Cain. We can find it, and you can go back."

She considered what he'd said but shook her head and sighed.

"My tribe." She seemed in a trance. "Do I have a tribe any longer? Or have I become part of your tribe? I sometimes feel like I have. No, if I'm going to stay here there's something I want to get out of it. And I am going to get it."

"What's that?"

"You'll see when I get it."

He pulled her closer. "Okay, then we're in the dark about too much of this. We need a clearer picture. You need to contact the Male who tipped you off, the Male who gave you that note. This Jack. Can you trust him?"

"Maybe, maybe not, but I can't approach him, he's implanted with a chip. Even if he doesn't want to turn me in, I'll be found out. Anything I say to him will go directly to Cain. And therefore, to Group. What were you thinking?"

"I'm thinking I need some coffee. I'm thinking I keep forgetting that everyone in your tribe has the friggin' chip."

Harlan sat at the dining table, leaned on his elbows, and dropped his head into his hands. Nothing was said until Angelica placed a mug of coffee in front of him and joined him at the table.

"Okay, hear this out and let me know what you think. I'm sure I can still get some time with the president, but we need to have a foolproof plan in place before I go to see him. Explaining it isn't going to be easy, but we need to start at the top. It would be fruitless to go any other route. MPS, Interpol, FBI, CIA. They don't have the ability to put a fire under the ass of the rest of the world. And that's what needs to be done. The Earth needs to be warned, and it must be done by the president."

"And what do you tell him that persuades him to make such a move?"

"I don't think telling him that I'm having a passionate love affair with an alien and don't want to screw it up, is the way to go."

"Probably not."

Harlan began drumming his fingers on the table and twitching his knees. Angelica placed her hands on his. "Would you sit still, it's annoying as hell."

He laughed. "I think I liked you better when you were an automaton. You're becoming too human."

"Should I buy some clothes?"

"Don't go overboard. Okay, assuming I can get this meeting with POTUS, I'll need to convince him on the spot, right then and there, that we've been visited by beings from Elsewhere and he needs to take immediate action. Like I said, it's not going to be easy. There's a fair chance he'll just throw me in the loony bin."

"Loony bin?"

"A place for crazy people."

"I can go with you. To see the president, not the loony bin. I can explain it better than you."

"I hate to break it to you this way, but you're worthless without the chip. You're just another beautiful woman with a wild story."

"I can show him where the chip was."

"It's just a scar. It proves nothing. I'm going to have to go full-Norcross on this. I'm going to need to kidnap Jack and drag him in. He has the chip. If he's in the Oval Office with me when I meet POTUS, Group will be able to monitor it all. It will convince them we're serious about turning things around. Maybe we can get a dialog started."

"You don't even know what Jack looks like."

"No. But you do."

TWENTY-FOUR

With summer ended, the Atlantic City beach was nearly deserted, though the ocean temperature was still moderately warm, and a few hearty souls were indulging themselves in an early morning swim. An overbearing mother shouted at her ten-year-old daughter, "Cordelia, get out of that water, you'll freeze to death."

Harlan and Angelica sat on a brightly painted, wooden boardwalk bench facing the sea. Pedestrians, rickshaws, and bicyclists passed in front of them as seagulls cleaned up whatever scraps of sugary tidbits tourists had dropped from their doughnuts and bagels. Angelica wore a pair of his old jeans, ripped at the knees, cinched at the waist, and splattered with yellow paint. She also wore his blue Georgetown hoodie, dark glasses, and a COVID mask. Only her jet-black hair was visible poking out of the hood.

For no discernable reason, Angelica began laughing. "I just realized, this is a total waste of time. Manny, Moe, and Jack were blackballed from the casinos. Security circulated their pictures. You could have just contacted them for a picture of Jack."

He thought this over for a minute and shook his head. "No, that kind of crap is all handled by a private firm, and they'll be too tight about what they share. It would require a FISA warrant, raise a flag, and take too much time. We'll stick with this plan."

"Damn, it sounded so easy."

She stared out across the wide beach. Clearly, she had some trepidation about running into Jack once more.

"Jack doesn't like the other two at all. He likes to pace the boardwalk alone in the morning so that he doesn't need to talk with the others. I think he makes up poetry, but only in his head because he never writes anything down on paper, and that's why his note startled me so much. I'm sure he'll walk by here sooner or later. It's interesting, with all of our technology, pen and paper have become the only safe way of communicating."

Harlan drew in the sea air. "I almost feel like taking a swim. I haven't been in the ocean for years."

"Funny, I never went in the water when I was holed up here. It does look tempting. Strange that people still wear clothing while in the water. That really makes no sense at all. Everything just gets wet." She took in a deep breath as well. "Though, this might be the first time in my life, as a counterfeit human, that I don't want to take my clothes off. I want to be covered up. I'm very nervous about being seen."

"Don't be."

Angelica sat up straight. A look of surprise quickly swept across her face.

"Wait, hold on, they do know you. They know what you look like. Why didn't I think of that before? You met Moe in Dallas. They all know what you look like. He submitted images of you and the two other investigators."

"Dodge and Arnold. They were examining the scene for Interpol and the FBI. Shit. How good is Jack's memory?"

"It doesn't make any difference. The images are stored in his chip. He may not consider scanning back, but if he thinks you look familiar, he might."

"Shit. Shit. Shit. I've got to think."

"Well, think quick, because here he comes. And he's got Manny with him. I didn't count on that. Jack's the short man wearing the green windbreaker. Manny's the round one. They're to the right, just behind the woman with the stroller."

Jack and Manny were about fifty feet away. Harlan shifted his position on the bench so that he had his back to them. "Okay, they won't recognize you with your face covered up. Tuck your hair into the hood."

After she had, he pulled the zipper up to her chin and tied the hood's drawstrings.

"Perfect. This will still work; it doesn't matter if they're both in the pic. When they're about ten feet away, nudge me with your knee. We'll then stand, turn our backs to them and the ocean, and I'll blow off a few selfies."

"Got it."

When they neared, Harlan and Angelica stood and positioned themselves. But Jack stopped directly in front of them, leaned on the iron railing, and looked yearningly out to the ocean, keeping his back to Harlan and Angelica. Manny kept walking down the boardwalk and ducked into a nearby Starbucks.

Without turning Harlan shouted, "Hey my man, what're you doin'? Lookin' for whales? We're trying to get a selfie here with the ocean. And without you in it."

Jack turned and faced them. "Oh, sorry. No, no whales, just pondering my future. And my past. Sorry." He then ambled down the boardwalk off to their left.

Once he was out of range, Angelica untied the hood and removed the COVID mask.

"He always was a bit of a dreamer. Did you get a shot?"

"I had it on video. We're good. I even got Manny before he walked off."

As they walked back to Harlan's car, he perused the video, paused it with Jack's face in full frame, and showed it to her.

"That's him, right?"

"Yes."

"Okay, back to DC."

"I thought you were going to apprehend him?"

"Not with you. And not with Manny. What if they put up a fight? Which I assume they will. What if they try to kill you right here and now?"

She laughed. "They can't kill me, only Cain can do that."

"And how far away is Cain?"

"I assume he's up there in room 608."

"Alright. Say, we take Jack, who has an implanted chip, which Cain is monitoring, we somehow get rid of Manny, and we—"

"Okay, okay, I see your point. What's your plan?"

"Let's get to the car. I don't feel you're safe here."

Once they were cruising down the Atlantic City Expressway and five miles out of town, Harlan opened up.

"There's an agent, Lou Walsh, at MPS. He can get me directly to the president. We need to explain all of this to him, which ain't gonna be easy. This is pretty far out there, even for me, and I'm living it. But he needs to be totally convinced. Then Lou and I will come back to A.C. and pick up Jack, drag him into the Oval Office, and try to convince the president to act. And hope that Group is listening in."

Angelica was quiet for a few minutes as she considered it all. Eventually, "It's not going to work."

"Why not?"

"The moment you take him, Cain will be on to you. Your location will be easily pinpointed because of Jack's chip. You won't get forty miles down the road before they take him back."

Harlan growled. "Shit. Shit. Shit. What if we keep him completely silent? Cain won't miss him until he fails to show up after one of his long walks?"

"No, that's not good enough. They can intercept you anywhere between here and DC. You need to be very vocal with Jack to get through to Group. But Cain will defend his turf. He'll cut you off if he can figure out how to do it."

Again, she was quiet as she thought it over.

"Okay, you can't drive him to Washington. You'll need to grab him, keep him absolutely quiet, put him on a helicopter, and take him directly to the White House Lawn. Perigee doesn't have the equipment here to intercept you in the air. Once you're in the air, and being monitored, you'll have the ability to talk freely and convince anyone who's listening in, that your motives are legitimate. The President needs to be on board before you bring Jack in. He needs to understand that Perigee is real, and their motives are real."

Harlan smiled. "Time to talk to Lou Walsh."

TWENTY-FIVE

After returning to DC Harlan and Angelica staked out a somewhat out-of-the-way spot on the steps of the Lincoln Memorial. The marble statue of Abe seemed to be watching their every move. The reflecting pool stretched out before them; the Washington Monument rested off in the distance. It was a touristy spot, but few tourists were wandering about on this morning, making it an innocent enough location for them to meet up with Lou Walsh. The sun was bright, and it warmed them both.

"That's Walsh coming toward us on the left side of the pool, with the black baseball hat." The hat read *Steel City Football* and sported a Pittsburgh Steelers logo. "Funny guy. I guess I should have told him you'd be with me."

She laughed once he got close enough for her to read the logo. "I forgot all about that Pittsburgh Steelers story. Did you believe me?"

"Not for a minute."

"I didn't think so. I've learned a lot since then. Do you think Lou's going to be embarrassed?"

"I sure hope so."

Walsh scaled the steps and sat on Harlan's left. "How's it going?"

"Good. Nice hat."

"I thought you'd get a kick out of it. I was going to bring you some cologne from Nordstrom."

Harlan cocked his head toward Angelica. "This is Angelica. The cheerleader and fragrance specialist."

"Oh, shit, sorry." He pulled the hat from his head. "Ahh. Wait. Is she the one? She's your reliable source? Your Deep Throat?"

"In a manner of speaking."

"Does this mean she's coming over? We're moving forward?"

"Angelica, meet Lou. Lou, meet Angelica."

They shook hands. Lou couldn't control his impatience. "Who are your people? Who do you work for? Who's behind all this? How do we reverse it?"

Harlan held up his hands like a prizefight referee separating two boxers.

"Okay, hold on. Relax and let me bring you up to speed. This isn't going to be easy for you to absorb, so bear with me."

He found himself speaking as if he were talking to a ten-year-old, but there seemed no other way to proceed, so he jumped right into it.

"First, and brace yourself for this, Angelica is an alien. Not an alien like someone from Ukraine or Afghanistan, but an honest to God, outer space, alien. You need to grasp that and understand it as a hardcore fact before we can move forward."

Lou laughed, but it wasn't a happy laugh. "You dragged my ass all the way over here to tell me that? You've spent too much time in the woods, buddy-boy."

He stood to leave, but Harlan grabbed hold of his jacket and also stood.

"I knew this wasn't going to be easy." He looked at Angelica. "Show him your scar."

She got to her feet and peeled off Harlan's Georgetown hoodie, leaving her naked from the waist up.

Harlan cleared his throat. "Ahh, yeah, I guess you could have just dropped it a bit in the back. Anyway, here we are." He pointed to the scar on Angelica's neck. "She's from a place called Perigee." He passed on explaining Perigee was conveniently made-up. "She was embedded with a microchip. Here." He pointed out the scar. "I removed it so her handlers couldn't track her or eavesdrop on her conversations."

"You are absolutely out of your friggin' mind, you know that? You expect me to believe this crap? Just because she has a scar?" He looked around. "Where's her flying saucer?"

"I kinda thought it was going to go this way. Listen, Lou, we're living in two entirely different dimensions. Think about everything that's gone on. What else could it be? Who else would have the capabilities of neutralizing every single piece of livestock on the entire globe? They're here."

"Bullshit. I've got better things to do."

He again made a move to walk off, but Harlan held onto his jacket.

"Come on, Lou, what else have you got?"

The three of them stood silently as Walsh thought this over. He finally gave in. "You've got a point. I'm just having trouble wrapping my head around this."

"I'm going to let Angelica paint the picture."

She went on to explain the entire situation to Lou, from top to bottom and ended by confirming that sterilization awaited the entire human race. It took the better part of half an hour.

When she'd finished Lou looked up to the sky and stretched his neck and shoulders. He then brought his gaze back to Harlan.

"Jesus. Is all this for real?"

Harlan spoke for the first time in twenty minutes. "It's for real."

Lou sat quietly for another minute. "I don't know. I'm not buying it. I'd feel better if you'd show me some little green men and a spaceship."

"For Christ's sake, Lou. What do we have to gain by making this up?"

"What's she got to gain if it's true? There's the question. Why doesn't she just go back to wherever she came from? She doesn't need to save the Earth if what she says is true."

"Angelica's chip is gone. She can't go home. She's stuck here."

He considered this for another long moment.

"Okay, okay, say I go along with all this lunacy. What's next? If she can't communicate with this Group, where do we go from here?"

"You want the short form or the long form?"

"Let's start with the short."

"We need to secure one of their operatives, walk him into the Oval Office, and hopefully set up a dialog between POTUS and Group. Angelica believes there's a slim chance we can buy some time before Phase Three is set in motion, but POTUS needs to get the world's polluters to come together and go cold turkey on fossil fuels for starters."

Walsh laughed. "I don't see that playing out."

"To be honest, neither do I."

"And if we can get the Old Man on board, where do we find one of their operatives?"

"That's the easy part. I know where to grab one."

"We need to brief POTUS beforehand. He doesn't absorb things that quickly. It's been hard enough for me to grasp it."

"Can you set us up with a meeting?"

"Yes. But you know how he is, it might help if we had a few little green men with ray guns and a flying saucer to grab his attention."

TWENTY-SIX

Harlan met Walsh at the White House security gates two days later. Lou looked past him down the walkway. "No Angelica?"

"No Angelica. You know how The Old Man is with good-looking women. He won't hear a word we're saying. And if we do convince him we've been visited, he'll have her locked up, and we need her out and accessible."

"Define accessible, lover-boy."

A Marine guard walked them into the White House and a staffer took them to the Oval Office. The room was empty, but they remained standing. The president arrived two minutes later.

"Nice to see you again, Harlan. Enjoying your vacation?"

"Not so's you'd notice, sir."

"I know the feeling. The world's gone crazy. I hope you boys have some answers for me. What have you got, Lou?"

He cleared his throat. "Some answers, but bizarre answers. And one long-shot solution."

"Bizarre seems to be the norm as of late."

Harlan and Lou briefed POTUS like two tennis pros lobbing a ball back and forth; never leaving him a moment to interrupt or get sidetracked. When they'd finished, he stood, turned, and looked out the window for a full three minutes. He then looked over his shoulder at them.

"Well, I'll be dipped in shit. You fellas are serious about all this crap, I take it."

"Yes, sir," Harlan answered.

"And for three months we've had the best scientists in the world trying to reverse this issue by experimenting with sound waves, blasting these bulls with everything from ambulance sirens to Lynyrd Skynyrd? And now you're telling me it was all done with UV light or some such shit?"

"Yes, sir."

"And how did you two sleuths come up with all this information?"

It was Harlan who answered. "We took one of their operatives. We then removed and destroyed a tracking chip they had implanted. Without being monitored, the operative was able to fill us in on the entire operation."

"What does this operative look like? And please don't tell me he's a little green man with a ray gun who arrived in a flying saucer."

"They're living in an entirely different time and space continuum," Harlan answered. "They can duplicate the human form. You might pass one of them on the street and you wouldn't know the difference. There's no telling how many of them there are across the globe."

"Why."

"Why what, sir?"

"Why is this operative so willing to help out? Turn against his own? Doesn't make sense."

"Well, sir, the operative is kind of screwed."

Walsh couldn't resist saying, "Literally."

Harlan gave Lou a sideways glance. "Thanks for clarifying, Lou. What Lou means by 'literally' is that the operative has come to understand that they can't return to a Perigee way of life; they're basically trapped here. So, yes, they're kind of screwed, and the operative has decided to make the best of a crappy situation."

"Why isn't he at this meeting?"

"The operative was afraid they'd be taken hostage, even held for ransom. I seem to be the only one they trust." Harlan thought, *Jesus, juggling pronouns can be a bitch.* But he knew he was being recorded and everything he said could be thrown back at him at some point and possibly lead to Angelica.

The president sat, placed his elbows on the desk, and drummed the fingers of his left hand on his chin. "Okay, Lou, what's your long-shot solution? Let's hear it."

"As I said, their next move is to sterilize humanity, but Harlan's contact says there's a grace period. It could be as long as five years; it could be less. There's no telling. We need to set up a line of communication with their Group, find out what their timetable is, and see if we can work with them. See if we can buy ourselves some time."

POTUS grumbled. "Great. And how do we set up a line of communications?"

"A week ago, Harlan picked up a visual on another one of their operatives who's still implanted with the microchip. He's holed up in Atlantic City and goes by the name of Jack. Our plan is to take him, load him on a chopper in AC, fly him straight to that lawn of yours, and march him in to see you. Group will be monitoring him the entire time by way of his chip. They'll hear everything we say to him, and by the time we get him to the White House we're hoping we will have convinced Group that we're willing to work with them."

"And then it's up to me to change the entire landscape of the Earth."

"Yep. That's kinda the plan, sir."

TWENTY-SEVEN

Harlan and Lou positioned themselves on the same Atlantic City boardwalk bench that he and Angelica had perched on a week earlier. It was a misty morning with dense fog rolling in from the ocean. No swimmers, just people in raingear strolling the beach and a few surf fishermen who seemed to be catching nothing. Angelica was essentially out of the picture; without her chip there was little left for her to do but watch. Neither Harlan nor Angelica was certain how Jack would react, and he wanted her safely out of harm's way. He believed there was a possibility Jack could become violent and resist, even though Angelica assured him that Jack was basically a poet.

Harlan brought up the photo of Jack on his phone and passed it to Lou.

"I didn't really get a face-to-face with him. This is all we have to go on. According to Angelica these guys aren't into changing their clothes that often. Hopefully he'll be wearing the same green windbreaker. And if Manny's with him, we'll need to improvise very quickly."

After a forty-five-minute wait, Jack appeared off to their right, no Manny. They remained still until he was ten feet away. They then rose and stepped directly into his path, stopping him dead in his tracks. The three stood there facing one another frozen for a moment. Then Harlan produced a three-by-five file card and held it up for Jack to see. It read: *We have liquidated Angelica. Do not say one single word. Not one. If you do, the same fate awaits you. We fed her to the fish.* Walsh had selected the wording. Harlan thought it was a bit heavy-handed, but it explained why Group could no longer track her chip, and that she was no longer in play. Jack appeared noticeably frightened and remained quiet.

Lou cocked his head toward the boardwalk off ramp, took Jack's elbow, and they walked him down the ramp and over to a waiting armored black Lincoln MKT with smoked windows. Another MPS agent, Rich Perez, sat at the steering wheel. Harlan, Lou and Jack slipped into the rear seat with Jack in the middle. They remained totally silent until they reached a waiting Marine Corp helicopter positioned at the military subsection of the Atlantic City International Airport. After they boarded the chopper, it lifted into the air. Harlan was the first to speak.

"First of all, Jack, I want to thank you for being cooperative. I assure you no harm will come to you. I only wish your other operative had been as obliging. We don't generally play it that rough. Too bad, she seemed likable enough."

Jack remained silent, his frightened eyes darting from one agent to another.

"It's okay, Jack, feel free to speak." Harlan shouted over the chopper's engine racket. "We know you're being monitored by Group. Obviously, we know your name. We know Group can hear everything we say. And Cain as well. We want Group to hear everything. We're trying to create a dialog with Group. We're taking you to meet the president of the United States. We need you to be our conduit between the president and

Group. We know Group's motives and desires. We're looking for a compromise."

Jack slowly shook his head from side to side.

"No harm will come to you, trust me."

He continued to shake his head. "It doesn't work the way you want it to work. I can't do what you ask."

Walsh was already growing impatient. "Well, Jack, I'm afraid you have no choice in the matter. We're going to open up this channel even if we need to cut that chip out of you with a chainsaw and toss you out of this chopper."

"Lou, take it easy. Don't worry, Jack. As I said, you're in no physical danger. You have my guarantee. Though I'm not sure how long I can control my colleague." Harlan found himself wondering if they also played good-cop-bad-cop in Perigee.

"I'm telling you it doesn't work the way you want," Jack repeated in a hushed voice. "Yes, Group is monitoring all of our speaking, but I can't relay any information coming from Group. My implant is not designed to do that. I don't receive incoming messages from Group. It's above my grade. I am just monitored. Only Cain receives messages from Group. And 'A' before him. Then they pass those messages on to operatives at my level ... If they choose. If you want a direct dialog with Group, you need to clutch Cain."

"Clutch?"

"Shit," Walsh growled, "Why didn't she—" He stopped himself, realizing that getting into a, "What really did happen to 'A' conversation" would be more than counterproductive.

"Basically, there's no way we can confirm whether Group is monitoring our chat or not, is that it, Jack?"

"Yes."

"Do they know you've been taken hostage? Or, I should say, taken for a visit to the White House?"

He only shrugged.

Harlan leaned back and ran his hands through his hair. "Can you contact Cain in some way? Do you have a device of some sort? Cell phone? Space-age communicator?"

Jack ignored the question, and asked, "Do you know why we are here at Earth?"

"Yes."

"Do you know what our plans are for your people that live on Earth?"

"Yes."

"Do you know how it will end?"

"Yes."

Jack made a motion with his hand indicating he wanted to write out his thoughts and not broadcast them. Perez produced a legal pad and a pen and handed them to him.

Jack was apparently not noted for his penmanship, and it took a while for the agents to clearly make out what he was trying to say. In the end it came down to this: *You don't want to talk to Cain. He's impatient and wants it to be over, and he will do anything he can to move things forward quickly.*

Harlan took the pad from him and wrote: *Can we get back to the Females' timetable? Maybe even extend it? This is what the president wants. We need more time. Probably even more than five years. Is there any way to get Group into direct contact with the president?*

Jack wrote: *There are words that can be spoken that will get the attention of Group's communication sensors. The USA is the main focus of their intentions—and Russia—White House, president of the United States, Oval Office are good words. Don't mention that you killed 'A.' Violence brings on more violence. Non-American capital cities—Paris, London, Tokyo, Rome, Berlin, Moscow—would be good to say. You need Group to send someone to the White House who's far more senior than Cain.*

How do we know we've got Group's attention?

You don't. But if you do have Group's attention, and they think you are honest in your intentions, they will maybe send someone else and block Cain. You will need to be communicating with a Functionary, *otherwise you will be wasting your time.*

"I think you're going to like meeting the president of the United States, Jack. At the White House. In Washington, DC."

TWENTY-EIGHT

The helicopter settled on the White House lawn shortly after noon. Jack, Harlan and Lou were quickly ushered into the Oval Office by a half dozen staffers. POTUS was waiting for them. It took them less than a minute to bring him up to speed. The president focused on Jack.

"He doesn't look like an alien to me. I was still expecting green. Or something like the guys in *The New Yorker* cartoons. He looks too much like a real person. Does he speak English?"

"Yes, sir."

"Then, he understands what I'm saying?"

"Ah. Yes, sir, I would suspect so."

There was a timid knock on the door and Mrs. Albright stepped in.

"Excuse me, sir, but there's a gentleman outside who insists on seeing you. No one quite knows how he bypassed security. He just seems to have appeared out of nowhere. The Secret Service has searched him thoroughly. He's unarmed. Since they're aware of the situation in here they haven't escorted him out of the building just yet. They're waiting for your orders."

"This could be an emissary from Group, sir. Hopefully, we've broken through." Harlan then looked at Jack. "Is that it, Jack? That's what's going on?"

He shook his head. "I don't know. I receive nothing. It could be Cain for all I know. But then maybe not. I think I should not speak any further."

"Jesus Christ, bring him in," POTUS shouted at Mrs. Albright, loud enough to be heard throughout the building.

She opened the door, and the visitor was escorted in by three large Secret Service agents. One on either side and another stood directly behind him; all looking like leopards ready to pounce and devour their prey. The visitor focused on Mrs. Albright.

"Thank you, Jesus Christ." He then turned to the president. "Call me Davenport."

Davenport stood six foot three, wore a tailored tan suit, and resembled a Puerto Rican right fielder more than anything else. The president looked from Davenport to Jack and back to Davenport.

"Do you represent Group?"

"Yes." Davenport then turned his attention to Jack. He pulled a small metallic card from his jacket and held it out for Jack to see. Jack reacted as if he had seen death itself.

"You are to leave this room. Your functioning is now no longer necessary at this location."

Without saying a word, Jack stood on shaky legs and left the Oval Office with Mrs. Albright.

The president focused on the three Secret Service Agents.

"You men can leave as well. Let's keep this a cordial little chat. We're all friends here."

The agents begrudgingly stepped out of the office.

"Thank you." Davenport surveyed the room. "We at Group are somewhat being confused. You appear to be well-informed about what our plans are. The operative who just walked away through the door with Jesus Christ told you nothing. We have been monitoring him, we know that is truth. This is our reason for being confused."

Lou jumped in before POTUS could derail things. "We've been able to tap into some of your communications. Our ability is limited, but we're the only nation on Earth that has developed this capability. It would be pointless for you to communicate with any other nation. They are all in the dark. Any logistical issues should be settled here, in this office, and nowhere else."

"Let us sit and talk to one another together."

Davenport moved between the two facing sofas in front of the Resolute Desk, sat, put his feet up on the coffee table and waited to be joined. "Nice setup you have here."

The president was dumbfounded by this lack of protocol, but he ultimately held up his hands in a friendly fashion.

"Okay, okay, sounds good to me, Davenport. Let's see where this gets us."

Harlan sat on the same sofa as Davenport, which gave him an oddly uneasy feeling. Almost the same feeling he got when Angelica first sat next to him on Amtrak. And Davenport gave him a curious glance, as though he was sensing something he didn't like in Harlan. The president and Walsh sat on the opposite sofa facing them.

"Before we talk about any possible solutions or compromises," Davenport started, "We had a Female operative who evaporated from our observances. Her name was Angelica. We are assuming she has been liquidated, or accidentally dispatched. If she had fled or been dispatched we would still be able to trace her. This we cannot do for some reason. Is this something you may have knowledge about?"

The president responded. "I assure you, Davenport, that's not how we operate. We are a peaceful people."

He laughed. "You forget that we have been monitoring humans for thousands of your years. On this land mass alone the first humans painted their bodies and slaughtered one another for trivial reasons. The white race then developed the technology to cross the big water and humans came from the east to slaughter the tribes in the west. You kill one another as a matter of routine, every day of your year. You enslave your own species. You terminate children in places of learning with weapons of war. Even with my limited understanding of your language, peaceful is not a word I would ever use when describing humans. As you have developed from the apes, you have only become more violent toward each other. You spend time and resources developing new ways to kill one another in larger numbers. The east side of your Mediterranean water spills innocent blood at the directive of imaginary idols that dance in human heads like hornets."

POTUS cleared his throat. "Well, all that aside, rest assured, we have no knowledge of the Female you're missing. People go missing all the time, and if she had no local history, so to speak, no identification documents, she could be lying in a morgue somewhere. Who would know? No one would be notified. She could be buried in a potter's field somewhere."

"As I said, we are possessing the ability to track this Female, alive or dead. Her embedded tracking mechanism has gone invisible."

Harlan instinctively reached into his pocket and crumpled the note he had handed to Jack, while POTUS smiled and slapped his knee. "You know, that reminds me of this mutt my granddaddy had. He used to run off, so old Pappy had the veterinarian put one of those damn microchips in him. Didn't stop him from running off, and he went missing one day. Never heard from that darn dog again, and that chip was a malfunctioning piece of crap. People put too much faith into those microchip thingies."

"Thank you, sir," Walsh chimed in to keep the shaggy dog story from consuming the entire afternoon. He couldn't help but notice, in staring at the bottom of Davenport's shoes that they looked as if they'd come straight out of the box. There were no scratches or any sign or wear and tear on the leather soles.

"Mr. Davenport, I think we all need to get on the same page and develop a way to proceed. Can you tell us what your timetable is? How long does the Earth have before you move into Phase Three? And to be totally honest, our objective is to avoid Phase Three altogether, which I suspect is more than obvious."

Davenport gave POTUS a serious glance. "Let me say that there are elements of our being that see no point in allowing the human race to continue beyond this afternoon. The hardliners want to eradicate the disease now. They see no benefit to studying diseases. They want to get the work here done quickly and proceed to other desires."

"Desires?"

Davenport looked beyond Walsh's shoulder as if focusing on an imaginary tablet. "Objectives."

"Ahh."

"There are other elements who are thinking differently. They want to save your house. But they are mostly the Females and artistic types, and we are losing our impatience with them."

"I think I'm following you. What would be the Females' thinking?"

"They believe there is a good thing to keep the humans as a biological experiment. To be observed. Then, we are educated if these equine leavings should grow up Elsewhere."

"Equine leavings?"

"I think he means horseshit, sir."

"Ahh, right."

"I was only playing with your words. I'm intrigued by the languages of diseases. Methods of communication. Your language is quite odd, but mildly entertaining to play with. Example: profanity. We do not indulge in profanity, and I find it fascinating. It seems to highlight a lack of vocabulary in those who use it. So many different uses for the word shit. I have yet to understand the meaning of, 'Are you shitting me?' At any rate, you are a small fraction of the problems we are facing," Davenport continued. "So few of you have the same understanding of space and time as we do. Where you are simply an atom's electron in our world, we understand that we are also only an atom in another's world. Though I've come to realize that some of you do understand."

Harlan, thanks to Angelica, was one of those who did. "You make this sound hopeless. Is that intentional? I'm more interested in what direction you personally are leaning. And if you have the authority to make changes."

Davenport shifted his eyes to Harlan. "You are speaking this language too?"

"Uh, yes."

"I had been believing you were a Dark Mechanic, here to observe, and not talking for that reason."

Harlan considered this for a long moment before responding. "I'm not positioned as a Dark Mechanic. My interests lie Elsewhere. But yes, I am here to observe. And I understand why you're confused by this shit."

"If you are not a Dark Mechanic, you have not needing to know why a Dark Mechanic would be necessary, so I will not speak further on this."

Harlan made a mental note to grill Angelica on this Dark Mechanic thing. "No, I'm not a Dark Mechanic. They're obsolete as far as we are concerned, have been for eons. We cleansed our society of that type ages ago. Let's just say, we're not alone in wanting to achieve an equitable solution here. For all participants."

"But you are not one of these—people. That much I sense inside."

"No, I'm not. I'm an observer. I arrived shortly before you. And as you mentioned, time and space are relevant. Or irrelevant, depending on one's perspective. But again, I am only here to observe, and report my findings. I think it fair to say, that everything transpiring here is being made note of and will be communicated to others. You are wise to understand that we are all simply an atom in another's world."

Both Walsh and the president were getting totally lost, but they had the good sense to keep their mouths shut.

Harlan added, "Let me only say that I represent a society that also has a strong interest in your timetable."

"I understand this. I'm not an easy one to be fooled. The shade you chose for your human exterior should have enlightened me. After all, I made the same decision. Superior thinking often follows the same path."

Davenport sat up a bit straighter and pulled his feet down from the coffee table. He now directed his comments toward Harlan rather than POTUS or Walsh.

"We are looking to the same goal, I'm sure: to stabilize this electron these two call Earth. And when I say stabilize, I am meaning permanently."

Davenport waved his hand toward Walsh and the president. "I am certain you know we have advanced a system where we can invade their matter with light. I'm sure it is unelaborate by your standards, perhaps even antwacky. In the short time our Females gained rule they developed a strategy using a new technology. They had universal backing for this plan."

"But from what information I have absorbed, I understand your Females are no longer in charge. In my sphere Males and Females are not categorized. There is total equality." *Eh, more bullshit, but why not plant a seed?*

"The Females are no longer in charge because they changed their plan without offering it up for debate. There were many tensions because of this changing. Rather than neutralizing the humans and have it over and done with, they decided to give them five of their years, and then monitor to see if there had been noticeable large adjustments to atmospheric conditions. If so, this globe would become a laboratory we could learn from. If no change was observed, then Phase Three would be set in motion."

POTUS was getting impatient. "So, hell, man, do we have five years of not?"

"It has been shortened to two years by the Males. And most of the first year has elapsed. But as was mentioned, there are those who would rather just get it over with at this point in your time. They believe diseases should not be toyed with. Disaster is certain to follow."

Harlan stood, walked behind the Resolute Desk and looked out the window. He stood there for a full minute while the others stared at his back. He then turned and faced Davenport.

"I have a larger view of this situation. Neutralizing the livestock here was not the correct route to take. You should have focused on human consumption of fossil fuel, but what's done is done. For reasons I don't care to go into, I would suggest that you return to your Females' original plan and give the humans five of their years to stabilize their atmosphere. This is a millisecond in your environment and far less in mine, and neither one of us will miss a moment of it. There is a larger picture which must be considered, one that I don't have the freedom to discuss. One that is most likely beyond your understanding. Let me simply say, that exterminating the humans would also be a mistake. They can be harvested and put to use. It has worked Elsewhere."

Davenport got to his feet and walked to Harlan as if no one else in the room existed. He spoke in a hushed, intense tone.

"Give me one example where allowing this disease to survive, or harvesting it as you say, has worked to benefit the lifestyle of any other creatures."

"It has worked outside of your realm. Often a cure for disease has been found within the disease itself. In areas you know nothing of."

"Even with my limited knowledge of this shit language I have learned the difference between chickenshit and bullshit. They will now have three of their years instead of two. No more. And again, the first one is nearly expired. I will not negotiate for any longer. Ultimately the final decision is not mine to make. We can't afford to play games with our way of life."

He then turned to leave, and as he walked out the three Secret Service Agents stepped into the office to escort him from the White House grounds.

Harlan held up a hand. "Let him leave on his own."

Davenport turned to Harlan. "I will take my pawn with me. The one they call Jack. I won't trust the humans with him and his belongings any longer."

The agents looked to the president who nodded, and Davenport was gone.

Walsh leaned back in the sofa and put his hands behind his head. "Jesus, Stone, that was one hell of a bluff."

POTUS looked from Walsh to Harlan and back. "Would one of you two MPS fellas like to tell me what the hell is going on?"

"It looks like Davenport mistook Harlan for an alien from Elsewhere."

"I prefer to think he saw me as a higher life form."

"We have a little over two years, sir. Do we have a plan?"

"I have a Cabinet meeting set for an hour, but I'm not in the least bit optimistic the world can pull this shit off."

TWENTY-NINE

"What the hell is a Dark Mechanic?" Harlan called to Angelica as he entered the loft that evening.

"You met a Dark Mechanic? That is so cool. I've never met one." She was truly excited.

He shook his head. "No Dark Mechanic, but the scheme worked. Group sent a guy named Davenport to meet POTUS. He was—"

"What's he appear like?"

Harlan began to describe Davenport, but Angelica stopped him.

"I don't mean physically. He can take any form he likes. How does he move? Where do his eyes go? How good is his English? Does he sit still? I have a pretty good idea who Group would send but give me his consciousness. Looks mean nothing. He can assume any physicality."

Harlan tried his best to attach a personality to Davenport and finished with, "Something was going on between us. I can't put my finger on it, but there was an energy that passed."

Whatever he had said, something clicked with Angelica. "Okay, I know who he is. I've met him. Davenport. Odd name, but I see why he chose it. And he appeared as a Black man?"

"Yes. In fact, he looked a lot like Roberto Clemente."

"I don't know who that is, but this Davenport I know of was a strong supporter of the Females' original plan in the beginning, and he's smart, very smart. He's not the ultimate decision maker, but he's up there. He knows how to play both sides to his own advantage."

"I could see that."

"And a Dark Mechanic? How'd you hear about them?"

"Davenport initially assumed I was a Dark Mechanic. What the hell is a—"

"Dark Mechanic?" She laughed at him. "It's kind of crazy that he mistook you for exactly what you are. An agent who only reports to Group's highest command. No one really knows who the Dark Mechanics are. I've never met one ... I don't think. I hope not. Like your MPS, I wasn't sure they even existed."

"Interesting that it was easier for me to pass for an alien, than it is for me to pass as a white guy at Lord and Taylor." Harlan walked to the refrigerator and took out a beer. "Want one?" He knew the answer but asked anyway.

She shook her head.

"Glass of water?"

"Okay."

"What I don't get is: You can tell who's from Perigee and who isn't just from the vibes. Why did Davenport think I was from Perigee? Or in the end, Elsewhere?"

"Did he say that?"

"No. But there was the Dark Mechanic thing. He seemed to think I wasn't human. Our skin shade is close, so maybe that's what threw him. I vaguely made on that I was from Elsewhere. Left him guessing as to where Elsewhere might be."

Angelica walked over to the window and looked down at the children in the playground across the street.

"We don't reproduce like you mammals on Earth do. I have to say I prefer your method even if nothing comes of it, but we don't make sex at Perigee. We are just created at Formula and everything is set. No one thinks that much about it. We have no childhood."

"Then why the necessity for Males and Females?"

"We're still harvested for reproductive elements. That part of propagation plays out the same as humans. But we are produced as adults, with preprogramed education, and positioned where that education will be most useful. I believed there was no changing that. Well, I guess there isn't. It's not like I can have a baby or anything. I'm now finding that sad. And who would know how to raise one, anyway? They're all so small. I'd probably break it."

Harlan approached her from behind and wrapped his arms around her.

"I assume you're going somewhere with this line of thought?"

"I don't think the same way I did three months ago. I don't smell the same. My head and body have changed. My temperature has changed. My brain travels in a funny direction. I'm forgetting things from my past. I'm thinking if I ran into Davenport at this moment, he might not know I'm from Perigee. He could be as confused about me as he was with you."

"And you're saying that somehow the reverse is true? That I've become some sort of alien mongoloid? A part of your being has invaded me? Through osmosis? And you are now half human? After all our time alone together?"

"No, that's not a possibility. We were so close in the cabin. I could sense you were thinking along those lines. I didn't want to scare you away. I didn't want to scare me away. But I've been enjoying this warmer life. Davenport was duped, he assumed you were neither from Earth nor Perigee and was left guessing as to where your Elsewhere might be."

She turned to face him. He smiled and kissed her. "I suppose it's better than catching the clap, but I'm still keenly aware that I'm a disease in your eyes."

"The clap?"

"Not important. It's a charming little ailment humans can be exposed to. Perigee maybe even sent it our way as a sadistic joke, who knows? You're probably immune to it. Lenny's?"

"Sure, there's nothing to eat here."

—

Rather than take a Lyft they walked to Lenny's. It was a cool autumn evening, with light traffic, and only a few dog walkers on the sidewalks. Harlan stopped to pat most of the dogs they passed as they strolled along. As he was giving a large black and brown tailless mutt a serious rubdown she couldn't resist laughing.

"Maybe you should get one of those things."

"I'm not home enough."

"You've been home for over two months."

"That's changing. The FBI is now convinced that Norcross was killed by a bad player and not me. I've been cleared. I'm back on payroll as of tomorrow."

Angelica gave him a dispirited look.

"I'd planned to tell you. I just thought I'd wait 'till later. Walsh and I will now share leadership of MPS."

"Well, that sucks."

—

Like every other bar and restaurant, Lenny's was still reduced to serving vegetarian, fish, and chicken dishes. Harlan and

Angelica settled into their regular booth and Mackie greeted them with a Guinness and a glass of water.

"Chef's been playing around with a shrimp and pasta recipe he saw on one of the food channels last week." Macky placed their drinks on two cardboard coasters. "That's if you want to stretch your horizons. Fair warning, it has coconut in it."

"Coconut?" Angelica asked.

Harlan laughed. "It's something people put in food to make it inedible."

She ordered it anyway.

"Hold the shrimp?"

"Hold the shrimp, but I'll take the sauce."

"Yep, you're definitely becoming more American, whatever that means. I hope you're not planning on breathing on me any time in the near future. I can't stand coconut." He looked at Mackie. "I'll have the fish and chips since it's back."

"Not for long."

"I can't afford the chicken. And let's have some taco chips and salsa."

"Live large."

After Mackie walked off, they sat quietly until Angelica said, "I was watching FOX News this afternoon. They keep referring to your president as a bonehead. Group leadership wouldn't put up with that in Perigee."

"Welcome to DC. But I see your point. FOX needs to be convinced that this is the real deal, a life and death-issue. They need to lay off the Old Man and get on his side if anything's going to change. It's not going to be an easy sell for POTUS if FOX starts undermining him."

"And telling them that they've been invaded by aliens that look like humans probably won't work. They're going to want flying saucers and little green men like everybody else."

Harlan drank a third of his Guinness in one swallow. "The plan is to keep the media in the dark about Perigee until the president can get other world leaders convinced. And get those same people on board and go cold turkey on fossil fuels within three years."

"I thought it was five years."

"Three and one is gone. It was all I could squeeze out of Davenport. He didn't even wait for me to make a counteroffer."

Angelica laughed at him. "I can't decide whether you Americans are very naïve or very arrogant or just dense. Probably it's arrogance."

"I hate that your English is getting so good. What are you talking about?"

Mackie placed a bowl of taco chips and salsa on the table and walked off without a word.

"You're the one who said you've been invaded. After the Dallas building collapsed what was next?"

"Argentina."

"And then what?"

"Arsons in Chicago, Denver, Albuquerque, et cetera."

"Mumbai, Yekaterinburg, Osaka, et cetera."

Harlan took another long sip from his Guinness and slowly set the glass back on the table.

"We obviously knew Perigee had placed operatives across the globe. What's your point?"

"Consider this: Perigee's new leadership turns against the Females. I don't know how many Females were put on Earth, but let's say that one of the Females knows it's a certain death for her to return to Perigee. She then finds a willing human to remove her microchip, she can no longer be traced, and she blends in with the populace."

"And that's what we did. You did."

"What makes you think it didn't also happen in Beijing or Moscow? I'm not saying it did because I can no longer communicate with other Females, but don't you think there's a chance that I'm not the only Female who moved in on a connected government person? My initial assignment was to get close to a person who had access to a world leader. As a spy. To be certain that they hadn't developed a method for disrupting our plans. Of course, I was tipped off by Jack, and that's why I'm still alive. Other Females may not have been so lucky."

"But there could be more of you?"

She shrugged. "I don't know. All I'm saying is that there's a slim chance that other countries have already opened a channel to Perigee. And they may have even been visited by some Davenport type. Your president's task may not be as hard as it seems."

"If that's the case, Davenport didn't say a word about it."

"As I said, he can play both sides."

"And you attribute this theory to the possibility that some rogue Females may still be alive?"

"Well, if there are any out there, they'd be Females. Males have no interest in preserving this place, and their language skills are for shit. And at this point, if any Females stayed behind, they would have needed to have ditched their chip."

"Seems far-fetched. Some world leaders would have spilled the beans by now if they'd been contacted. The CIA would have sniffed it out and walked it into the Oval Office. And not to be blunt, but any operative, Male or Female, without their chip is essentially worthless to either side of this dilemma."

"Then prove me wrong."

"I'd like to prove you right. We can use all the help we can get."

THIRTY

Norcross's former office had been rearranged to accommodate enough space for both Harlan and Lou—two computer monitors, and teak desks placed opposite one another, which positioned the two agents sitting back-to-back between the two desks. It was a bit awkward at first, but it allowed them to swing their chairs and easily read the other's computer screen. They left the speedbag hanging in place.

"You never know when that damn thing may come in handy," was Lou's rationale. Harlan wasn't so sure, though it turned out that he was the only one who would use it.

It wasn't the function of a MPS agent to give advice to the president. His or her job was simply to gather information that had been requested by The Old Man, be absolutely certain it was truthful and accurate, and then present it to him without any frills or opinions. Accuracy was the key. Truth was the key. If they learned more than requested, all the better. POTUS had political hacks, aides, congressmen and congresswomen, lobbyists, big-time campaign donors, et cetera to give him more advice than he ever needed or wanted. Unfortunately, if these people didn't like the facts discovered and presented by MPS, the facts were changed to fit their preferred narrative; this became known as, Alternative Facts.

"You know, even if Angelica's theory about the possibility of there being more Females like her turns out to be on the money, it doesn't necessarily mean any other international leaders have been contacted. These babes may just be lying on a beach in Curaçao working on their tans and thanking their lucky stars Group never caught up with them. Also, this extension was only negotiated yesterday with Davenport in the Oval Office. There's no way in hell any other nation is up to speed on this. You, and your Darth Vader act, pretty much confirmed that."

"If Perigee had contacts with other world leaders, Davenport would need to bring them up-to-speed, which he could do in nanoseconds. He has those communication capabilities."

They sat quietly for three or four minutes, rolling all this through their heads.

"No." Harlan finally broke the silence. "I'm siding with you. My money's on the fact that Angelica's wrong about this. The deal was cut right then and there in the Oval Office. No other nation was afforded the opportunity to put in their two cents. And you were very specific that we were the only nation with the capability of intercepting Perigee communications. If he recognized that as bullshit, he would have called you on it."

Harlan leaned back in his chair and placed his hands behind his head.

"To say that all of this kept us up last night would be an understatement. Angelica seems a bit fixated on the topic. It may just be wishful thinking; she's uneasy about being the Lone Ranger."

Harlan rubbed the back of his neck in an attempt to loosen up. "I hate to say this, but I think we're going to have to make another trip to Atlantic City. Talk to this guy, Cain. Maybe he has the ability to communicate with any possible Female counterparts. We need to have a definitive answer on this shit before we do something really stupid."

"I can't believe Davenport just rode off into the sunset without leaving us a way to touch base with him."

"The ball's in our court. The only ones left are Cain and whatever counterparts he may have. We need to take Cain if we have any hope of opening future dialog with Davenport and Group."

Lou shook his head. "Jack said Cain was the impatient type. I'm guessing he's not even on board with Davenport's two-year deal. Or any deal. He may want to do some damage just for kicks."

"Davenport didn't look like anyone Cain would want to cross."

"You're forgetting that Davenport's look wasn't his real look, it was pinched from Roberto Clemente."

—

They left early the following morning. The drive to Atlantic City took a little over four hours, and they positioned themselves on the same boardwalk bench. The idea was to wait for Jack, be upfront with him, approach in a friendly way and ask to see Cain. They knew whatever they said would be transmitted to Cain and Group.

After a two-and-a-half-hour wait, and no Jack, they opted to go directly to the hotel room where Manny, Moe, and Jack had been residing for the past few months.

The hotel was a seedy place even by Atlantic City standards. The ground floor windows were covered with heavy security bars. The casino sparkled like a Hollywood set, but there was no real lobby to speak of, no breakfast room, no carpeting, a cracked linoleum floor with a bare-bones front desk. It was as if the lobby sat in a different world than the buffet restaurant and garish casino. When they entered the hotel, they walked directly to the elevators but were stopped by the desk clerk; a man in his twenties, grossly over-weight, wearing shorts and a far too tight orange Philadelphia Flyers Orlon T-shirt.

"Can I help you gentlemen?" He didn't bother to look up from his *People Magazine*.

"We have friends in 608. We're just paying a visit. They're expecting us."

"Well, gents, that's not how things work around here. First, no one goes up to the rooms unannounced because this section of our operation has no metal detectors, and you fellas don't look like the type that would pass through a metal detector without making a shitload of noise. And second, the three men in 608 checked out yesterday, so I wouldn't say they were exactly expecting anyone."

"They checked out and paid their bill?"

"In cash. Left a hefty tip; kinda like they had no use for the money. Ya know, something tells me this visit of yours isn't totally on the up-and-up. Call me psychic." He lifted his gaze, gave them a disapproving look, and reached for the telephone. "I'm going to ask you to leave or I'm calling the police. This is a clean hotel."

Lou walked up to the man, slapped his I.D. on the counter and said, "We are the goddam police, dickhead."

Harlan laughed and took Lou by the arm and led him out onto the sidewalk. "Nicely done, cowboy."

"I've always wanted to do that. No telling if the opportunity will ever come up again. I thought he was going to shit his pants."

"I'm glad you got it out of your system."

They stood in place for five minutes before Walsh said, "Now what?"

"Let me call Angelica. She may have an idea where they might have gone."

Lou stared out at the ocean while Harlan made the call. Angelica answered after the third ring, and he explained the situation.

"Makes sense when you think about it," was her response. "I suspected this might happen. You negotiated the two-year deal. Group probably pulled everyone out ... around the world ... if anyone existed Elsewhere."

"Why would they do that?"

"'Why wouldn't they do that?' is the real question. They'll be coming back in two years to analyze progress. The clock's ticking. And that's if they don't double back on their promise. They hold all the cards. Why hang around? It's Atlantic City. It sucks. They're not going to destroy any more buildings. Davenport left an ultimatum. Earth either passes or fails. That's the reality. You should be proud of yourself for pressuring the Males at Group to revert to the Females' original plan, otherwise you might have no time at all."

"Little consolation, two years isn't a boatload of time."

"I'm guessing that if, and it's a big if, as you've pointed out, any other world leaders are aware of what's going on, they probably have been contacted and told that the time frame is two years, the US will run the show, and wait for directives. We communicate much more quickly and efficiently than you do. As I said, Davenport works both sides. He's clearly Group's front man."

"There's too much shit hanging in mid-air. I'll be back in a few hours."

THIRTY-ONE

Harlan and Lou were in DC in time to scramble up a 4:00 p.m. meeting with The Old Man. After they had briefed him, POTUS only offered one word.

"Shit."

"Apparently they're all gone and won't be back for two years." Harlan glanced at an empty chair hoping an offer to sit would come his way. It didn't.

"I have it on good authority that they won't even be looking over our shoulders to see how we're coming along. In two years, they'll return and run some sort of environmental tests; we've either pulled it off or we haven't. Honestly, sir, I don't think they care one way or the other if we live or die. Their single mission is to preserve the planet and its airspace. They've identified us as a disease. A disease that needs to be controlled or eradicated, and they'd be happy with either outcome."

Lou tried to put a rosier face on it.

"Sir, it is possible that some other world leaders have been contacted. And that they know as much as we do. And have been told by Perigee to remain mum about it. In which case it wouldn't take much to get them on board. They will listen to you. Of course, that's a huge if. And to be honest, it's a stretch. Neither Harlan nor I think that's happened. No one's come forward yet, and there's been no chatter out there. And—"

"And, what?"

"The eternal question: who do you trust? If no other nation has touched base with you, there are only a few scenarios: one, they've been contacted by Perigee and have been told to stand by; two, they haven't been contacted at all; or three, they don't trust you, i.e. the US. And if England, France, Italy or Germany were aware of Perigee, I don't see them remaining mum about it under any circumstances."

"And if they know nothing about this invasion, I'm going to look like I've lost my goddam marbles. Talking about aliens, who at this point, no longer exist. And even if they did still exist, they look like Roberto Clemente. What are the odds that some rogue alien, like the one who's been feeding you information, exists in some place like China? India? People are going to want some tangible proof, or I'll be hung out to dry. The entire world will see me as a doddering old fool."

Harlan resisted the temptation to say, *Yeah, but only for two more years.*

"Sir, the fact that all the breeding livestock on earth has been neutralized, people are selling their souls for shrimp burgers and chicken salad sandwiches, and no rogue nation has surfaced to take responsibility, must make everyone wonder what the hell is going on. People are panicked. It's dragged on too long. What else could it be but a visit from another society? The world may very well be ready for a plausible explanation, even if it is aliens."

POTUS seemed to think this over. This time he answered with three words. "The goddam Russians."

And he was right about that. It was one thing to convince educated, clear thinking, world leaders that there was a serious threat knocking at the door, and if they didn't immediately institute strict regulations on fossil fuel consumption and generate more green energy overnight it would be devastating to the human way of life. It was another thing to convince a nation of paranoid people with an off-the-rocker dictator, who has an arrest warrant hanging over his head, that this wasn't some American president's attempt to scare them into pulling out of Ukraine and closing down the only cash-cow they had left: oil.

POTUS rubbed his brow and continued.

"I have to convince ExxonMobil, Shell, BP, Chevron, King Coal, the Saudis, the Other Side of the Aisle, all these piss-ant hostile nations, FOX News, the Average Joe, and the Russians, the goddam Russians, that this shit's real. And do it all with no evidence other than the fact that a bunch of bulls are shooting blanks and flashing a Roberto Clemente rookie card."

They were silent for what seemed an eternity. Harlan finally broke it. "We have a meeting set up with Bayless and Dodge at Interpol for tomorrow."

He looked at his watch and stared at the seconds ticking away as if they were lemmings jumping off a cliff.

"Obviously Interpol worldwide has been following this closely since the buildings were destroyed and Norcross was killed. Clearly, they know something's happening, and as per protocol, their NCB offices have been in touch with most ambassadors. Bayless and Dodge are aware that they've been tailed by someone, they just don't know who or why. As far as we know they haven't considered that it might be aliens. At this point Interpol is convinced that most world leaders will be compliant with any US masterplan, or counterattack. They're still beating the bushes looking for some nonexistent bad guys."

"The goddam Russians?"

"Well, yes, sir, that's going to be a problem. But everyone else is sweating bullets waiting for some other shoe to drop and they're anxious to make a move. It's Big Business, your detractors, social media, and some news outlets that are going to be the tough nut to crack. And, as you put it, the goddam Russians. There are a bunch of people out there who are out to get you, sir."

"Ya think?"

Harlan cleared his throat. "Sir, I know that as MPS agents it's not our place to offer advice but..."

"Let's hear it, Stone. You've already got me two years. Should have been five, but two's better than nothing."

"Yes, sir. We tossed this idea around on the way back from Atlantic City. I know this is going to sound a bit loopy, far-fetched, and questionable on a legal, and constitutional basis, but, well, it wouldn't be the first time an administration has pulled a stunt like this." He took a deep breath. "To begin with, let's assume that China, India, Indonesia, et cetera, the big polluters, will work with us. Well, maybe not China, that may require some finesse."

"I see you've conveniently left the goddam Russians out of this stunt?"

"Yes, sir. The Stunt is this: we don't have any aliens, but the Pentagon can fabricate them for us. Maybe not little green men and flying saucers, but effects and images created by holographic projection, or AI, that can fool anyone. What if the Russians are set up to break the story? What if they're the first to learn of an alien invasion? What if they discover who it was who sabotaged the livestock industry, and why? What if we spoon-feed it to one of their FSB goons via a double agent? What if it looks like the Russians start pressuring the US to do something about climate change? Yuri Polushin gets to look like a savior of the world. What if we let them start pushing the green energy angle?"

"It's a thought." POTUS stood and paced the office for a minute. "No, I don't like it. It makes us look weak. I like the idea of fabricating little green men because otherwise we have nothing, but I'm not giving the goddam Russians the upper hand on this. If we do this, we do this in-house. Screw the Russians. They can't be trusted."

All was quiet for a moment. Eventually, the president said, "Let me sleep on it." He began flipping through a stack of papers as if he were looking for the supermarket circulars. After another two minutes, he said, "Okay, okay, to hell with sleeping on it. We need to move. The clock's ticking away. For this fake alien thing to work we're going to need to produce something so terrifyingly real, it scares the shit out of everyone. I'm going to need to get General Dixon of the Joint Chiefs to put this together. He loves this kind of crap. He's such a child sometimes. You two have worked with him before, I take it?"

"Ahh, yes, sir, we have." Harlan resisted saying, *Oh man, General Dixon. This could go off the rails real quick.*

Walsh simply nodded, thinking the same thing as Harlan while POTUS picked up where he had left off.

"I like this idea. I think. But if the truth gets out in any way, that I'm making up phony aliens, I'm totally screwed. I want Doug Dixon to run it. No one's better at this sort of shit. He runs a tight operation; there will be no leaks. He'll need free rein to hand-pick his players, though."

Harlan cleared his throat. "Agreed, sir, if we go this route, I believe the approach must be kept totally in-house, as you say."

"Totally."

"And, sir, you're right. We're hog-tied, we have no choice but to go it alone. It needs to be a US operation, and US only. No other nations involved, no Interpol, not even the FBI, and no NSA or CIA. It must not leave this office. The entire world needs to be convinced that the images we create are the real deal, and the less people in the know the better. One leak and we're—"

"Screwed."

"Yes, sir. I'm sure the general would agree. We can wait for his input if you like."

POTUS ran the palms of his hands over his balding head. "Yes. I'll get him in here tonight after dinner. Be back here at eight. He'll go for anything if it involves screwing the Russians. He wants an enemy he can target, and right now we don't have one."

"Yes, sir. We'll play it cautiously with Interpol tomorrow, but we're still going to need to work with them in some fashion. In the end it's a much faster way to read the international temperature. Diplomatic channels won't move fast enough at this point. And we must know if any of these other nations have been contacted by the aliens, and Interpol will have a finger on all of that too. Fake aliens only work if no one else has had contact with Perigee operatives. It only plays out if absolutely no one knows what the visitors from Perigee really look like."

The president leaned back in his chair. "Also, we're going to need to handle FOX News. When it comes to blowback on this administration, they're worse than the goddam Russians."

THIRTY-TWO

"God dammit, I love this shit."

From the look on his face, Harlan surmised that General Doug Dixon hadn't been this excited in decades.

"And all this alien crap is for real?"

"Yes, sir."

He was truly amazed at how easy it was to explain to the general that the Earth had been invaded by creatures from Elsewhere. Dixon's complexion had gone bright red with the anticipation of battle, and the bristles of his close-cropped hair seemed to stand straight up and grow longer. Even his chest full of campaign ribbons appeared to expand. The briefing had gone so smoothly it made Harlan wonder if Dixon had been personally contacted by Perigee operatives, so he asked.

"General, have you touched base with any aliens? They would appear as normal men, not as some sci-fi creature. Could even be a woman. Any strange people walk into your life recently?"

"Hell, no. But the Joint Chiefs haven't been sitting on our duffs playing Texas Hold 'Em for the last two months. Someone had to blow up the cattle industry. I'm a meat and potatoes kind of guy and I don't like this crap one bit. We've been chasing down every piss-ant lead and rumor that's out there. Everything has taken us down a dead-end street. Christ, we knew it was a huge-ass operation. The only question was who had the resources? Once we cleared the Chinese, North Korea, the goddam Russians and the Saudi money twits, no one was left. Of course, the North Koreans are just pissin' in the wind, so we wrote them off early." He laughed out loud. "Aliens. This is beyond beautiful."

"But, general, you do understand the basic problem," Lou chimed in, "We don't really have any aliens."

"I get it. Who gives a shit? Like Stone said, we make them the hell up. We can do this. Cooking up little green men and flying saucers is child's play. We've got a whole damn division—"

"Ah, sir, we're trying to stay away from cliché." Harlan added, hoping not to push his buttons. Fortunately, things were moving too fast for POTUS to keep up, or interrupt. "We're trying to stay away from green men with ray guns and flying saucers. We need them to look human with a soft focus because that's the form they took. They didn't come here with weapons."

"Right, no little green men. We need to scare the shit out of people. Those *New Yorker* aliens are about as scary as a gopher taking a dump. But you all are missing the big picture. Like Pershing said, 'Infantry wins battles, logistics wins wars.' Scaring people into going cold turkey on gasoline ain't gonna cut it. We'll do it of course, and it will be a hoot watching the general population react, but we need to win over the suppliers. India may well believe in all the perogie-people hype, but we—"

"It's Perigee, sir. And technically they're not people. And technically that's not the name of their domain. I made it up."

"Right. But my point is, you're never going to scare the folks in India off gasoline." He crossed over to the globe on a sideboard and stabbed at India, as if no one knew what country he was referencing. "It won't fly. They've already told us to piss off when we sanctioned Russian oil years ago. And The Hague's arrest warrant for that shithead Polushin hasn't fazed them a bit. If the gas is there, they're going to suck it up until it's gone bone dry. All those little scooters and shit they drive around? We need to cut them off from the goddam Russians. Same with Venezuela, the Saudis and the rest of those middle eastern clowns. Their supply routes need to be shut down."

"Texas? Oklahoma? South Dakota? Them too?" POTUS managed to get it.

Dixon stopped and gave him a questionable look. "With all due respect, sir, did you take those states in the last election cycle?"

"Well, no."

"Then screw them. This is war. You play to win. They'll come around when they see what's at stake. They all like kids as much as the next guy. It's not going to crush their economy. A bunch of fat cats will take a hit, sure, but they can afford it, and they pump their political handouts into the other side of the aisle anyway. And in the end, the Venezuelans, Indians, and Arabs will ultimately come around as well, because you know why?"

POTUS shook his head.

"Same reason. Because of the kiddies. It's all about the children. They focus their entire life's attention on having babies. Legacy means everything to them, and for legacy to endure you need a bunch of friggin' kids. And grandkids. We studied this shit at The Point. Even in chapel, 'Children's children are the crown of old men,' Proverbs seventeen-six. It's the goddam Russians that will be the tough nut to crack, especially that piss-ant Polushin. All they care about is money, getting shit-faced and reading depressing literature."

He turned his focus to Harlan.

"What do you have on those bastards? Do we know if they've been contacted by Perigee? It would be just like that jackass Yuri to have been contacted and not give a flying shit. He's the same as all these other wannabe, narcissistic dictators. They don't give a good God damn about the guy on the street or saving humanity. It's me, me, me with all those clowns. As long as Polushin and his kind are lining their pockets with gold napkin rings, cigarette lighters and perching on gold toilets, they could care less about what's going on with the people starving in the streets."

"Ever since the Ukraine invasion we're getting nothing out of Russia. Lou and I have a meeting set up with Interpol tomorrow. We haven't filled them in on Perigee, but we're hoping their senses have taken them to the possibility of an alien existence. It'll make explaining this a lot easier. We'll see tomorrow."

Dixon looked at the Old Man. "What about the CIA?"

POTUS cleared his throat. "They haven't come to me with anything on this either, which leads us to believe there's been no Perigee contact with any governments outside of the US. If the CIA did have anything, they would have walked the story into the Oval Office the moment they had a clue as to what was going on. I just spoke with Director Collins yesterday morning, and he mentioned nothing about the goddam Russians. Same with the FBI and NSA. No cabinet members have touched on it either."

Dixon began pacing the office, head down, hands in his pockets.

"I'm going to need to personally put together the team charged with creating these aliens. And, yes, scare the crap out of people right off the bat, that's definitely the way to go. It's the fastest way to wake everyone and get the media salivating. The last thing we need is to have one of those FOX News turds question any of this."

"I just thought of something." The president had an unconvincing smile on his face. "Let me contact Jerry Bosworth. He produced *Alien Road Trip*. Did anyone see it?"

They all shook their heads.

"Great film. I saw it three times. Even my grandson loves it. He's watched it five times I'll bet. Never tires of it. I think he likes the scenes with the topless babes more than anything. You all should check it out. Anyway, Jerry's a heavy donor. Lives in Santa Monica. Those creatures in that movie were frightening as hell."

The general furrowed his brow.

"Is this the guy who was picked up for carting underage women off to his ranch in Calabasas? That Jerry Bosworth?"

"It ended in a mistrial. Nobody proved anything. He's always good for a few laughs."

"He's a sexual predator."

"He settled down, from what I hear."

"Sir, and again, with all due respect, we need to keep this between my team and the four of us in this room. We can't let Hollywood anywhere near this. And I suggest not even bringing the VP in on it. If it somehow leaks to the news that our aliens aren't the real deal, this falls flatter than a pre-op guest at a Mar-a-Lago fundraiser."

POTUS smiled. He'd made a good choice in Dixon.

"Okay, fine. Besides, I haven't spoken to the VP in weeks. I don't even know where the hell he is right now. I think Canada, maybe Manitoba? He likes to shoot moose. What kind of a sadistic son-of-a-bitch gets his jollies off by shooting a moose?

I was a big fan of Rocky and Bullwinkle in my younger days, and—"

"Ah, sir, I think the general is right about keeping film people out of it."

"Yeah. Right. No Hollywood, no VP. How long will it take you to fabricate some aliens, Doug?"

"I think we can get something cooking within a week. Someone's got us on a stopwatch, and the second hand's ticking away. Once we get some terrifying images produced, we can share them, along with the Perigee demands, with other governments. We'll need to give them a week's jump-start so they can prepare their national guard, military, and law enforcement. There may be large-scale panic. They need to be on top of their game."

POTUS raised his hands. "Just a thought but there might be a better way to play this. I like your thinking, Doug, but what if we take it that far and no farther."

"Meaning?"

"Meaning we follow your timetable exactly and then let it ride. We don't make any big announcement indicating that we've been invaded by aliens. Sit on it for a month or two and see if someone leaks it. Or feed it to some Russian FSB agents through a double agent?"

"I don't get it."

"I'm going back to something I thought of earlier today. Leaking it surreptitiously. Within a month, some mole or slippery insider in some out-of-the-way nation is going to leak it. He's going to try to sell the story and images to some rag or TV show. The whole world will then come clamoring to us demanding the truth, even the goddam Russians. All the media will swallow it, FOX News is cut off at the knees, and it puts us in the driver's seat. They'll think they have a scoop. They'll believe that they dug up the story all on their own. It makes it all far more believable."

General Dixon let this soak in for a moment and eventually nodded.

"I like that, sir. It works. Though we're still going to need to let other international intelligence agencies know that the aliens exist so they can be prepared. We'll insist that they keep a lid on it. They'll eat up the fact that we've trusted them with class-A sensitive information. And along those same lines I suggest we give nothing to the goddam Russians, no images, nothing. Leaving them in the dark works better. Their FSB agents will pick it up on the street. Then we wait and see how they handle it. We need to employ the long game."

"That's how I saw it."

"Let's be careful about the long game," Harlan added. "Let's not play it too long. The clock's rolling and Perigee isn't honor bound to hold onto their timetable."

—

As Harlan and Lou passed through the White House security gate on their way home, Lou let out a small chuckle. "Nifty idea POTUS had, someone leaking it to the goddam Russians. Wonder how he came up with it?"

"He's sharp as a tack."

THIRTY-THREE

"It's not surprising. Interpol had bounced the alien concept around at our meeting in Lyon two weeks ago. Even though there was no hardcore evidence." Bayless filled his coffee mug for a third time. "It was a well-considered possibility, basically because we were at a loss for any other logical explanation. Interesting how much the Webb Telescope has influenced all the naysayers."

As with General Dixon, Jordan Bayless and Christian Dodge realized that no nation had the wherewithal to handle an operation as large as the one they'd been witnessing. As a result, Harlan and Lou had little difficulty convincing them that Earth had been visited by creatures form Elsewhere. The MPS agents did however leave out two critical facts from their briefing: Perigee operatives had left and wouldn't be back for two years, and the aliens Interpol would eventually see would be totally fabricated. General Dixon had promised to serve them up, but that was still a week off.

"I gather no other nation has reported any direct contact with Perigee?"

Harlan was now certain the answer would be 'no', but he wanted Interpol to confirm it.

"No. Nothing's out there. By what you've told us, it seems the White House has been the only entity to communicate with them directly. If Perigee did any deep analysis of the current world-order, they wouldn't waste their time with anyone else."

"Including the Russians?"

Dodge laughed. "Neither Russian Interpol NCB, nor their agents, have ever been upfront about anything that goes on internally. Still, they seemed particularly edgy at this last meeting. Something's going on, but Polushin has an iron grip on everyone and everything in Russia. Their agents have been pretty much locked out since Yuri made his move on Ukraine, but it's even tighter now that it's dragged on. A certain amount of them hail from Ukraine. Still, they were very tight-lipped. And then there was the Egorkov thing."

Harlan and Lou sat up a bit straighter in their chairs.

"What's up with Egorkov?"

"He wasn't there."

Dmitri Egorkov was the senior Russian Interpol officer. Nearly everyone in the intelligence community had crossed his path, at one point or another. He'd held the top position in Moscow for over ten years and he had a reputation much like Norcross; the law was everything to him and he never rested until a case was solved. Though it was well known that he had recently developed disdain and frustration with Moscow's ongoing corruption. And his family roots were also in Ukraine, a situation for which he held a good deal of contempt for Polushin's heavy hand. He had also never missed an Interpol meeting in Lyon. Ever. He was a foodie who liked good wine and *foie gras* too much to pass on a trip to Lyon on the Kremlin's dime.

"He wasn't there?"

"He wasn't there. None of the other Russian agents were willing to talk about his absence, but it didn't go unnoticed—by anyone."

"I'll get the CIA on it, see if anyone's spotted him recently."

"We're ahead of you, Harlan. That's how much his absence shook up the meeting. I contacted my people at the CIA that very evening. It's like Egorkov has evaporated. He hasn't been to the Moscow NCB office or shown up at any of his usual hangouts in a few weeks."

Lou crossed his arms over his chest and slouched back in the chair.

"Well, it wouldn't be the first time Yuri disappeared someone. Just seems odd he'd go for a person so high up. And why? He's used Egorkov time and again to extradite his enemies back into Moscow. Egorkov's one of his most valuable assets. Why neutralize him?"

"In the end, it's just one more piece of internal Moscow bullshit," Dodge added. "We've got a much bigger issue to deal with than Polushin's paranoia and fragile ego. How do we handle Perigee? Does POTUS have a plan?"

Harlan resisted the temptation to laugh. "The answer to the first question is easy. We don't handle Perigee, or can't, until they resurface, and there's no telling when that might be. We're on their timetable. They could resurface today, tomorrow, next week, next year. But we're on an extremely short fuse, I can tell you that much. Right now, we're left with the immediate task of meeting their demands. We need to create a serious worldwide effort to drastically reduce greenhouse gas emissions. Every nation, every individual needs to be on board. Perigee has put the screws to us."

Bayless grunted. "Okay, okay, let's hold on a minute. Sorry, Christian, but I'm scaling this back before it gets out of hand."

Dodge was put off at being contradicted, but he was out ranked and let Bayless continue, giving him a noncommittal shrug.

"I don't see this as within Interpol's mandate. If aliens are responsible for this mess, and there's basically no evidence of human criminal activity, and the aliens have left, none of this falls into our backyard. This is strictly State Department stuff, and Interpol's going to have to move on. You know that, Harlan. We're law enforcement, we're not alien hunters. Why the pitch to drag Interpol into this?"

"For that very reason." Harlan paused to consider how much of General Dixon's charade he should give up. "The State Department and their foreign counterparts will move too slow on this. The clock is ticking faster than we think. We don't have the time to watch diplomats wring their hands and look for political solutions or score points. None of this is up for debate any longer. And in the end, they don't know who's telling the truth; trust has been eroded. When this gets out, and I'm sure it will, individual governments are going to need to be prepared ... from a law enforcement perspective. Interpol can get that message out more efficiently than anyone. And your NCBs tend to trust one another."

"I don't know ..."

"This can't go through diplomatic channels. Nobody trusts anyone. The world needs a serious wake-up call and Interpol is the only organization that will be listened to. And taken at their word. You guys don't answer to anyone politically. Any credibility the State Department had was pissed away with the last administration. You know that."

"Aliens. Christ, we don't even know what we're looking for."

Harlan was tempted to say, *Well, this is your lucky day, bucko*, but held it.

"The Pentagon has Oval Office CCTV images of Perigee operatives communicating directly with POTUS, and some other images they picked up in Northern Virginia and Mississippi. General Dixon would like to see these images distributed to world leaders via Interpol and not diplomatic channels. He feels this reduces the possibility of leaks."

Lou stood, which positioned him above the Interpol agents.

"Nonetheless, it will be leaked. It's the way the world works. And when it does leak, we need to be prepared for the possibility of a worldwide panic. And to be honest, Interpol is going to be dealing with the usual jackasses who surface in a situation like this. If oil becomes an international black-market commodity it's going to go the same way beef has. It will just be on a more global and larger scale. Tankers will be hijacked and held for ransom or sold to the highest bidder. You've got to see that coming."

Bayless also stood and perched himself on the corner of the desk, though directed his comments specifically to Harlan.

"This will have to go to the secretary-general. How soon can you get me those images? I know him, he won't authorize anything without running it past the general secretariat, and he'll want—need, hard evidence."

"The Pentagon is compiling 3-D images now. They should have readable digital files within a week. I'll get them to you on a thumb drive. None of this should go out electronically, only hand-to-hand. Can you get the secretary-general on board by then?"

"Not so fast. Get me the images."

THIRTY-FOUR

"I know, I know, you said no little green men. But I think you'll agree that this shade of green works, and nothing says they need to be little. This is all adjustable. Nobody ever said the Army isn't flexible. We'll make them stand taller than POTUS, if you want."

General Dixon was right. Making the aliens green gave them an eco-look, something he felt matched their demands for transforming Earth into a greener planet.

"Christ, they're tree-huggin' aliens. Make them friggin' green, right? We also ditched the idea of too scary. I mean, shit, just their existence alone is going to scare the crap out of people. Why overdo it? Nobody ever said the Army can't be subtle. Besides, these characters do come with a track record. Neutralizing the livestock, the building collapses, the arsons. People have been primed to be frightened. These dudes have already exhibited their ability to do a boatload of damage. And kill people."

"Gills?" Harlan asked.

"These clowns are from Perigee. They don't have our atmosphere. Have you ever been to Perigee?"

"Not recently."

"They've gotta breathe, right? You don't want them walking around in flippers and scuba gear like a bunch of damn Navy

SEALS. Anyhow, these are just the rough sketches. I didn't want to have my boys move forward with the animation and special effects until I had the go-ahead from you guys on the initial design. We had considered making a few women and giving them tits, but it proved to be too distracting. The boys did have fun with it though. The variety of options surprised the hell out of me. Five engineers, five different breast preferences."

Harlan shook his head. "Can't they just breathe out of their mouths? I think the gills are overkill."

"Okay, screw it. I wasn't married to the gills anyway. We've got to make them believable. That's why I shied away from being too frightening. We don't want people wondering why the president didn't crap his pants when he first saw them."

Dixon produced three more drawings and handed them to Harlan and Lou.

"Are you okay with what we did with the eyes and ears? We didn't want to make them look like they walked off the set of Star Trek. Which, by the way, was no easy task. Hollywood's already covered just about every freaky look we came up with. Researching this was a real ball-buster. The last thing we need is for someone to say, 'Didn't I see these creatures in that Jerry Bosworth movie?'"

"No." Lou studied one of the drawings. "I think this works for me. If you get rid of the gills. Is it possible to give them some chameleon-like features? Making it so that they change colors for no obvious reason? That might intrigue people. Maybe make the eyes glow a bit? Ultimately, they are out of their element."

"Piece of cake. And you're okay with three fingers? We could throw in a few more. But I wanted to stay away from five."

"Three works."

"Although, we're not going to be able to really arm them in any way. No ray guns, no lobbing balls of fire, that kind of shit. Remember, this is all smoke and mirrors. Having them physically destroy things is going to be a tough nut for us to pull off. Especially within a week's time. And you don't want that shit happening in the Oval Office, anyway. Nobody wants to see the Resolute Desk go up in flames."

"Yes, my wife is very fond of this furniture."

"Right, sir, that was my thinking. They will be able to walk through walls and all that crap but even picking up a piece of paper may be a hard thing to graph out and make look realistic with just three fingers. Less is more, that's the Army way. There's a big difference between Hollywood bullshit and realism. The Army isn't big on bullshit. These guys need to be plausible."

"We didn't want to make them look too violent, anyway, so that's good. What about clothes?" Harlan said, mostly thinking out loud. "Do you see them wearing some sort of otherworldly outfits, or human clothing. Which is what they wore when they were here meeting POTUS."

The general laughed.

"Yeah, we weren't sure how you wanted to play that, so we didn't deal with any clothing. And that's why we didn't waste time giving them peckers swingin' in the breeze. We figured that part would be covered over. Any suggestions?"

"I'm thinking we go with contemporary human clothing. Three creatures are all we need, and if they look pretty much the same, we'll want to distinguish them from one another, and clothing should be the best way to do that—trousers, shirts and jackets—no ties."

POTUS let out a long laugh.

"That reminds me of a party me and FLOTUS were invited to a few years back. On the invite, the lady had handwritten 'No ties.' But her handwriting was so sloppy, we thought it read 'Noties.' Couldn't figure out what the hell she meant."

"Thank you, sir." Harlan took a moment before continuing. "Anyway, if the aliens are going to change colors the clothing should be affected by the change. Maybe glow a bit around the edges. It'd be a good effect. We want one of them to stand out as the leader and the other two to look as if they're his lieutenants or possibly silent bodyguards. This way they speak with one voice. And I don't want to get anyone in on this to do costumes. The fewer people involved the better. Can your team handle that? You can probably find all you need in a Land's End catalog. Stay away from Brooks Brothers, okay?"

"Right." Dixon began gathering up his presentation. "I'm going to have these jokers just fade in and fade out. No spaceships. No transporters. None of that crap. It's been done to death by Hollywood. Again, less is more. The evidence of Perigee's power is already out there we don't need to hit people over the head. The more I analyzed the situation I realized we already have a primed and captive audience. Our fish are on the line, we just need to get them into the frying pan."

Harlan and Lou stood to leave. "What's your timeline, general? When can we expect a finished preview?"

"Five or six days, max."

"Great. Keep us posted."

When they reached the door, Dixon called out to them. "Hey, Harlan, can I ask you a question?"

"Shoot."

"Will I ever eat a steak again?"

TICK_ TICK_ TICK_

"General, if we pull this off, I'll get you a T-bone, even if I have to personally steal it from Yuri Polushin's home freezer."

THIRTY-FIVE

For three days, General Dixon had given Harlan updates on his progress. With each morning, he became more and more enthusiastic about the images his team had developed. Every conversation seemed to end with, "You're gonna love this shit." Harlan in turn kept The Old Man informed at their briefings each day at 5:00 p.m. It had become a waiting game; nothing could move forward until the general delivered the goods. He was a perfectionist. It wasn't going to happen overnight.

Angelica and Harlan took advantage of the downtime by kayaking from the Bridge Street Boathouse or taking long strolls through Rock Creek Park, where Harlan had developed strong relationships with several shaggy mutts. But they couldn't escape the fact that time was ticking away while he was playing with dogs.

"I'm still seeing a lot of puppies."

Angelica smiled at him. "We didn't neutralize the canines if that's what you're getting at. They're scavengers. If it turns out that Perigee decides to neutralize the humans, canines will become useful when it's time to scrub up the mess that's left behind, the dead bodies. We're not going to get our hands dirty disposing of your carcasses, and we're not going to run the risk that a new disease emerges from rotting human tissue."

Harlan laughed. "Right, I never thought of that. What happens when all the undertakers and gravediggers are dead? Not a pretty picture. Watching a bunch of feeble humans in their nineties, dying of starvation because there are no 'illegal immigrants' picking spinach and broccoli for them, while at the same time fighting off packs of ravenous rottweilers."

About twenty yards ahead of them Harlan noticed a bedraggled woman sitting on one of the park benches humming to herself. Alongside her sat a small traveling case. She was in her mid-twenties, and even though she seemed down on her luck and sporting disheveled clothing, it was clear she was, or had been, a very attractive person.

"Looks like someone's having a tough time of it."

As they got closer to her, he reached into his pocket and pulled out twenty dollars. The woman was humming what sounded like Paul Simon's *Slip Slidin' Away*, but it was an otherworldly rendition if that was what it was intended to be.

As he moved to hand her the cash, Angelica stepped between them, lifted the woman's face, and let out a soft humming sound of her own. The woman stood, turned her back to Angelica, and allowed her blouse to fall over her shoulders, exposing a scar at the base of her neck. It very much resembled the scar Angelica had retained after Harlan had removed her tracking chip. Angelica placed the woman's blouse back over her shoulders and the three of them sat on the bench; Angelica in the middle, the woman clutching her case tightly on her lap.

"She's from Perigee. She doesn't speak English."

Harlan looked at her and said, "*Kahk-vahs-zah-voot?*"

"Svetlana."

Harlan smiled at her. "Well, she speaks Russian. Is that how you communicate in Perigee? By humming poorly arranged Paul Simon songs?"

"It's a much simpler language than English. And we can share far more information and share it a lot more quickly. How did you know she spoke Russian?"

"The shoes."

Angelica shook her head. "Why do I bother asking you questions? Your answers make no sense." She then took Svetlana's hand and began to speak to her in their Perigee humming, but Harlan held up his hand, putting an end to it.

"Okay, let's stop this right here. Let's take Svetlana back to the loft and get her cleaned up. We can discuss everything there. I don't know who can decipher your musings, but we shouldn't take chances. At any given moment twenty percent of the people walking through Rock Creek Park are wearing some sort of listening device. It makes Gorky Park look like a toddler's sandbox."

Svetlana perked up noticeably at the mention of Gorky Park. They stood and walked to Harlan's car in silence.

After they arrived at the loft, Angelica led Svetlana to the bathroom, handed her a fresh towel and closed the door.

"We can do this one of two ways," he said after she joined him on the couch. "Either you debrief her in your language and then bring me up to speed, or I debrief her in Russian and I bring you up to speed. Which would be my preference."

Angelica shook her head. "No, she's in a fragile state. She's lost and she doesn't know who to trust. She's in an alien land. All she has is a case full of rubles and no language skills. No clothes, no friends, nothing. It will be much easier for me to gain her confidence. I'm the only one who speaks her native language."

"Okay, but I reserve the right to step in. And one other thing, call it my inherent distrust of all things Russian, don't mention anything about what my function is, Davenport, or what the White House is cooking up. Gather what information you can from her, but don't spill any beans."

"Beans?"

"Just let her do the talking."

"She's not Russian, she's from Perigee."

"We don't know that for sure. A scar is just a scar. Be careful. There's too much at stake. Until we have this all sorted out, I want her to believe what Davenport believes: I'm not human, I'm from Elsewhere."

She gave him a kiss. "This will work out, don't worry. We need to move slowly."

"Fine, but an hour ago you were warning me that time was ticking away."

They sat quietly for thirty minutes until Svetlana emerged from the bathroom holding the towel in her left hand. It had the effect of taking Harlan's breath away.

"This … nakedness. Is it a thing with all Perigee Females?"

Angelica laughed. "We don't share your attachment or enthusiasm for clothing. It gets in the way."

"Apparently. Maybe I'll retire to the bedroom and read *War and Peace* while you two chat."

"*War and Peace?*"

"It's a book. I have it in the original Russian. Война и мир, *Peace and War* was the preferred title by Tolstoy. The beginning part's easy. It's in French."

"Sometimes you confuse me."

"Uh-uh. Sometimes the Females of Perigee confuse me. Speaking of Females, try to confirm with her that there aren't any more of your Females out there."

The chat between Angelica and Svetlana lasted less than twenty minutes. When they'd finished Angelica called out to Harlan. He returned to the living room to find them both naked.

Angelica smiled. "I'm just trying to make her feel more at home."

"Is it working?"

"I think so."

"Good, we wouldn't want to appear inhospitable. Pierre hasn't improved much since the last time I read *War and Peace*. He's hopeless. Actually, they all are. I think that's why people read Tolstoy, they can be happy they're not living in one of his books. And on a slightly different note, what have you found out?"

"Svetlana's experience has been pretty much the same as mine, except she was placed in Russia. She worked her way into the life of a Russian agent a few months ago. One who had access to their president, Yuri Polushin."

"And his name is Dmitri Egorkov." It wasn't a question.

"Yes. How did you know?"

"Lucky guess. I mean, how many Russians can there be out there? And let me make another wild guess, he's now dead."

"She doesn't know for sure. He was arrested and taken to a penal colony outside of Moscow. She was no longer able to communicate with him. She feels he was too much of an asset to Polushin to be exterminated."

"Where have I heard that before?"

Svetlana perked up when she heard Dmitri's name, but it was clear she didn't have any knowledge of English.

"Like I said, her story is much like mine, except she studied Russian at Group. Just like me, she was also told by a Male, who'd been conscripted, that Perigee was eliminating all Females upon their return. So, she got Egorkov to cut out her microchip, and destroy it, and she stayed behind. She said she's in love with Egorkov. Apparently love is some sort of infection humans can get. You never told me about it."

"You'll know if you catch it. And how did she end up in Rock Creek Park with a suitcase full of rubles?"

"As it played out with you and with POTUS, Egorkov explained everything to Polushin. Polushin took it all in and indicated he would investigate options. But Svetlana says Yuri's a frightened little man only concerned about his own personal wealth and image, his brand."

"The world's full of them."

"Egorkov knew this about Polushin and didn't trust him, he's double-crossed too many people in the past. He got Svetlana a fake passport, gave her a hundred thousand dollars in rubles, and got her a plane ticket to Washington, DC, by way of Brussels. They both expected that Perigee would have placed an operative in the States, and she'd be safe if she could make contact. After Egorkov was arrested by the FSB, whoever they are?"

"Russian goon squad."

"Anyway, the FSB ransacked Egorkov's apartment. Svetlana told them she was the cleaning lady and they let her go. She slept three nights camped out in Egorkov's dacha outside of Moscow, but when she realized he wasn't going to be released, she panicked, took his advice, and flew to the US. Though she believes he's still alive."

"I wouldn't count on it. Polushin has too much to lose, no matter how much of a fixer Egorkov is." Harlan leaned back in his chair and studied Angelica. He then stood and said, "Let's step into the bedroom for a second."

He glanced at Svetlana, "*Prah-stee-tyen-meh-nya,*" and they left her sitting alone in the kitchen.

After they were out of earshot, he gave Angelica a hard look, "Okay, I'm going to need a definitive answer here. How many more of these Svetlanas are going to show up? When General Dixon comes up with a model, we can't afford any additional surprises. We're dead meat if there are any more Females out there."

"She can't understand us. She only speaks Russian. We didn't need to leave the room."

Harlan shrugged.

"Okay, fine, Group's original plan was to only approach the countries that had nuclear capabilities, figuring that was where the power was. But language became the issue. None of the Females could handle the Chinese or Hindi way of talking. And Group didn't see the smaller powers as worth monitoring." She rubbed at her temples. "My head is losing so many history facts every day. There's no guarantee the Males didn't alter plans. They can't be trusted, but there's no way they had the time to train more operatives in human languages, especially if they've restricted themselves to Males. I remember a decision to leave the British people alone, too. Since they speak the same language as the US people. We assumed the US and the UK was all one species."

"You missed that thing in 1776?"

"We were focusing on diseases. You're a disease. Mutations happen all the time. We didn't consider it alarming, or something to make note of. Just another variant. And remember the Females drew up this plan, not the Males, who seem to enjoy analyzing war, and such things, much more than we do."

"Nice to know that the founding of my country was simply a variant of sorts."

"Don't take it so personally."

"So that's it? It's only you and Svetlana who are here from Perigee? Can you guarantee that? Only Russia and the US?"

"Yes, we're the only ones, at this point I'm certain. Svetlana is of the same opinion. And can you guarantee me that she will be safe? Here in your loft?"

He smiled at her. "Yes. But I think we should consider purchasing some more bathrobes. I wouldn't want anyone to get a chill."

THIRTY-SIX

General Dixon was smiling like the Cheshire Cat when Harlan and Lou were escorted into the Oval Office. The first words out of his mouth were, "You guys are gonna love this shit."

POTUS walked in five minutes later, looked at the general, and said, "What have you got, Doug?"

"You're gonna love this shit, sir."

And the president did; they all did. Dixon and his team had created creatures that appeared menacing while at the same time intelligent. They spoke English in a deeply accented baritone voice and stood upright like human beings. They were dressed in contemporary clothing with only their bald heads and hands noticeable, and what 'skin' could be seen was an iridescent green which changed in texture and hue as they moved about on the projection screen. Their eyes were a radiant white-blue and had the illusion of cutting into everything they were focused on.

"I told my boys I want formidable but not too frightening. Realism was the key. People need to say, 'Holy shit,' the moment they see them. And if we made them too scary it just looked like more crap from Hollywood."

"Good work, Doug. Now how do we show them in conversation with me? That's what we need to send out to other world leaders. They must know that I've been contacted personally."

"Already done, sir."

Dixon removed his presentation drive and connected a second drive to his computer. The next film clip showed his creatures and the president and Harlan sitting on the couches in front of the Resolute Desk. Harlan's face had been fuzzed out, so that he couldn't be identified, and they were engaged in conversation. However, there was no audio, which seemed to bother The Old Man.

"What do you have us saying?"

"Nothing."

"Why's that? Why no sound on this clip?"

"That's the beauty of this, sir. The creatures' lips and yours are formulated in abstract AI movements. I only had them speaking in the other version to show you it can be done if necessary. This presentation will go out with no audio, and we want to ensure no one can be able to read your lips. Remember this is all top secret, the highest categorization. We need to create a type of worldwide paranoia so that everyone will be required to look to Uncle Sam for leadership. And when this gets leaked to the public, and it will get leaked, you can bet your sweet ass on that, we will be in the driver's seat. The world will follow your directives. The abstract lip movement also gives you the ability to create whatever conversation you like. No one will be able to confirm or deny what was said between you and the aliens. Plus, the display will be offered as being not the full extent of your conversation. If we want to add any dialog, we can do it with subtitles. We can also create a second and third visit if necessary. Flexibility and subtlety, they're what make the Army sing."

POTUS stood and began to pace the room. "Why's Harlan in there? Why a MPS Agent? Why not the VP?"

Dixon rolled his eyes. "Sir, with all due respect, do you really want the Veep in on this? We've already covered this. Do you want to let him get anywhere near a microphone? Remember the Girl Scout fiasco?"

"Good point."

"Stone is in there, and blurred, to create more shock and confusion. He's the Mystery Man, the secret agent, and he's also your witness; someone who can reinforce your story if called upon to do so. Notice he doesn't speak, no lip movement, more mystery. Just by Harlan being there people will know you aren't the only one who's met the aliens. That's for the general public, but if Davenport gets a hold of one of our drives, we want him guessing if Harlan's the same alien from Elsewhere that he met when he was here. And that the dudes with him are Harlan's dudes, and not from Perigee."

"General," Harlan interjected, "Davenport will know these images are fake."

"Not so sure about that. In all likelihood, he thinks these clowns come from wherever you're supposed to be from and are working with us. At some point, he might even scan the images from the Dallas collapse and see you. We need to cover our asses on that too. Keep them guessing, that's the Army way. Besides, we played around with POTUS being alone with our aliens, but it looked too staged. People would see it as BS right off the top."

The president stopped pacing, leaned against his desk, and folded his arms across his chest. "So, this is it? We're ready to rock and roll? I can send this out through diplomatic channels?"

Harlan cleared his throat. "Ah, sir, again, we're going to distribute this through Interpol, not diplomats. This needs to go directly to world leaders and not be circumnavigated by some policy wonk who thinks he has all the answers. Don't forget some of those people are still glued to the past administration and are hellbent on making you look like a fool. We don't want some opinionated politico tossing in his two cents. The fastest and most efficient way to distribute this is through Interpol, and keep politics out of it." He looked at Dixon. "General, is there any way, any possible way, that some bad player will be able to parse these images and determine that they are fabricated?"

"Not in a million years. My boys are brilliant." He smiled. "Now that I say that ... two of them are women, they don't really count as boys. In fact, they're sharper than some of the boys. They weren't distracted when we were thinking about giving the creatures tits. Though they did think it was a somewhat juvenile exercise."

"Right," the president said, but his mind was on something else. "Can we go back to something we discussed earlier, are we going to get these images to the goddam Russians or leave them in the dark?"

Harlan had brought Lou up to speed on what Svetlana had reported so he let him respond to the president.

"There's a bit of a problem there, sir. We have it on excellent intelligence that the Kremlin, at least Polushin, has been informed about the visitors, and what Perigee's intentions are. Polushin was given the information personally by a senior Russian Interpol Agent, a man named Dmitri Egorkov. Egorkov has since disappeared, and Polushin, from what we can determine, has totally ignored the situation. Our source guarantees that Yuri has never had a face-to-face with any Perigee operatives, so he won't know our images are fabricated. The plan now is to give the information to the Russian Interpol office on a flash drive, but the likelihood of another agent having the gonads to deliver it to Polushin is remote. We're going to have to assume that when the images get leaked, and given worldwide exposure, it will inspire other Russian politicos to call Yuri out on it."

Things were moving a little too fast for the president. "Let me get this straight, we're still going with my original plan, right?"

"Yes, sir," Dixon answered. "These thumb drives are going to go out to every nation, marked as top secret, the highest level of confidentiality, and then we're going to just sit on our tails and take for granted that some jackass leaks it to the press?"

Both Harlan and General Dixon stood at the same time, looked at one another, and shrugged.

"You take it from here, Stone. I came through with the goods. Making it fly is your department."

"Thanks." He then focused on POTUS. "Sir, not only are we sending the drives out worldwide, we're taking it a step further. General Dixon will be distributing them to every US military commander here and abroad. It will also go out to every police department in the country. Canada, Mexico, and NATO Nations will be given special consideration. It'll be an early heads-up to be certain North America and Western Europe are doubly prepared and stabilized. Lou Walsh has drafted cover letters, written by you, of course, with detailed information on Perigee, their demands, and the best way to handle the public outcry once we make our announcement."

"What announcement is that?"

"There is no announcement, sir."

"No announcement?"

"It won't get that far. Next week we will be sending out thousands of copies of the general's flash drive to every corner of the Earth, to every unstable government and small-town police department. All labeled *Top Secret, For Your Eyes only*. Your theory of sitting on it for a month will never materialize. If it isn't leaked to FOX News within twenty-four hours, I think we're all going to be astounded."

THIRTY-SEVEN

It all went exactly as planned. FOX News pundits, CNN pundits, CBS, NBC, ABC; pundits for every major television network in every corner of the Earth were on the story within forty-eight hours of the release of the *Top Secret, For Your Eyes Only* thumb drives. No one knew for sure who was the first to leak the story because it was leaked by countless sources worldwide. No one got the scoop, and everyone got the scoop. To a person, the pundits dumped on POTUS for not being forthcoming, for which he was prepared. They accused him of everything under the sun, from not being transparent with the public, to treason, to conspiring with aliens, which was an allegation unfamiliar to most legal experts and had yet to be enshrined in the Constitution. There were calls for his resignation. Opposing members of Congress demanded his impeachment.

Though, oddly, the mass public hysteria that Harlan and the entire team had predicted, never materialized to any significant degree, much to the dismay of the news outlets. By and large, people seemed intrigued more than anything, because, after all, it made perfect sense. The public came away with a, "Well, what else could it have been?" attitude. They were disappointed that they hadn't personally observed any signs of the aliens or their spaceships and were anxious to see and hear more about the president's encounters.

Their curiosity prompted them to ask more rational questions than any journalists had considered. POTUS began holding town hall meetings and personally supplying answers to their questions. Courtesy of General Dixon, he was able to provide more visual proof of his encounters and the specific details of their conversations. And once the Old Man made clear the seriousness of the situation, and the potential consequences, most men and women sided with him. He was in his element; he became that loveable old granddad who was going to make it all turn out right in the end, and communities began focusing on solutions rather than simply pointing fingers.

Electric vehicle production and sales soared. Farm equipment manufacturers scrambled to develop practical solar and electric alternatives. In urban areas, electric trollies, bicycles, and rickshaws quickly became the favored mode of personal transportation. People driving gasoline-powered vehicles were given withering looks. Sure, in the beginning, oil tankers were hijacked, but there were very few buyers for their hot cargo. Hydro, solar, and wind energy production was ramped up. And no one ever questioned the validity of the leaked thumb drives.

But the clock was still ticking, and these advancements were chewing up time. The energy required to build a new infrastructure contributed more CO_2 emissions than the Earth was eliminating. In the long run, the picture was fairly rosy, in the short run, not so much. A few Asian countries didn't seem to be pulling their weight. And after eighteen months, no significant dent had been made in the reduction of greenhouse gasses, certainly not a dent that registered on any human monitoring devices. There was anguished hope that Perigee instruments would detect a more noticeable change. However, a year and a half had passed, and most of the world was taking it as a challenge. That much was clear. People were pulling together.

"Except Polushin and the goddam Russians."

General Dixon nodded in total agreement with the president.

"Yes, sir. And the OPEC jackasses, don't forget them. For the most part, the world is doing all it can, but the real culprits are China and India for not scaling back usage. They're sucking up that crude like spiked punch at a Baptist New Year's Eve party. There's a whole corner of the globe that's nothing more than a carbon monoxide cesspool. And here I was totally convinced they'd be on board to establish their legacy, keep their offspring, offspringing. Man, did I miss that call."

"Doug, I've tried everything to win over those twits. They're married to Moscow's crude, and they rationalize their consumption by maintaining that if the rest of the world knuckles under they don't have to. Greenhouse gasses will be reduced enough to satisfy Perigee's demands without their participation."

"That's rolling the dice, sir, and we all know it." Harlan paced the Oval Office, half wishing POTUS had installed a speedbag. "Perigee isn't going to see it that way. Even if our emissions have been significantly reduced, it's going to be all or nothing with them. According to them, we're all part of the same disease. There's no distinguishing by race or nationality."

"Goddam Idi Amin had it right all along," Dixon grumbled under his breath.

"Idi Amin? What the hell's he got to do with this?"

"In 1972 he told all those Indian shitheads to pack up and get the hell out of Uganda. Then he took control of their piss-ant, bullshit businesses and turned them over to the Ugandans. The place ran like a top after that."

Harlan shook his head. "General, resurrecting Idi Amin and his methods aren't going to garner a great deal of compassion from anyone."

"Screw compassion. It worked."

"I think our situation is a little different."

"Hell, no. We negotiate with Perigee. Be honest with them. When they return, we tell them what's going on, and have them go sterilize the crap out of all those Asian bastards and leave us alone. See how all the Indians like that bullshit. And neuter the damn Chinese while they're at it. They're making a mess of Uganda as I speak with their goddam Belt and Road Initiative. They're chewing up Uganda like Christmas cookies in July. They need Idi to come back and crack the whip. He ran a tight ship. I like a man like that."

"Calm down, Doug. There's got to be a diplomatic way out of this."

"I agree with the president. We've got to turn it off at the spigot. If we can shut down the Russian supply lines, OPEC will follow suit. They won't want to go it alone. And they can't go it alone logistically, anyway. We can blockade the Gulf, but it's the Russian pipelines we need to shut down."

Dixon smiled. "Okay. I'm on board with that. Yeah, that's the way to go. I assume you mean we bomb the piss out of the Russian pipelines."

"I didn't say that, general. I don't think starting a nuclear war with Russia is going to clean up the atmosphere that quickly. We need to find a way around Polushin. We need to either win him over or foment a palace coup. I don't see any other way. And we have zippo time to do it."

"No way you win over that shithead; he's such a clown. Look, I'm not talking about bombs, as in real bombs and jets and missiles and shit, when I say bomb the piss out of them, I'm talking about what you told me about Norcross and cow farts and eco-terrorists."

"I'm not following you, Doug."

"It's simple, sir. We set up the eco-terrorists to bomb the Russian pipelines. We run the operation; we supply the explosives. But to Polushin it looks like those flunkies did the grunt work, which, of course, they will."

Harlan cleared his throat. "I've been to Russia, more than once. There are no eco-terrorists left. Anyone who thought along those lines was eliminated by Polushin years ago. The real dissidents are out of the country or dead or locked up for life. He's now going after their families."

Dixon laughed. "Jesus, you think I'd let a bunch of shitheads like eco-terrorists or Greenpeace handle something this big? We'll use Special Forces troopers. Dress them up in peasant clothes and make up a bunch of hand-painted signs for them to leave behind. The idea is to make it so that Polushin can't trace it to any government. It needs to look civilian. I can put any one of my boys anywhere on this globe and Old Yuri wouldn't know shit, wouldn't even look up from his girlie mag."

"I'm sure you are capable of doing that, general, but anyone you drop into Russia is going to need to speak flawless Russian, otherwise they will be traced right back to this office. I speak Russian, Lou Walsh speaks Russian, and we speak it flawlessly, but not well enough to fool any FSB agent. We have accents, no way around it. I like your approach, but you'd need to recruit dissidents inside Russia to make it work. Russians would have to be the ones to handle it for there to be a chance of success. And they're going to need to pull it off using Russian explosives because the FSB forensic people will be able to trace anything back to its source. Sorry, general, but I don't see us making a plan like that work in such a short period of time."

Dixon slammed his fist on the coffee table. "Jesus, I hate these goddam Russians." And then as if a light bulb had gone off over his head, "What about this Interpol agent who Yuri threw in the slammer way back when?"

"Dmitri Egorkov?"

"Yeah, that's guy. Where the hell is he?"

"Six feet under would be my guess."

"Do we know that for sure? What's the CIA skinny on that, sir?"

POTUS picked up the phone. "I'll get Director Collins on it. What did you have in mind, Doug?"

"If we can find out where he is, my boys can get him out. Piece of cake. We do this shit all the time. Remember Noriega?"

Harlan ran his fingers through his hair and shook his head.

"General, that operation didn't exactly go by unnoticed. Our invasion of Panama and the snatching of Noriega were hardly subtle. We were ostracized by the UN for it."

"Okay, okay, bad example, but I can make this work. I can get Egorkov out without anyone knowing shit. And after I do, it shouldn't take much to bring him over if he's been treated like any other Polushin enemy. Then all we need is cash. He can recruit his old Interpol buddies, he can buy what he needs, he can get it done. That's if he's as good as you say he is, Stone."

"He's good at what he does, general, or was at one point. But what you're asking isn't what he does. He's an Interpol Agent. He solves crimes, he doesn't commit them. And in the end, I sincerely doubt he's still alive, and if he is alive, there probably isn't much left of him."

THIRTY-EIGHT

Initially, Svetlana was surprisingly cool to the idea of returning to Moscow, rescuing her inamorato, Dmitri Egorkov, and cooking up some hair-brained revolutionary oil pipeline bombing operation. And in reality, there was no solid plan to do so. Harlan had returned to his loft from his meeting with POTUS and General Dixon, sat down with a glass of wine, and told Angelica and Svetlana about the plan to get Dmitri out. In the year-and-a-half, since they had found her on a bench in Rock Creek Park with a boatload of rubles, Svetlana had learned to speak English and had settled in as if she was native to DC, if such a thing was remotely possible. Though, she, and Davenport, still believed Harlan was from Elsewhere.

Harlan had briefed her on POTUS's meeting with the aliens, knowing full well she was bound to see General Dixon's images on TV or social media. Where those aliens were from was never made clear to her, and it only served to make her fearful. She refused to move out and live on her own. Oddly, Harlan thought the idea of her returning to Russia wasn't a half-bad one, mainly because eighteen months of having two stunning women lounging around his loft butt-naked was beginning to become slightly distracting.

"I wouldn't count on this *Great Escape* idea of General Dixon's coming to fruition. First, the CIA needs to confirm Dmitri's exact location and confirm that he's still alive. I hate to say this, but I know how Yuri Polushin operates. The chances that Dmitri is still breathing are slim to none."

"But I told you where they took him. How hard could it be to find him?"

"I passed that location on to the CIA months ago. Before this latest development, but they were pretty cool on the idea of finding him. That's where they'll start their search now that there's renewed interest. But people get moved around in Russia, you know that. The fact that no one has reported his death is a good sign, but again, it's no guarantee. We'll just have to wait and see what the spooks come up with."

Svetlana slapped the palms of her hands on the table and forcefully stood. The move nearly toppled Harlan's wine glass. She sounded like a spoiled five-year-old.

"Okay, screw it, if I need to go back to Moscow to help free him, so be it."

Harlan sat quietly for a full minute. The silence was broken by Angelica.

"Well, why not? Why can't she go back?"

"Let me think this through."

Another long silence followed before he said, "You have a Russian passport. You can go back any time you like. No one's stopping you. The reason I'd always advised against it was because we all realized there was no purpose. You'd be miserable and eventually, you'd end up just like Dmitri. And you were okay with that."

"I don't care. That was yesterday. Today is today. I'm going tomorrow. Let's set it up."

Harlan held up his hand. There was something in Svetlana's tone that made him think she was bluffing, and that she had no desire to return to Russia, and who could blame her? Still, there was something disingenuous about her tone.

"Okay, hold on, slow down. If you want to see Dmitri, you're going to need to work closely with the CIA and General Dixon. There's no other way to do it safely. Obviously, you can, and would be, a very useful asset in any operation they might work out; trusted female Russians are hard to come by. But you can't just take off on your own and expect the pieces to fall into place."

"I have all that money. I saw how things work in Moscow. This doesn't need to be some over-the-top military operation. People are easily bribed."

Harlan sighed. "The only reason you got those rubles into the US in the first place is because you smiled at some lovelorn customs agent who thought he had a chance to make it with you. And that's why he didn't bother to check your luggage. If he had, you'd still be in the slammer. It's not going to work the other way around. Russian passport or not, they're going to search you and your belongings, discover the cash, and some Russian customs agent is going to get himself a new Bentley out of the deal. And you're going to be sitting next to Dmitri sooner than you think—in some Siberian *gulag*."

Svetlana's newfound enthusiasm was instantly, and very easily, deflated. She sat and rested her head on the table, not bothering to respond. Angelica placed her arm over her shoulder.

"At this point, everyone wants to get Dmitri freed and involve him with whatever operation we can organize, if it comes to that. And personally, I'm not one hundred percent sold on the idea. I've met him, Svetlana. I've traveled to Russia. Love him or not, you know he's not a real leader; he likes to work solo. But let's see what the CIA finds out. If Dmitri is alive, he'll be pinpointed. Your idea of bribing someone may well be their best option. It would be quiet, attract little attention and anyone who accepts a bribe keeps their mouth shut. They'd probably want a body, though."

Svetlana lifted her head. "A body? What kind of body?"

"Preferably human."

Both Females gave him a quizzical look.

"If Dmitri is alive, and if he can be located, and if they can get to him, and if they can negotiate a bribe, then the person accepting the bribe will be forced to explain an empty cell. The easiest way to explain an empty cell is to not have an empty cell. The CIA gets him out, and the next morning they find him dead in his cell."

"But it would be another man's body. Won't they perform some tests to be certain it's him?"

"They'll be too busy covering everything up. The quicker Dmitri Egorkov disappears from everyone's memory the better."

"But the CIA would have to kill another man to make it work?"

Harlan laughed. "It wouldn't be the first time they've done that. But no, trust me, finding dead Russians in Moscow isn't as hard as you might think."

THIRTY-NINE

Once again Harlan and Lou found themselves cooling their heels in the Oval Office waiting for POTUS to make an appearance. When he finally walked in, after twenty minutes, he was followed by the CIA Director Bradley Collins.

"Have a seat, boys. I'm happy to report that Director Collins has located Dmitri Egorkov."

The president sat. Collins pulled a file folder from his case and handed it to Harlan, then dropped into a nearby armchair. Harlan thumbed through the papers and handed the folder to Lou. Collins waited for him to scan the information before he spoke.

"We've confirmed that they're holding Egorkov in Prison IK-1 in Yaroslavl."

"Jesus," Harlan muttered. "And he's still alive? He might be the only one who is. That tank has a special reputation."

"Our sources indicate that they've cleaned up the place since all that nasty stuff was leaked in 2018. But that doesn't mean it's a model of modern-day prison reform. It is still Russia after all—and he's on Yuri's shitlist. But, yes, Egorkov is alive. You're positive he's the one who brought Polushin up to speed on this entire Perigee situation?"

"Yes, sir, that's been confirmed. He did so a year and a half ago, at about the same time we distributed General Dixon's flash drives. Polushin obviously ignored everything and had Egorkov thrown in the can to keep him from speaking out. But there's no way your average Russian doesn't know what the hell's going on by this point. The general's drives have been a YouTube and TikTok sensation from the start. Even with the Russian blocking apps, shit gets through, bet on it. So, the question remains, can you get Egorkov out? And is it worth it?"

"Is it worth it, is the bigger question. I did a background check on him. He's not a team player, even by Moscow standards."

Collins drummed his fingers on the armrest for a full minute. He wasn't smiling, but that wasn't unusual for Collins. He enjoyed playing the role of chief spook to a much greater extent than his predecessors. He was more of a greasy politician than a man who'd risen through the agency's ranks.

"Yes. I'm confident we can get him out, but we've never done something like this so deep into Russia before. It's risky on an international and, dare I say, political level. If Yuri ever suspected the US of springing Egorkov, the shit is really going to hit the fan. There's no telling how he'll respond. He's unhinged at this point. Plus, to be perfectly honest, I think this plan of Dixon's is beyond boneheaded. It'll never work. Cutting off the pipelines does nothing. They'll have them up and running within a week, and Egorkov, and whoever he recruits, will be hunted down like dogs. And when they're rounded up and tortured, everything comes right back to this office. All this is assuming he will sign on and work with us in the first place. A lot of his type are married to Mother Russia, no matter how much they despise Polushin, or how Ukrainian they profess they might be. They can't be brought over."

Harlan sat still. He had boxed himself into a corner. There were only five individuals on Earth who had actually interacted with an operative from Perigee and knew for sure what they really looked like: POTUS, Harlan, Lou Walsh, Rich Perez, and Egorkov. Thanks to Svetlana, Harlan, and Lou were the only ones who truly knew Egorkov's detailed history and his personal connection to Perigee.

Lou had met Svetlana, and the two MPS agents agreed that revealing that she'd been sent from Perigee to Russia by Group would only expose her, and Angelica by association, to unnecessary scrutiny by the CIA, FBI, NSA, and the like. Both Females would have been dragged in for questioning long ago, and quite possibly never released. Their images would be made public and expose Dixon's drives as fabrications. Added to the mix was the fact that Svetlana still believed that Dixon's aliens were not from Perigee, but came from Harlan's Elsewhere.

Fortunately, no one had investigated how Egorkov might have known about Perigee before the Dixon presentation was leaked. And apparently it was never tortured out of him. No doubt because of his concern for Svetlana, he clammed up.

Collins directed the conversation to POTUS. "Sir, I know you've never liked this, but I think the only solution here is regime change. If not in Russia, it would need to be in India or maybe China. I don't see any other way out. Fossil fuel consumption in that part of the globe needs to be halted ASAP. We can't stop the clock from ticking. We need to move in on these people."

"I don't know, Bradley. Regime change starts getting us into some real muddy waters. I'm thinking back to that time when we—"

"If I may, sir?" Harlan interjected. "I believe the director is on the right path. General Dixon's idea would never play out. Though I think we have a better chance for regime change in

Russia than anywhere else. And it could happen more quickly there. Time is of the essence at this point. The people of Russia are extremely frustrated with leadership. They've had their sons and husbands come home in plastic bags ever since Polushin's been in power. The ISIS-K terror attack landed in his lap. We warned him, he didn't listen. He's lost any sense of reality. The people know what's going on. And in the end, very few Russian livelihoods are directly affected by oil and gas; that money goes straight to the oligarchs. And they've grown weary of being shunned by The West. They may be primed for a quick change."

"It's really the only way, sir."

"I don't like being ganged up on."

"Nobody does, sir."

Collins said this as if he were speaking to a sulky teenager and Harlan rubbed at his eyes to keep from laughing. Walsh nudged him in his side just to make him more miserable.

The president leaned back in his chair and shook his head from side to side. "Okay, I give up. How do we proceed?"

Collins offered one of his thin smiles.

"First things first, do we really need Egorkov? There are plenty of other dissidents in exile who are far more familiar and respected by the Russian people than a disgraced Interpol Agent. He could be more trouble than he's worth. He's not some guru who can jumpstart a crusade."

"That's true," Lou said. "He's not a politician. He'll never be the leader of any type of movement, but he's highly respected within Interpol, inside and outside of Russia. He produces results. It's the main reason we distributed Dixon's drives through Interpol. If he could unite Russian Interpol against Polushin, who knows? There might be something there? Whoever leads the effort will need some muscle."

The director wasn't impressed. "I don't have to tell you, no one in the intelligence community has ever been dazzled by Interpol. We see them as nothing more than a bunch of glorified beat cops who think too highly of themselves. They've bungled more operations than I can count."

Lou and Harlan shared a look. It wasn't the first time they had had to deal with inter-agency rivalries. And even though Interpol itself was not strictly a US agency, there was clearly no love lost between them and the CIA. Harlan and Lou were sitting on a huge asset that no one else was privy to: Angelica and Svetlana. They'd been playing it close to the vest for a long time. It was Harlan who responded to Collins.

"Director, here's something MPS has been trying to sort out. And I'm aware that you may not think very highly of us at MPS either. Since we pretty much only deal with domestic issues. Of course, at the behest of the president of the United States."

Might as well remind him who we report to, Harlan thought. *And it's not the friggin' CIA.*

"But consider this, Egorkov was jailed before we released General Dixon's flash drives, which proved to the world that there had been an alien invasion. This can only mean one thing; that he also, somehow, must have caught on to the fact that it was Perigee who had orchestrated the livestock issues, and caught on at an earlier stage than the rest of the world. Maybe even us."

"What's your point?"

"Sir, the point is, Egorkov must have somehow also made contact with a Perigee operative. Perhaps it played out the same way as it did with us. He found a low-level Perigee flunky, kidnapped him, and used him as bait to drag Davenport into the Kremlin. Perhaps Polushin himself has even met with Davenport."

"Who the hell is Davenport?"

"Ah, right. Davenport. Davenport is the alien you see speaking with me and the president in General Dixon's footage. I forgot there was no audio."

"I should have been brought up to speed on this Davenport business a long time ago."

"Well, he's gone and won't be back for a while. There didn't seem to be much point in identifying the creature by name."

"And Egorkov?"

"He's the only one who can answer our questions. No matter how you plan to implement regime change in Russia, Egorkov is a valuable asset. We need to get him out and find out what he knows. He'll have the best insight by far on how to deal with Polushin."

After a long pause, Collins mumbled, "I'll work on it."

FORTY

Harlan and Lou waited until they were well down Pennsylvania Avenue and clear of any listening devices before they said anything significant. They weren't about to talk about fake aliens and organized leaks near any government buildings or embassies. It was a cool spring evening. The cherry blossoms were just beginning to pop, though neither agent noticed.

"Nice cover-up on your Davenport gaff. I'm just thinking," Lou put forward as they walked toward Harlan's car. "Do you think Yuri has actually met with Davenport?"

"Well, if he has, he's known that the Dixon production was bullshit from day one. Russia, the Kremlin, and Polushin were the first to receive it." They walked in silence for another two minutes. "No, Polushin would have called us out on all this a year and a half ago if he knew what Davenport looked like. He hasn't met him. And I doubt Egorkov's ever seen any of the thumb drives. He was jailed too early in the game."

"No telling what can seep through prison walls, but if he's stuck on Svetlana, and wants to see her again, he'll keep his mouth shut. She is a bit of a fox, by the way. I was thinking of putting a move on her one of these days. Screw Egorkov."

"Spoken like a true romantic."

"I learned it all from you." They walked another thirty feet. "Have you ever stopped to consider that these otherworldly women might be capable of some sort of mind control? That maybe they have something else going on, other than the foxiness thing? You've twisted a hell of a lot of policy people, and policy rules, when it comes to your handling of Angelica. Just sayin'."

Harlan laughed. "It's worked out for the best. It was the only way I could have handled it. We would have learned nothing, otherwise. And without their chips, there's no information any hardliners could squeeze from them." After another thirty feet. "There's no way in hell Collins is going to work with Interpol on this. He's too much of a prig. I doubt if he'll even contact them, let alone bring them on board. We need to set up another meeting with Bayless and Dodge and get them up to speed. They know Egorkov better than any of us."

"Collins ain't gonna like that. Especially if we go behind his back."

They had reached Harlan's car. Lou slid into the passenger's seat and Harlan crossed over to the other side where he saw a piece of paper under his windshield wiper. At first, he thought it was a parking ticket. He removed the piece of paper and moaned, "Shit." He unfolded the paper. It was a note from Angelica; her handwriting was unmistakable. It read, *Meet me at Lenny's when you're done—alone, no matter what the time. I'll be there.*

Harlan dropped into the car. "Where can I drop you?" He handed the paper to Lou. "I'm not sure what's up, but whenever she insists on being alone with me it can only mean one of two things."

"And they are?"

"Something has freaked her out, and you can use your imagination for reason number two."

"Drop me at Peyton Place. I'll see if I can set something set up with Bayless and Dodge for tomorrow. For your sake, I hope nothing's freaked her out. You look like you could use a little TLC."

—

After Harlan dropped off Lou, he went straight to Lenny's. Angelica was waiting for him in their usual booth. He sat opposite her, leaned across the table and touched her cheek.

"Are you okay? You couldn't have just called me?"

"I think something's going on. I don't know who's monitoring what. There's this thing in the back of my head telling me to be cautious. Don't use the phone, don't talk to strangers."

"I thought we removed that ... thing," he said, trying to lighten the atmosphere. It didn't work.

"I'm serious."

"Yes, well, I'm picking up on that. What's going on?"

"I was playing with your computer. I got bored and decided to do a little research on Dmitri Egorkov."

Mackie came over and they ordered a Guinness, a glass of water, and two fish and chips, one with no fish.

"With all the potatoes you eat, it's amazing you don't weigh three hundred pounds."

"This body isn't designed for weight gain."

"Jesus, if we could patent that we'd own an island in the Bahamas right now. Anyway, I doubt you learned much about Dmitri Egorkov without going into Interpol records. You should have waited for me to get home, because to access that stuff you'd need a few passwords."

"Has anyone ever told you that you have absolutely no imagination when it comes to creating passwords?"

"You hacked your way into my computer, into Interpol?"

"Your sister's middle name followed by the year she was born is hardly a secure password."

"It is as if I can never remember what year she was born or her middle name."

"And this is why you list all your passwords in your address book under your sister's name? Just so you can retrieve them easily if you need to? That's nuts. It's a good thing she hasn't married anyone, you'd probably forget her new last name and never find your passwords."

"Nobody likes a snoop." He took her hand. "I forgive you, but only because I'm so fond of you. So, what did you find out about Egorkov that's so earthshattering that we needed to have this clandestine meeting where no one is monitoring us?"

"Guess what his mother's name is?"

"You're serious, I take it?"

"Yes. Her name is, or was, Svetlana."

Harlan let her hand go and sat up a bit straighter in his seat.

"Well, it's not an unusual Russian name, Stalin's daughter and all, but I see where you're going with this. It's a little coincidental."

"That's what I was thinking. And think of this, just because she has a scar on the back of her neck doesn't prove that anything was removed, just like you once said."

"She's been living with us for over a year. She's done nothing unusual. She hasn't given herself away and hasn't tried to interfere with the process at all. And why wouldn't Perigee give her a name Egorkov would recognize and be attracted to?"

Mackie arrived with their drinks, set them up with napkins and utensils, and strolled off.

"No, I would buy that she's moved on to acting as a Russian spy," Harlan muttered. "That's plausible. But otherwise it makes no sense. Why would she still be embedded with a Perigee chip and just hang out and do nothing? What's the point?"

"She's the Elf on the Shelf. The thing that really doesn't make any sense is that Davenport would just evaporate, and plan to return in two years, without planting a listening device somewhere. Group would still want to monitor the situation here no matter what; if for nothing else, to make sure the Earth was making a concentrated attempt to turn things around. And what better place to plant a device than with an agent who communicates daily with the president? If Earth hadn't taken any drastic steps immediately, they would have shut this experiment down within a week and the story would be over. You'd be left grappling with Phase Three already. Obviously, Svetlana knew Russia was balking and reported it, but she also knew the rest of the world was taking action and she passed that all on to Perigee, too."

"Let me think this through."

"What makes this all logical is Egorkov. He was her source. Once Polushin's men hauled him off to prison she lost any hope of gaining inside information. She either had to find another Russian contact, or come here and latch on to you ... Or maybe Lou. It would have made no sense for her to find another Russian because she knew it would play out exactly the same as it did with Egorkov—the poor sap would have been jailed, and she'd be back to square one. She was probably totally blown away when she saw me. She never expected that."

"If that's the case, why hasn't she tried to knock you out of the picture?"

"I don't know, but I'm all of a sudden annoyed at being observed. If that's the case. And if she did turn me in, she'd lose her connection to you, and at the same time, out herself. Plus, she still thinks you're from Elsewhere. Davenport would want to watch you like a hawk."

Mackie arrived with their food and Angelica dowsed her fries with ketchup.

Harlan smiled and shook his head. "Having a spy in the house is kind of creepy. And it would explain why she backed off returning to Russia so easily. How do we determine if she still has a chip in her?"

"If she still does have the chip, it means she was lying about being in love with Egorkov."

"What makes you say that?"

"I don't believe it's an infection we can contract."

"I wish you wouldn't keep referring to love as an infectious disease. Some humans are into that sort of thing. I wouldn't want to insult them."

"Be glad I'm not calling you a disease anymore. So, what's the true test of love? There must be a test, what is it? There's a test for everything. You've been at this longer than me, what's the test?"

Harlan slid into the corner of the booth. "Come over to this side and sit next to me."

Angelica moved to the other side of the booth and sat with her thigh touching his. She brought her plate of French fries with her. He laughed. "See, there's the true test of love: you were unwilling to leave your fries behind."

"Okay, fine, I get it. I love fries. But that's all inside—inside of me. How do we know what's going on inside Svetlana?"

"We don't. We're looking at this from the wrong angle. And French fries aren't the best of metaphors for love. It's close, but I'd go with onion rings. It may be easier to determine if Svetlana doesn't love Egorkov, rather than trying to prove that she does love him."

"And how do we do that?"

"Go back and try to think of yourself with the chip still implanted. Then think of one of your colleagues in Perigee, one that you especially liked, and then think of how you'd react if they turned up dead or disappeared. How would you process that?"

"We don't react to things like that. Acquaintances move on, they leave us. It's a byproduct of time. They outlive their usefulness and are replaced. It happens. It doesn't call for a reaction; none is expressed."

Harlan pulled her even closer. "Then, the answer is fairly simple."

"Is it?"

"When we get home, we tell Svetlana that Egorkov's dead and see how she reacts."

FORTY-ONE

Lou Walsh had set up the meeting with Christian Dodge at DC Interpol NCB for 10:00 a.m. the next morning. Harlan met Lou fifteen minutes earlier on a bench near the National Gallery.

"It turns out Svetlana never had the Perigee chip removed. I'm pretty sure she's been reporting everything back to Group on a regular basis."

"Beautiful," Lou responded facetiously. "How'd you come up with that tidbit?"

"She doesn't love Egorkov."

"Well, damn, that sure as shit explains everything."

Harlan laughed. "It's a somewhat iffy diagnosis, but I trust Angelica's instincts on this. She's who caught on to Svetlana, not me. It makes perfect sense that Group would want to monitor the situation here by keeping someone on the ground."

"And that's why Davenport never suggested that they were missing any Females besides Angelica. The only other Female left behind wasn't missing at all."

"Right. But in the end, it doesn't change anything. Perigee hasn't stepped in yet, which can only mean they've been apprised of our progress by Svetlana and approve of what's been accomplished so far."

"You forget that they really don't give a shit if we pull this off or not. They hold all the cards. They also hold the damn stopwatch, which is quickly ticking away to zero hour while we sit on a friggin' bench."

In an almost subconscious response, Harlan checked the time on his cell phone. They stood and began walking toward Interpol NCB.

"How much of this new tidbit of yours do we share, and who do we share it with?" Lou said as he kicked a discarded coffee cup off the sidewalk. It was full of coffee and soaked into his shoe. "Shit."

Harlan laughed. "I would have left that baby alone. Okay, unless some dire need comes up for POTUS to contact Group, I say we wait and see how the CIA plans to handle this and share nothing with POTUS and Dixon. To be honest, I'm not convinced regime change is the best route anymore, or even a viable one. We're down to about six months to turn Asia around. Crap doesn't move that fast in Russia. Even if you disappear Polushin today, there'd need to be a radical about-face under committed new leadership. I'm not optimistic that will happen. The corruption's too deep. The ball will just keep rolling with a Polushin wannabe."

"China and India are just as bad. I still think we're best focusing on Russia. There's a ruling class that has the muscle to step in. The oligarchs aren't stupid. There's a good chance they'll work with us if Yuri's out. We have a lot of their money tied up."

They'd reached Interpol headquarters on E Street. After they entered, they were greeted by the same staffer and were escorted directly to Dodge's office. Dodge welcomed them in the typical strictly business manner many Interpol agents were known for.

"Bayless is back in The Hague. What's so important? I'll see that he's informed."

Clearly, he wasn't ready for small talk, so Harlan cut straight to the chase.

"The CIA is working on a plan to get Dmitri Egorkov out of IK-1 in Yaroslavl."

Dodge leaned back in his chair and laughed. "You're shitting me? What the hell do they want with him?"

Lou responded. "We figured the CIA wouldn't take the time to bring Interpol in on this. I guess we were right. Collins is a real work of art. Big mistake given Egorkov's an Interpol agent. You needed to be in the know."

"Fine, I'm now in the know. But again, why? Who gives a shit about him?"

Harlan laid out the CIA's entire regime change concept. Dodge listened but spent most of the time shaking his head. Nevertheless, he let Harlan finish.

"Granted, Egorkov's a good agent, he's respected, but he's as corrupt as every other Russian, and that includes the ones who work for this agency. They're all mini-Polushins. They'll line their pockets as fast as they can, just like Yuri has. Then buy a penthouse in Lisbon, and say, 'Screw the world. Who needs kids, anyway?'"

"I don't know Egorkov as well as you do, and you're probably right about all that. I suspect he has no leadership abilities. We thought you should be informed as to what the CIA is planning. General Dixon's in on it too. I would like to see Egorkov out of that hole. I want him in a safe house somewhere. I want to debrief him. I want to know how much contact he's had with Perigee. I want to know what he knows ... and exactly where Polushin stands."

"Well, thanks for the update, but this isn't what Interpol does and you know it. I'll see that none of our people get in the way. And that's about all I can promise. Let the spooks do what they want. If they get him out? Fine. But he better not set foot in Russia again. Second chances aren't in Yuri's playbook."

FORTY-TWO

It took a month, but surprisingly the CIA pulled it off. They had gotten Dmitri Egorkov out of Russia, into Finland, and then on to London where they'd parked him in a safe house in the Chelsea section of the city. He now resided in a full-floor, three-bedroom apartment overlooking the Thames. It was guarded twenty-four-seven by Russian-speaking MI6 agents. The operation was pulled off exactly as Svetlana had suggested. They bribed the crap out of every IK-1 prison official and almost the entire town of Yaroslavl, threw rubles around like confetti. In all likelihood, the depressing image of their future had become clear, and most had opted to cash out while they could. They owed Polushin nothing.

There had been virtually no public reaction whatsoever from the Kremlin or Polushin. They weren't going to admit that they had been had by anyone. Polushin clearly realized that Egorkov knew nothing more than what had been laid out in General Dixon's thumb drives, so why sweat it? On the other hand, the Russian people, not just the ones in Yaroslavl, knew the truth. They were getting restless, protests were becoming more frequent and boisterous, they could see into the future, and they didn't like what they saw. But for the most part, the FSB had things under control. Yuri wasn't remotely focused on

Egorkov. He didn't know who had grabbed him or why, and he most likely only mildly wondered why anyone would want the guy in the first place.

When he arrived at the safe house Egorkov was exhausted, confused, and hungry. No one had explained why he had been spirited away to England. Physically there wasn't much left of him, but his mind was still sharp. He carefully studied the entire apartment inch by inch, looking for listening devices more than anything. The closet and dresser had been outfitted with conservative British clothing; the bathroom was fully stocked with the essentials. The refrigerator had been furnished with a week's worth of food, wine, beer, and Russian Standard Vodka, all secured from a nearby Waitrose market.

After Egorkov had eaten three bowls of Rice Krispies laced with sour cream and capers, and a vodka chaser, he attempted to make some phone calls. He was denied access to an outside line. He had not been given a cell phone, so he turned on the television. There were no Russian stations available, but his English was good enough to follow the British sit-coms. It made no difference; he was asleep on the couch within five minutes. He slept for two days.

Harlan waited a week before he paid Egorkov a visit, opting to give him some time to get his strength back. This was the first time he'd been to London since before the Perigee arrival on Earth. It hadn't changed much; it never did. He brought Angelica with him, mostly to convince her that the UK and US were not the same country any longer. It was a fruitless endeavor. She saw no difference. Everyone spoke English.

Svetlana was left in DC. He had ceased speaking about the CIA plan while in the loft, purposefully keeping her out of the loop. The time for her to reunite with Egorkov would have to wait.

When he arrived at the apartment the guard at the door tapped twice and let him enter with no announcement. He closed and locked the door behind him. The guard was expecting Harlan. Egorkov wasn't.

The Russian looked him up and down and said, "I gather this is the time when I learn what this shit is all about?" He spoke in English.

Harlan replied in Russian. "My name is Harlan Stone. I work for the president of the United States. Personally. Anything you say will be transmitted directly to the president. This can work in your favor or against you. I'd like to ask you a few questions. You're in no danger. You can trust me on that. We're trying to iron out this situation."

They stayed with Russian throughout their entire conversation.

"Situation?"

"This visit from Elsewhere. Alien invasion, if you like."

No surprised look appeared on Egorkov's face at the mention of an alien invasion. He would have been more shocked if Harlan had mentioned there was a Stilton shortage at Harrod's. He simply said, "What do you want to know?"

"Have you watched the film footage on the thumb drive the MI6 agent gave you?"

Egorkov laughed. "That was better than half the crappy TV shows that thing plays endlessly." He pointed at the television. "One of the guards at IK-1 told me about these drives and the film, but I hadn't seen it. What a bunch of bullshit. Best laugh I've had in years. I take it the entire world has seen it, and has absorbed it as some sort of fact?"

Harlan gave him a smile. "It's served its purpose. Do I need to explain to you why it was fabricated?"

"No, it's obvious. From my point of view, it's too obvious, but I gather there aren't many in the world that have my point of view."

"Only a few. In English we've given the space that our visitors inhabit, their home so to speak, the name of Perigee, just so we all have a point of reference, communications-wise. And you're right, as far as we can tell, only five people have had any direct conversations with creatures from Perigee: me, two of my fellow agents, the president of the United States, and you."

"Which means you've met Svetlana. How is she?"

"Still not into wearing much in the way of clothing."

He smiled. "I found that part of her personality rather charming. It also kept my mind busy in IK-1. And now I gather she is your plaything?"

"No. I've offered her housing to keep a close watch on her. I have a plaything of my own."

"I'm sure you do. I imagine you handle yourself rather well in that area. And I did wonder if there had been more than one Svetlana sent to Earth. Sending one to the States makes perfect sense." He glanced at the refrigerator as if it was calling his name. "I suppose I should tell you, there is one other person who has had contact with, as you say, a creature from Perigee."

"Who's that?"

"Sergei Volkov. He's the doctor who removed Svetlana's tracking chip. Though there's no possible way that he would have known she was from your Perigee. I told him the chip was planted by the FSB."

Harlan cleared his throat. "Yeah, well, your friend Volkov did a shitty job. The chip was never taken out of her. She's been reporting back to Perigee on a regular basis."

Egorkov took a moment to let this sink in. "I never went there, but now that you mention it, yes, that makes perfect sense. I expected a change within her once the chip was gone, but none came. Though Volkov did cut into her. There's a scar."

"I've seen her scar. He took nothing out. Why would that be, do you think? Wouldn't he be more loyal to you than her?"

Egorkov again paused as he pondered this. "Like I said, I told Volkov it was an FSB monitoring device, and we didn't want to be monitored. I never let on that she was from Elsewhere. She must have changed the story on his operating table, maybe told him that she was an FSB agent or something like that, which would have scared the crap out of him. Maybe he followed her orders and not mine, created the scar and left the chip where it was. Or ..."

"Or?"

"She had a second chip. Somewhere else on her body. If so, I never noticed a second mark. And, trust me, I've been all over her body."

Harlan sat quietly for a moment absorbing the possibility of a second chip. "I suppose that could be a possibility. Were you in love with her?"

Again, he laughed. "Hell, no. She was unlovable. Good in bed, but that's about it. The relationship only lasted three or four months. Group had already neutralized all the livestock by the time she showed up. They were well into Phase Two. After I learned what was going on, I set up a meeting with Polushin. Told him exactly what Group's plans were and implored him to begin scaling back on gas and oil exports. He's a greedy little Napoleon. Only thinks about himself, doesn't want any more kids, and could care less about grandchildren because he won't be around to see them as adults, or be around to observe the future of humanity for that matter. Though he does believe he's immortal, so who knows? He just wants to finish out his days rolling in rubles, juicing himself up with Viagra cocktails, and nailing every high-end Slovenian hooker. Classic narcissist. His response was predictable. And the arrest warrant means nothing to him. He's ignored it. Like every other narcissistic petty wannabe dictator, he has no interest in traveling out of his element, going to another country. In fact, it frightens him. Foreign languages heighten his paranoia. They're all the same, Erdogan, Assad, your Trump. They all have their safe compounds, and venturing outside of their little Mar-a-Lagos and mingling with real people scares them shitless." After a minute he added, "Jesus, I still find it hard to believe I was screwing an alien."

Harlan laughed. "Yeah, well, sometimes you need to take one for the team. I can sympathize with you."

Egorkov laughed as well. He stood, walked to the kitchen, and pulled a beer from the refrigerator. "Want one."

"Sure, why not?"

"Glass?"

"Bottle's fine."

After he returned with the beers Harlan asked, "Are you up to speed as to where we are with all this, globally?"

"I think so. All the polluters have been narrowed down to China and India and Polushin's their gas station. It's that simple."

"I gather you know nothing about Perigee's timetable?"

"Great, they've got a Timetable?"

"Yep."

"And time's running out, of course."

"We've got five months to swing this ship around. We need to get China and India off fossil fuel and get Russia to cut off their oil supply."

"And you're going to do that in five months? Good luck, my friend."

"We don't have a choice."

"And you somehow think I can make that happen? That I have some magical influence over that crazy little shit?"

Harlan took a while before answering. "You know Polushin. We don't have any more time to bring him around. We now believe the only viable and expedient solution would be regime change in Russia."

He laughed again. "Political regime change, or assassination?" He held up his hand. "Wait, don't answer. I'm not thinking clearly. Assassination accomplishes nothing; they push back with everything, and he's simply replaced by a like-minded hack. And I know exactly who it would be. You need a serious dissident factor to take the governmental reins and steer it in a different direction. Tragically, Navalny, and people like him, have all been eliminated. You need to aggressively stir the pot and do so quickly. Oddly, I think the oligarchs would be better off getting their claws into dissidents than seasoned political hacks like Polushin. They'd be willing to work with the right person. And there's a big cash-out for them in the end for them."

He walked to the kitchen and pulled a bottle of the Russian Standard Vodka from the freezer. He then glanced at Harlan who shook his head.

"I'm good. I've had this discussion with the US president. He's come to the same conclusion. We think we have the right person, Mikhail Preobrazhensky."

Harlan waited for a reaction from Egorkov, but he seemed to take it in stride.

"I hadn't thought about him, but, yes, I can see that working." Egorkov said after some consideration. "He's respected by almost everyone and he knows the system from the inside."

"Good. But he will need to have serious security. An infrastructure needs to be established before any move is made. That's where we need your support. We need muscle, and Russian Interpol is the logical route. Not the FSB."

After Egorkov returned with his vodka, he sat on the couch and shook his head.

"Look, I appreciate you getting me out of IK-1, and I don't know what you had in mind for me, or what you expected from me. You wouldn't have pulled me out if you hadn't studied me and how I operate. Support? Infrastructure and teamwork aren't my thing. Perhaps if you cause a major uproar in Moscow and Saint Petersburg, something might take place. If it does, I can keep Russian Interpol agents from foiling any plans you might have, and I'll go a step further—I'll secure their cooperation for you and give Preobrazhensky a security detail. But manpower-wise, our numbers are small, no match for the FSB or the military."

"Can you get to some generals?"

"Hold on, back up, don't get carried away. There's no way in hell I'm going back to Russia … under any circumstances."

"What if I offered some incentives?"

"Not interested."

"I can make things uncomfortable for you."

He laughed once more.

"Worse than IK-1?"

"I have the authority to get you packed off to Guantanamo this afternoon, but at this point, that serves no purpose. We've reached the breakpoint. The clock is ticking down. How about a list of names? Other dissidents? You know who these people are. We need to set up an operational support base."

He laughed.

"And you know who these people are as well as I do. Christ, you just said you've already convinced Preobrazhensky to throw his life on the line. The CIA has better contacts than me, and you know it. You're banging your head against a brick wall, my friend. It's too late. Time is running out. Time has run out. Get used to it. It's all over."

Egorkov switched to English. "You're shit out of luck, and you know it. Be glad your Perigee creatures haven't decided to eat you alive."

FORTY-THREE

Harlan and Angelica spent their last day in London strolling the streets of Chelsea admiring the perfectly-maintained houses. They ended up on the banks of the Thames walking amongst the houseboats.

"Okay, now I like this London place better than Washington DC," Angelica said with a slight frown. "It's more civilized. Is that why the Americans decided they no longer wanted to be connected to the UK? They didn't like the civilized behavior? They're more comfortable making noise?"

"I never looked at it that way, but you may have a point."

They sat on a low brick wall close to one another, looking out over the river. Angelica glanced up at the approaching black storm clouds.

"Looks like we're in for nasty weather."

"In more ways than one. Dmitri Egorkov's a dead-end street. In the long run, he's a lot like Polushin, another disgruntled, overly-depressed Russian. He's going to sit it out until the end. He has no kids. He doesn't give a shit about anything but his morning cup of de-presto, his cigarettes, and the stash of vodka he has tucked away in the freezer. He has no interest in saving mankind. I told him I could fly Svetlana over to London for a few days if he wanted. All he said was, 'Keep her.'"

Angelica wrapped her arm in his. "Yes, there is Svetlana. Like I said, I'm getting a little tired of having a boarder. I know she's your only link to Davenport, but can't she be parked Elsewhere? I want to live like we did in the mountains. I don't want to be monitored twenty-four-seven by Perigee. I guess I've become too human."

Harlan let out a small laugh. "Hey, they're your people."

"For the forty-eighth time, they are not people. They won't be happy until you all have been eliminated."

Harlan didn't respond for a full minute.

"It sure is tempting to toss in the towel and head to the mountains. Of course, that means me leaving MPS, and society, really. And that's another reason to resolve the Svetlana situation. Lou and I are the only ones who know anything about her. I can't just walk away without deciding what to do with her. We can't trust her to be on her own. She needs to be watched. It's all so odd, we need to be watching the one who is in fact, watching us."

Angelica opened her mouth to say something, but he stopped her.

"No. This is an issue I need to work out. There are very few options. One, we just out her and hand her to the NSA. In which case they place her in some sort of holding facility and grill her endlessly."

She laughed. "Sometimes I'm amazed at how naive you can be. You don't see what's right in front of your face. What do you think has been going on for the last two-and-half years? Do you honestly think walls are going to stop Davenport? Svetlana? Or any Perigee operation? He'll simply pull her back to Group. Or place her Elsewhere. Don't forget she can move about in any fashion she chooses. So could I when I had the chip. Manny, Moe, and Jack? Same thing. I wasn't hampered by something as inconsequential as a wall. And Davenport will take any attempt at jailing her as an aggressive move on the part of the US. There's no telling what Perigee would do. Aggression begets aggression with Males. They could just shut everything down, initiate Phase Three tomorrow, and go home. Obviously, they're on to me, have been for nearly two years. Ever since Svetlana arrived. I'm only guessing they've left me alone in an effort to conceal Svetlana's identity and keep an eye on you. Svetlana is your barometer. When she leaves—" Angelica stopped mid-sentence.

"Yes?"

"When she leaves it's over. If Davenport returns, meets with POTUS, offers up a new timeline, and leaves, and Svetlana stays, Earth has passed the test, and Group will stand by a new timeline. If Svetlana leaves on her own without an appearance by Davenport, it's all over. Phase Three will kick in the next morning. Like I said, she's your barometer. What's your second brilliant option? Because the first one stinks."

"Okay. Obviously exposing her puts you in danger. But that can be resolved by us simply moving to another location. She can have my loft."

"And you don't think a Perigee operative will follow you the first night you walk to your new home?"

"Good point. So, it's back to Svetlana option two. We try to reason with her, see if we can work out an arrangement that works for us all. Do you think she's in the same position you were once in? Will she be terminated once she returns to Perigee?"

Angelica considered this for a few minutes. Harlan could see the wheels turning, so he gave her time to work it out.

Finally, she said, "No. Svetlana's clearly a much more trusted operative than I ever was. I'm convinced she's centuries older than me and has experienced far more activity than I will ever see. If the Females were still running things, I'd guess she'd hold the position Davenport now holds or maybe even higher. She's been entrusted with too much. Trusted to work alone here on Earth, with no backup. And if that's true, it would be much easier to work out an arrangement with her."

"What makes you say that?"

"She'd be able to make her own decisions. She wouldn't be required to get Group's input for any logistical decisions she makes. She can come and go as she pleases. She can most likely make the final decision. And woe betide the day she turns her back and leaves on her own."

"And this is why she never allowed Volkov to remove her chip."

"Right, she was probably able to return to Perigee after the Egorkov connection fell through, feeling safe that she wouldn't be eliminated. After all, that was something she had no control over, but she somehow knew she was safe. She was then instructed to come to Washington, DC to monitor Earth's progress from the angle of a White House insider, since getting into the Kremlin was out. Group knew that any effective changes must be driven by the US. I must admit, Svetlana pulled that off flawlessly."

"She sure did. And I never checked to see if she used that plane ticket, got on a commercial flight, and flew from Moscow to DC as she maintained."

"She probably worked out her own transportation. I see now that she has that capability. She just didn't count on the fact that I was still around. And she couldn't eliminate me because it would have sent up a big red flag."

"Who knew I'd be so irresistible to all these Perigee Females?"

She laughed. "Don't flatter yourself, if Lou Walsh had passed by her first in Rock Creek Park, they'd be having us over for dinner once a week. And neither one of you would know what was going on."

Harlan focused on a pair of runners across the river in Battersea Park for no particular reason.

"No, Lou's a jogger. He probably wouldn't have even slowed down for Svetlana."

"You slowed down for me."

"Hah. You trapped me, what was I supposed to do? Jump out of the train's window?"

"I didn't see you try. And again, don't flatter yourself. Lou speaks Russian. She would have grabbed him in a second. Wanna bet on it? He's even an easier mark than you. I know how Females work. I helped write the playbook."

Harlan stood, faced her, put his hands on her shoulders, and kissed her. "Jesus, that's it. That's how we get rid of her. That's the answer."

"What's the answer?"

"Once we get home, we hook Lou up with Svetlana. Get her to move in with him and out of the loft. It's so friggin' simple. He knows as much as I do. He has the same link to POTUS as I do, the same link to General Dixon and the Joint Chiefs. He's as much in the loop as me. He was there for the Davenport meeting, so that's all a green light. And she knows all this. She'd still be close enough to keep an eye on me, Lou and the president. You said it yourself, she'd be just as happy using Lou as her conduit. And it comes with fringe benefits."

"Benefits?"

"Sex."

"Ah, right, but Lou's met her. Nothing clicked for him."

"Nothing clicked because Lou was dating that bimbo from Rockville. That's all over and done with. All he does now is moan about not getting laid. And he thinks Svetlana's a fox."

"A fox? Like a dog?"

"It's a compliment, trust me. And this can all be accomplished without outing Svetlana. She'll never suspect we're on to her and things will roll along as usual."

"It might work. Do you think Lou will go for it?"

Harlan laughed. "Are you kidding me? He's hot for her. And God knows, Lou's a trooper. I'm sure he'll take one for the team."

"How romantic."

FORTY-FOUR

"Well, I have to admit, she's a hell of a lot smarter than that bimbo from Rockville. And for an alien, she's not half bad in bed. I've taken to calling her Lana lately. She likes it. Works better in bed. Three syllables are too much when you're on a roll. Though, she can't cook worth a damn."

Harlan laughed. "You've got to remove Svetlana's chip for there to be any hope of domestic prowess coming your way. Which ain't gonna happen. We need her as much as she needs us. And we need her with that chip in place if we have any hope of further communication with Davenport, or Group."

"No worries there. She's still under the impression that I think the chip was removed by Volkov."

Harlan and Lou were sitting on stools, gazing out the window of the Fenton Street Whole Foods, across the street from a CVS, eating take-out salads. Harlan had been back from London for a month. And Polushin and the Kremlin hadn't budged an inch despite mounting pressure from the Russian masses.

"Ninety days ... Time's running out," Harlan said, almost to himself.

"Well, there's a news flash. I've been spoon-feeding everything to Lana in hopes it gets passed along to Davenport, and in hopes we get a positive response. We've got zippo time to get these clowns to knuckle under and drop fossil fuel. And even then, it wouldn't make a blip on the greenhouse gas radar screen for a decade. Lana offers up nothing, but it is getting through, I'm sure of it. They know we're working overtime to meet their demands. Group monitors everything. Which I gotta tell you is a little unnerving when you're humping like bunnies and knowing all the while there's an entire universe out there getting a free porn show."

Harlan laughed. "Don't worry, I don't think they have a video component. It's just audio and still photos."

Lou shook his head. "How do you know that? You're just making shit up."

"I can check with Angelica if you want. She never mentioned it to me. But then I was oblivious to what was going on until I took out her chip. Things don't play out that way in Perigee, sex-wise. I gather they're just made in a lab somewhere and come out of test tubes as adults. If they're watching you, they probably don't know what the hell you're doing."

"You know what your problem is? You're too much of a goddam romantic. If Perigee has been monitoring us for over two thousand years, don't you think they would have figured out what screwing is all about by now? And all the reasons why we do it? Jesus, they're about to sterilize every dude in the world. Clearly, they've learned the science behind it."

"Well, yeah, all I'm saying is, the porno angle is far-fetched."

They were quiet for a full five minutes.

Finally, Harlan said, "This shit is going nowhere. The Old Man's cabinet is worthless. Even the Secretary of State, who prides himself as a Russia expert, can't get that turd Yuri to pick up the phone, or generate any kind of a revolution in the streets. The entire Preobrazhensky operation failed miserably, and Mikhail barely made it out of Russia and into Finland with the clothes on his back. And General Dixon bounces back and forth between bombing the piss out of the Russians, and his Idi Amin concept of having Perigee give everyone in Asia a limp dick and leaving the rest of us alone. Speaking of which, do you like Thai food?"

"Yeah, it's okay. Except for all the damn coconut."

"Why don't you and Svetlana come over to the loft for dinner? Bangkok West has a decent take-out menu, and they'll lay off the coconut if you push it. And there's a lot of vegetarian stuff. Angelica likes it. Maybe if it's three against one, we can squeeze something out of Svetlana? See where we stand?"

"Sure. Not a bad idea, and if POTUS has anything remotely substantial at today's briefing, we can feed it to Svetlana with her *Som Tum.*"

FORTY-FIVE
TICK... TICK... TICK...

Their 5:00 p.m. briefing with POTUS revealed absolutely nothing earthshattering. Polushin was as determined as ever to keep the oil flowing eastward, and any CIA attempts to get him ousted had gone nowhere. China and India were beginning to make an outward display of scaling back on fossil fuel, but their disclosures were strictly for the media, and Davenport surely saw right through it. Everything appeared good on paper, and in the papers, but ultimately, they were accomplishing nothing significant, certainly not enough to convince Group that they'd seen the way. Oil and gas consumption had tapered off to a certain degree, and the needle had moved, but at the same time, both countries were opening up new coal mines and burning through it like tomorrow didn't exist.

Lou and Svetlana arrived at the loft at 7:30 p.m. Angelica, as usual, was wearing no clothing, and Svetlana followed suit the moment she stepped into the loft. Harlan and Lou had become pretty much inured to this routine. After they'd settled in, Harlan ordered seven entrees from Bangkok West—all vegetarian. Three contained coconut milk and were facetiously marked on the lid with skulls and crossbones. The people at Bangkok West had a sense of humor and knew Harlan all too well.

"Everything's vegetarian?" Lou grumbled as he pawed through the paper containers. "You're shitting me."

"The only alternatives are dishes with chicken, fish or shrimp and some of us here still aren't on board with seafood. Or chicken, for that matter, which is a small blessing because I can't afford chicken."

Lou wasn't done grumbling. "You know, Lana, I totally get why you won't eat other living creatures, but do you know what fish eat?"

"*Nyet.* What?"

"Other fish. They're not vegetarians. It's a dog-eat-dog world down in the deep blue sea. By eating fish you're just getting even. Making the greedy ones pay for their evil ways. You should see it as a service to the fish world. Eliminating a few of the predators."

She smiled. "I don't really see the difference. It looks the same whether there's shrimps in the food or not."

"Right. I was thinking more of the flavor angle, not the looks angle."

Harlan opened a bottle of Pinot Grigio and poured a glass for Lou and himself. Angelica and Svetlana were happy with water.

The agents had worked out several scenarios which were intended to get Svetlana to open up about how Perigee perceived Earth's progress. But they couldn't settle on one specific plan. She was clearly ten steps ahead of them. There was nothing she didn't know, so they opted to only talk about what had gone on in the Oval Office a few hours earlier. This would be information they believed she couldn't verify and thus they felt free to improvise on the facts. Time was ticking away, and POTUS wanted Group to provide some answers. The Old Man was sweating bullets at this point.

They left it to Angelica to get the ball rolling, though she had strong misgivings about their approach, and suggested that they would be better off letting things play out until their time was up. But like the Males of Perigee, Harlan and Lou were much too impatient. Sitting pat and watching the clock wind down wasn't their style. Angelica felt their chances would be better if they were dealing directly with Davenport face-to-face, and she had said so. The only way to do that was to wait for his return. Pushing the envelope had a very strong chance of backfiring.

If Harlan had learned anything at all, it was that the Females of Perigee were much too patient and wedded to the truth. He was also aware that Svetlana could communicate directly with Davenport at any time. The moment had come to ask for an extension of time. Ninety days wasn't going to cut it. Everyone knew that, and those facts needed to be conveyed to Davenport.

"How'd your meeting go with POTUS this afternoon?" Angelica asked to neither one of them in particular, as she casually took one of the take-out containers and ladled out some vegetarian *Khao Pad*.

"The president believes there's been some very significant improvements in his relationship with Polushin as of late. There was a brief conversation between the two today. Russia's coming round, albeit slowly," Harlan lied. "And CIA Director Collins reported that India and China seem to be working overtime in an attempt to scale back the use of petroleum and gas, but coal is another issue. Of course, there's no telling if they're being honest with us, or if Collins' information is accurate. I'm not certain they're going to meet anyone's timetable. Ideally, POTUS would like to have another year. I'm sure Group, and

Davenport, would be able to pinpoint progress much better if we could swing a little more time. Everything's in place, we just need time to see if our efforts are working."

Lou added, "It's too bad neither one of you still has your chip. We'd like to be able to report all of this to Davenport firsthand, and do it now, rather than wait another three months. It would be helpful if he could personally put some additional pressure on Russia, India, and China while we're still on the clock. We're finding it tough going it alone. We could use his assistance."

Lou took a large, somewhat shaky, swallow of wine. "It now seems the only way to get these countries to come around is to set them up with a face-to-face with Davenport." After a long pause, "Am I wasting my breath, here? I feel like I'm talking to the damn wall. I'm repeating the same friggin' argument over and over, like Davenport's standing in the room next to me. I'm not handling all this frustration well."

Svetlana spooned a portion of Red Curry onto her plate.

"Davenport gets around. Just because you don't see him, it does not mean he is also blind. He knows nothing of Angelica and me, which is counting as a good thing, but he knows what things look like. What is true fact and what isn't true fact. You won't be able to fool him. Don't make a mistake of lying to him, or pushing too hard. Remember, he has nothing to lose."

"Nobody's trying to fool anyone, and nobody'd be lying. He doesn't even know what the hell we're talking about here." Lou said somewhat defensively. "Jesus, we're running out of time, and we just want him to know where we stand. We need a meeting, and we need to hammer out some sort of compromise."

"He will always know what is authentic and what is fabricated. And in the end, we, or I should say, he, still recognizes human beings as what they are, a dangerous disease, a threat to our existence. He doesn't distinguish between Canadian, Nigerian, or Russian variants; it's all the same disorder from his point of view. Even your own scientists know there is no difference between individual humans other than skin shades. Some diseases, under the microscope, can take on slightly different outward appearances, but in the end, their interiors are identical. Their impact is equally deadly for us; rather, him. People in India are able to breed with people in Brazil—they're all the same infectious disease, and that's what makes any disease so dangerous."

She took a long drink of water and focused on Lou.

"Let me ask you this, if your scientists had pin-pointed a deadly cancer, would they sit and watch it if they had a way of eradicating it? Would they wait to see if it would grow larger? Spread to other areas? No, they would try as hard as they possibly could to destroy it. And your disease experts have consistently done this time and time again. This is Davenport's frame of mind as well. It's the Perigee frame of mind." She looked at Harlan. "You know this. You should explain it better to him."

Harlan wasn't sure whether to take this as a threat or not. *Did she know the actual truth? Did she know there had been absolutely no progress whatsoever? No phone conversation between POTUS and Polushin? Did she know he wasn't from Elsewhere?*

Lou, pushing back added, "How could Davenport possibly know what the president said to Polushin in their call this afternoon? Only Harlan, General Dixon and I were briefed on it. All we want to do is bring him up-to-speed. He needs to know we're trying. He needs to back off."

She shrugged. "By now you should know what Davenport can monitor, and what he cannot. The Males don't respond well to pressure. Look at yourself in the mirror right now. You're angry. Your face is red. It's not a winning position. You need to be more careful in your approach. You have no bargaining power. Ultimately, you're impotent."

Angelica read Svetlana's shrug for what it was. Svetlana knew damn well there was no call between Polushin and POTUS. Davenport knew there was no call. And if he did feel pressured, he'd call it all off. Game over.

And Harlan felt the change in the air. He knew he had to put his cards on the table before it was too late. "Listen, Svetlana, we know you still have the chip. You haven't fooled any of us. We know you can communicate with Davenport. We need to have a meeting now. Lou and I have the authority to okay any bargain he wants, and we can do it right here, in this room, now. We do not need presidential approval for any deal we cut. You have us by the balls, and we know it. We need more time, and we need Davenport's help in securing an agreement with India and China."

"Help? You need help?"

"Yes, help."

"Help ..."

Svetlana leaned back in her chair and stared at the celling for a full minute. She then brought her gaze back to Harlan.

"For the longest time Davenport and Group believed you were from Elsewhere and had some compelling motive to ensure that these humans would survive, that they contributed to your way of life in some form; that they could be harvested. You had fooled us all, but now you ask for help from us. I can now see we were mistaken. You are only human."

Angelica took Harlan's hand and gave it a soft squeeze. She then looked at Svetlana. She had no readable expression left on her face; even the color had faded from her cheeks and body. She was staring over Lou's shoulder as if there was a television monitor on the far wall. Her look was so intense that Lou turned in his chair to see where she was looking. There was nothing there but the bathroom door.

Angelica squeezed Harlan's hand once more, leaned back in her chair and studied Svetlana for a full minute. "How's the curry?"

"Good. I like it."

"Aren't you going to miss it? Aren't you going to miss Thai food?"

"I suppose I will. If I remember it."

Svetlana finished her glass of water and gave Angelica a small smile.

"I'm happy you understand. You will have a lifetime as you comprehend it now. I'm surprised you still have some wherewithal to read me without words. I thought you would have lost that ability. Davenport and I will check back with you at some point. The Females at Group have admired how well you have acclimated yourself. I personally don't believe any other Female would have had the resolve, or the strength, really. We are all impressed. So much so that several months ago there was a consideration to outfit your body with ovaries so we could observe that phenomenon better. It was a Female initiative, and as a result, it didn't go far. But it is something that has always intrigued the Group technicians."

Angelica finished her water as well. "There is a part of me that was hoping I would be able to negotiate that. I would like to have created something here, not just torn it all down."

"We know that. However, it was too risky. From a disease standpoint. If the disease were to escape and mutate, if it could learn to live among us—no, we couldn't take that chance. It was too unpredictable." She looked at Harlan. "And of course, all of that would have been pointless at this moment. The ovaries would have gone to total waste. I thank you for being so good to her, if nothing else. Truer words were never spoken. Yes, we do in fact, literally, 'have you by the balls.' If you'll all excuse me, I'm late for a train."

She stood, crossed the loft, and stepped into the bathroom.

"What the hell is going on?" Harlan made no attempt to hide the confusion that had swept across his face, and he repeated himself. "Dammit Angelica, what the hell is going on? What's she up to?"

She took a moment to answer. "It's over. She knows everything you just said was fabricated. Davenport's monitoring. He knows it's bullshit. They both saw it as a setup. You pushed too hard."

"Shit. It wasn't a setup. We need a direct meeting. We need more time."

"I know that, but that's not how they see it. Remember that they are frightened to a certain extent. Actually, to a large extent. Cancer is frightening, right? It's frightening for you. Any aggressive disease is frightening. They're fighting for their lives. You look at Group and Perigee as if they're some all-powerful entity. That's not the case. They are trying to stop a disease in its tracks. They're not willing to take a wait-and-see approach. And if Davenport felt pressured, if he felt the disease was becoming too aggressive—"

In a hushed voice, Lou cut in, "Hold it down, she can hear all this."

"No. No, she can't hear anything. She's gone."

He sprang from his chair and charged over to the bathroom. He flung the door open. The bathroom was empty.

"What the hell?"

"In the end, I don't think it makes any difference. You were out of time, and they weren't about to give you more. Consider the reality: if you found a cure, you'd be a fool not to implement it. It had become far too risky for Perigee. Ninety more days weren't going to change anything. You could see that yourselves. And Group could see that. They just pulled the plug. They're playing it safe. Can you blame them?"

"Jesus."

"I told you she would be your barometer. She's gone. It's over. Human beings have effectively pushed the Earth to a breaking point, and now they're going to pay the ultimate price." She smiled at Harlan. "But as I've been saying all along—it will be painless."

And Angelica poured herself a glass of Pinot Grigio.

PHASE THREE
TICK... TICK... TOCK...

FINIS

ACKNOWLEDGEMENTS

Tick... Tick... Tick... would have never come to life without the great support of the Vine Leaves Press team, particularly Jessica Bell and my extraordinary editor Amie McCracken. Many thanks to Christian Dietrich for some inside assistance, and Michael Fryd and Sharon Haynie for their valuable input. Much love to my wife, Cordelia Biddle, who brings me endless joy, as does my muse, Pearlie. And a special shout out to the EPA, NIH, FDA & CDC-NCEH and the dedicated individuals who work at these institutions. And for those who would choose to defund these agencies, or walk out on the Paris climate agreement, you would be well advised to wake the hell up.

ALSO BY STEVE ZETTLER

Two for the Money
Careless Love
12 Titles in the Nero Blanc Mystery Series
Ronin
Double Identity
The Second Man

VINE LEAVES PRESS

Enjoyed this book?
Go to *vineleavespress.com* to find more.
Subscribe to our newsletter: